ELLYN

Rachel Erin Worley

PHOENIX PRESS LTD

Published 2024
First Edition
PHOENIX PRESS LTD
New Haven Publishing Children's Books Imprint
www.newhavenpublishingltd.com
newhavenpublishing@gmail.com

Cover art © John M. Burns
Editors: Erica Worley and Ivan Frasure

Dedicated to Charlie and Eden

Content

1. The Northmen Attack — 7
2. Battle in the Village — 18
3. The Kings' Council — 24
4. Attack on the Castle — 30
5. Seeking Safety — 35
6. Welcome to Brystol — 45
7. The Alliance — 53
8. A Royal Wedding — 63
9. Ellyn's New Life — 71
10. A Stranger in the Night — 79
11. Peronell's Story — 86
12. Maerynn of Wyndham — 93
13. Maerynn's Proposition — 102
14. Corineus Makes Trouble — 111
15. Michaelmas — 117
16. Riding in the Woods — 126
17. Corbin and Julius — 134
18. Corbin's Hunt — 142
19. Corbin Confronts Ellyn — 154
20. In the Dungeon — 161
21. Ellyn's Letter — 168
22. Secrets Revealed — 179
23. The Assassin — 187
24. Dark Schemes — 199
25. Moonlight Escape — 211
26. Captured — 220
27. The Duel — 228
28. At Home in Lyntirith — 236
About The Author — 243

Chapter 1 - The Northmen Attack

A tense stillness hovering over a village on the shore of Eurasia was broken by the steady, low-pitched wail of a bull-horn. As the sound cut through the air, even sleeping dogs raised their heads, and rabbits in the forest looked up from the roots they were nibbling and sniffed the air with nervously twitching noses.

The moment it reached their ears, each person who heard that ominous warning looked up from their work. Blacksmiths froze, hammers in mid-air. Housewives paused, hands in the middle of kneading a lump of dough. Children scattered from the cobblestone streets where they had been running and playing. All knew the meaning of the alarm too well: the Northmen were coming.

The sounds of farmers and merchants going about their business and children laughing and playing in the midsummer heat were replaced with threatening silence before the note died away. A child's muffled cry was the only sign of life in an otherwise empty and seemingly abandoned place. Time stood still as each home waited and listened and prayed.

A few miles off the eastern shore, a young woman was riding side-saddle down a forest path. She was dressed in a long, green riding dress and black boots. Her skin was fair and smooth, and dotted with light freckles. Her light blonde hair had been neatly pinned up, but a few ringlets had escaped and were falling down her back. She raised her blue eyes at the sound of the bullhorn and turned to look at her companion several strides behind. Both halted their horses and looked at each other apprehensively. The first of the young women was Princess Ellyn, the oldest daughter of Eurasia's ruler, King Wulfred. She looked wise beyond her seventeen years, and while she possessed the qualities of grace and sensibility expected of her rank, she was always adventurous, and would not be contained in her chambers for too long. She was escorted by Alys, her maidservant. Although the young women were separated by several years and a great distance in class, there was a unique and longstanding friendship between them.

"What unfortunate timing," Ellyn sighed as they turned their horses back towards the way they had come. They began travelling at a swift pace down the forest path. Sunlight dappled through the leafy canopy and danced off of Ellyn's long blonde hair and pale face.

"Do you think we will have time to return safely, Your Highness?" Alys wondered aloud. "We are so far into the woods."

"I am sure we're in no danger, Alys," Ellyn assured her. "We're far enough from the shore that the warriors will not have any chance of reaching us before we return. But we must hurry, or Mother will fret. She was hesitant to let me go riding at all."

Both spurred their horses to a steady canter, but did not wish to go any faster over the rough and rocky path, for fear of bringing harm to their horses. Both animals seemed to recognize that something was wrong and their ears were pulled slightly back, alert to every sight and sound. Ellyn sensed that her horse, Borin, was tense, and spoke gently to calm him. They had only been riding for a quarter of an hour when Alys gave a small gasp and said, "Do you hear something, Your Highness?"

Ellyn pulled Borin to a halt and held her breath, listening. The only sounds she heard were the occasional twittering of a bird, and the rustling of branches swaying in the breeze.

"I can't hear a thing, Alys. You must have imagined it," Ellyn replied. She had hardly finished her sentence when a stick cracked just beyond the brush lining the path. They both whipped their heads around toward the noise.

"There!" said Alys in a hushed voice. "Someone is nearby."

Ellyn strained her eyes, but the trees were so thick that, for several moments, she saw nothing unusual. But then there was a flash of color through the branches and brambles, and her eyes widened as two young children emerged from the trees into sight, and froze in terror when they saw Ellyn and Alys.

"Don't worry, we won't hurt you," Ellyn said gently. She dismounted Borin and approached carefully, trying not to startle them. "Are you harmed?" she asked, kneeling to their level.

The younger child, a boy of about four, covered his face and began to sob. The little girl wrapped her arms protectively around him and buried her head behind her arm so that both of their grubby faces were hidden from sight.

"Those evil men are in our village," the little girl said, lifting her head and looking at Ellyn, her small voice quavering. "We heard them coming and Father told us to run and hide in the forest. I'm afraid they'll find our family because he had to stay and protect Mother and the new baby," she said. Then she broke down into tears.

Ellyn was overcome with compassion for the two children. Stroking the girl's brown, tousled hair and laying her other hand on the little boy's shoulder, she said gently, "Don't be afraid, we will keep you safe. What are your names?"

"I am Leela and my brother is Lucan," the girl replied.

"Leela, you can ride with me; I'll help you into my saddle. Lucan, this kind lady's name is Alys. You can sit with her and we will keep you safe until the danger has passed. Don't worry; we have many strong and brave soldiers. They will make sure the Northmen aren't allowed to hurt you."

Lucan was hesitant to leave his sister's side, but Ellyn was able to convince him to climb into Alys's saddle. The maidservant did her best to soothe the frightened boy, glancing left and right, looking for any possible danger.

"There, is that alright?" Ellyn asked after she lifted Leela into her own saddle and pulled herself up behind her.

"Yes," the girl replied. "But I hate the evil men. I am afraid of them. They may find us! And they will want to kill us."

"Well, there is no need to be frightened; you're safe with us. Are you ready, Alys?"

The two horses and their riders set off once again. Ellyn kept a keen watch and a wary ear to the sights and sounds around them. Nothing seemed to be out of the ordinary. Her hopes continued to rise the closer they got to the castle. Far before they reached the forest's edge, she began to hear activity through the trees. Even though there was at least a quarter of a mile of the path to cover before they reached the castle, the air was very calm, and sounds travelled easily through the woodlands. She could hear her father's voice above the commotion of clanking armor, horses whinnying and men calling back and forth to one another. She couldn't make out any words, but knew that many soldiers had already departed to meet the Northmen, and her father was organizing even more groups of armed men to join them. The soldiers had been prepared to depart for battle at any moment, and in recent months, they had needed to do so more frequently.

"We're almost there," Ellyn announced, slowing Borin to a walk so she could address Alys. "I hope Mother is not too worried about us."

But Alys did not reply. Instead, she whispered urgently, "Listen, Your Highness!" Both horses were pulled to a halt once again as they sat in utter silence, listening.

"Yes, it is the soldiers preparing to go out to fight the Northmen," Ellyn replied, breaking the tense silence.

"No, look!" Alys insisted. Ellyn looked back at her maidservant and was about to speak, but the horrified look on her face caused her to stop. Alys pointed a trembling finger off to the right of the path toward the edge of a small clearing. She was clasping her throat, trying to gasp for air. Ellyn followed her gaze, and suddenly felt as though she was being smothered with fear. Behind a cluster of trees, she could see the glint of two spears and the tops of two helmets, almost completely concealed by the thick foliage. The red symbol on each of their helmets was immediately recognizable to Ellyn as one which struck terror into any inhabitant of Eurasia who saw it. She swallowed hard and tried to calm her pounding heart.

The sound of two gruff voices speaking loudly in a foreign language reached her ears, and she could tell they were speaking to one another, but could not understand their words.

"How is that possible?" she finally gasped out, in a hoarse whisper. "How did they come inland so quickly? We are almost two miles from shore!"

"I'm scared," Leela whimpered, burying her face in Borin's mane.

"Hush, we must be silent," Ellyn whispered, stroking the girl's hair. Then, turning to Alys, she said, "We haven't been seen yet, I don't think. Come, we are almost to safety. We must hurry!"

Ellyn and Alys urged their horses into a walk, both keeping their eyes on the path in front of them, not daring to turn their heads. Ellyn held her breath, praying silently. Just as she thought they were out of the warriors' line of sight, she heard a shout and looked behind her with dismay. Two large men were looking straight in their direction. Their bodies were covered with layers of steel and they had long swords sheathed at their sides. Their faces were hidden behind bushy facial hair and thick eyebrows. One was pointing threateningly at them and the other held his spear outstretched towards them.

"We are dead, we are dead," Alys wailed hoarsely, although only the words "dead, dead!" were able to escape from her lips.

"We are not dead," Ellyn said, spurring Borin into a run. In an instant, both horses were racing along the narrow forest trail, their hooves beating over the rough woodland path. Ellyn could hear yelling behind her but did not turn her head, keeping her eyes fixed on the path ahead. She did not attempt to lead Borin. He knew they were in trouble and that he must lead his mistress to safety. Every muscle in his powerful body was tensed as he lunged through the woods, with Alys's horse only a stride behind. Ellyn wrapped her arms around Leela and twisted her fingers through Borin's mane, trying to keep from tumbling from the saddle. Occasionally, she heard a cry, or shout from their pursuers. A warm trickle of blood ran down the side of her neck as an arrow whizzed past, grazing her ear. She squeezed her eyes shut, hiding her face in Leela's hair.

With every leap, Borin ran with growing determination. Ellyn only opened her eyes once, but all she could see was a blur of trees, and Leela's hair streaming into her face. She could not tell how far they had to go, or how close the warriors were. She could only hear the furious thunder of hooves, an occasional shout from their pursuers and the pounding of her own heart.

Borin suddenly gave an earsplitting neigh and reared onto his hind legs, nearly throwing his passengers from the saddle. Wrapping her arms around Leela and gasping for breath, Ellyn looked ahead, wondering what had made Borin halt so abruptly. When she looked up, her stomach sank, and she groaned in dismay. Another Northman had appeared from behind a line of trees in front of them, about thirty yards ahead. He stood directly in their path, aiming his spear toward them. Ellyn heard a stifled scream behind her from Alys. She considered turning to the left, off the path and into the concealing trees in an attempt to lose their enemies in the thick foliage. But the two Northmen from behind were closing in, running around a bend of the path not far behind with surprising agility in their heavy armor. They were trapped. Ellyn's eyes darted from left to right as her mind sped even faster than her heart was beating. She was running out of time to make her decision, but her own life and those of three others depended on her to make the right one.

A screeching whinny cut through the air as Borin was struck with a flying spear and he tumbled to the ground. Ellyn clutched at midair as he fell, trying to break her own fall. Everything was a whirl of sounds and flying colors and the next moment Borin's heavy body fell on top of her legs.

"Ellyn!" Alys screamed as her mistress was hurled to the ground. The air was pounded from Ellyn's lungs and she lay, stunned, waiting to receive her death blow. She heard the shouts of the Northmen as they grew nearer, and tried to free herself from under her wounded horse writhing in pain on top of her. Then Alys's cries stopped. Borin was silent. Ellyn held her breath and braced herself, waiting to die.

But death never came. Instead there was a yell of pain, followed by a muffled groan. Then Ellyn winced as, only a few yards away, she heard a howl of agony such as she had never heard before, followed by a chorus of shrieks and wails, which lasted only a few moments before they ended with a final roar.

Ellyn became aware of a gentle hand on her head and she heard someone saying, "Are you injured? Can you hear me?" The voice was indistinct and its tone and volume too vague for her to decipher. She blinked several times, trying to clear the ringing sound from her ears, and the dirt from her eyes. She tried to free her legs from underneath her horse's body and turn her body over so that she could see who the speaker was. Slowly, her vision began to clear, and she could tell it was a man, and thought at first that it was her older brother, Ivor. But then she realized that the voice was not his, and belonged to someone she had never seen before.

"I will try to lift the horse slightly and see if you can pull yourself free," he said. She was finally able to turn towards the speaker and, through blurred vision, could barely make out his form, but could not distinguish his features.

Ellyn felt the extreme pressure on her legs slightly lessen, as the horse was lifted. She curled her fingers through the dense grass that lined the path and pulled with what little strength she could muster. Once freed, she sat, stunned, leaning against a tree as she tried to collect her thoughts.

"Are you alright?" the young man asked. At last, Ellyn looked up and was able to see her rescuer kneeling beside her. He was dressed in the simple attire of a peasant and she guessed him to be a few years older than herself. He had dusty blonde hair and his eyes were full of concern as he looked down at her.

"I – I am alright, thank you," Ellyn was finally able to whisper. She tenderly rubbed her scratched arms and felt her sore head. The feeling in her legs was finally returning.

"Good. Wait here and I will examine your friends. Call out if you need me."

Ellyn looked around, surveying the scene. Three warriors lay within only a few yards of her. One had an arrow jutting directly out of his heart and the other was pierced through his temple, the arrow protruding through the other side of his head. The third was lying in a mangled and bloody heap, a filthy sword next to him. Ellyn gasped when she saw Alys lying in the middle of the path, her eyes closed. She could not see Lucan, but heard his muffled sobs nearby and could tell that the young man was speaking gently to him. Then Ellyn turned her head and looked to her left. Leela was lying in a crumpled heap next to Ellyn. She could not see the girl's face, as it was turned away from her, and reached over to rest her hand on Leela's body. Her chest was moving, very slightly, up and down, and Ellyn felt the rhythm of her beating heart. She was still alive, but her little body was so mangled and twisted that Ellyn knew she could not have escaped without serious harm. She looked away, biting her lip. Then the most distressing sight met Ellyn's eyes. Borin had collapsed in the middle of the path with a spear sticking out of his side. His eyes were open but lifeless. The faithful horse's last moments had been devoted to rescuing his mistress, and he had perished in the attempt to reach safety. Tears came to her eyes.

"I'm sorry about your horse." Ellyn started when she realized the young man was standing next to her again. "I can tell he was special to you."

"Poor Borin. He has been my horse since he was a little colt." She took a deep breath to keep the tears from falling. Then, the danger of the situation struck her again, and, forcing herself to be calm, she asked, "How are the others? Is Alys alright? And the little ones?"

"The young woman is fine," he replied. "She sustained no injuries and I believe she fainted from pure fear. The little boy only has a few small scratches from when he slid off the horse. The little girl, however, was much less fortunate. She is still alive, but I am no physician and cannot properly examine her. I can tell that she has several broken bones, and she struck her head when she landed on the ground. She will be in severe pain if she regains consciousness.

We must reach safety and find a physician for her. Come, there may be more danger on the way. Are you able to walk?"

"Yes, thank you. I am feeling better, but still a bit dizzy."

"Then I will help you onto Farthinger and give you the little girl," he said, indicating his horse standing nearby. "I think your maidservant will be able to ride once she awakens, along with the boy. Her horse sustained no injury. Do you think you will be over-exerting yourself?"

"No, I am feeling better already," Ellyn said. She grimaced as a streak of pain shot through her leg in her attempt to stand. The young man helped Ellyn to her feet, and she leaned against the tree for a moment before he helped her into the saddle. Then, with extreme care, he lifted Leela from the ground and handed her to Ellyn. She winced as she saw the little child's face that looked so pale and deathly that she checked her pulse again for reassurance. She was hardly recognizable, covered with bruises and scratches. Blood trickled down a large gash across her temple, but her little chest continued to rise and fall. Ellyn leaned down and softly kissed the little girl's forehead, trying to hold back more tears.

Turning, she saw that Alys had finally begun to revive and was now looking around, dazed and afraid. The rescuer was kneeling at her side and began to help her onto her horse. The maidservant was still trembling and was looking through the trees, as if expecting to see more men appear.

"Here you are, my boy," the man said to Lucan as he helped him in the saddle with Alys.

He cautiously led the two horses down the path carrying the four frightened and scarred victims. Ellyn noticed he was very alert, his hand resting on the hilt of his sword. Whenever he turned to glance at her, she saw that his eyebrows were furrowed together, and his jaw was set firmly.

While the journey to the castle seemed like an eternity, it was less than a quarter of an hour later when they emerged from the woods, wounded and sore. A nervous, unnatural silence surrounded the grounds. The soldiers had already left to meet the Northmen, led by their king and his oldest son. Hardly a bird twittered from the trees and there was not a soul in sight. The young man halted and glanced from the deserted stables and outbuildings to the castle, looking for any sign of inhabitants. They did not have to wait long. From the barn, two stable boys and a servant appeared. The young man began giving orders and the servant helped Alys and Lucan down from the horse, which was led into the stable.

"We can take the children inside for now," Ellyn said. "We have a physician we can send for."

It then occurred to Ellyn that the young man had known exactly where to lead the horses and did not seem in the least bit fazed that the castle was home to Ellyn. She had not introduced herself and had never met him. Did he know who she was? He was only a peasant, and Ellyn had always avoided the villages, and had little to no interactions with anyone who was not royalty. But these thoughts immediately left her as the young man lifted Leela from her lap and began carrying her towards the castle.

"Take this young man's horse to the stable as well," Ellyn ordered the second stable boy as she dismounted.

"Ellyn, my child! What has happened?" Ellyn's worried mother exclaimed as soon as she laid eyes on her daughter. "Who are these people? I was so worried about you!"

"I'm so sorry, Mother!" Ellyn exclaimed. "I will tell you everything later. This little girl needs help. We must send for the physician."

"I fear he may not be able to come with those vile men rampaging the land. But we will send for him nonetheless," Queen Cordelia said. "Oh, my child, you are harmed! Are you in pain?"

She led them from the foyer into a nearby sitting room. Lucan was set on a chair and given a cup of water. He soon had the blood and dirt wiped from his face. The little girl was laid on a couch, where little else could be done except to wait for the arrival of the physician.

"What happened, my dear? You must tell me quickly! It was the Northmen, wasn't it? And who is this?" the Queen asked as servants bustled about, tending to Leela and Lucan.

"Yes, we found these children running from their home for safety and were on our way here when three Northmen intercepted us. This is our rescuer who found us just in time and saved us before they could do any real harm."

The young man bowed his greetings but Queen Cordelia was too flustered to extend the usual formalities of introductions.

"You could have easily been killed!" she exclaimed. "Are you sure you are unharmed? Perhaps you should go rest in your room."

"I'm not hurt, Mother," Ellyn assured her. "But I am so worried about Leela. I want to sit with her until the physician arrives."

Queen Cordelia wrapped her arms around Ellyn. "Both of the children will be well tended to. Go change your clothes and wash your face. Then you can tell me more later on. I will see that the children are properly tended to."

"Yes, Mother," Ellyn said. She opened the door and hurried down the hall and up the winding staircase to her room.

When she entered, Alys had already changed from her soiled dress and was wiping dirt from her face.

"Are you alright, Your Highness?" she asked, hurrying to the door as Ellyn entered.

"Yes, I am perfectly fine. I have no serious injuries and I'm sure I will feel refreshed once I have changed. But I was so worried when I saw you lying senseless on the path. Are you sure you are well?"

"Besides a few scratches and bruises, I am perfectly fine. Now let me change you from your torn riding clothes."

"Those poor children," Ellyn said as Alys helped her into fresh clothes. "I fear for their parents.

The Northmen have been known to inflict serious destruction on villages."

Just as Alys was clearing the dirt and blood from her face and arms, there was a light knock on the door and Regan, Ellyn's fifteen-year-old sister, entered the room.

"Mother told me what happened, Ellyn, and I wanted to see how you are," she said. "I am perfectly alright, Regan. How are Leela and Lucan?"

"The physician has just arrived and is inspecting the little girl. I hope she's alright; she is so young."

"Yes, poor little girl."

The sisters fell to a solemn silence for a moment. Then Regan smiled impishly and said, "What did he look like?"

Ellyn stared at her blankly for a moment, then, trying to conceal a smile, said, "What does it matter? There are more serious things to be concerned with at this time, besides peasant boys. Of course I am eternally grateful to him, but our country is in danger. Besides, I will never see him again. He was merely a peasant who happened to be passing through at the right time. But did you not see him downstairs in the sitting room?"

"No, he has already gone."

"Gone?"

"Yes. Mother assured him that the children would be taken care of and he has left. I think he was concerned that he would be in the way, and probably wanted to see if his family is safe. He must live in the village where the Northmen are attacking. I heard from one of the servants that a very handsome peasant boy had led you here, and I was wishing I had been able to see him."

Ellyn said nothing, but wished she had at least learned the young man's name, or thanked him before he departed.

"Let's go down and see if we can help. Mother will be worrying about Father and Ivor," Ellyn said after a brief silence.

"I wish I could understand these invaders," Regan said as they turned to leave the room. "They have caused so much grief and destruction for so many people for no rational reason."

"Evil people are willing to do more than you could imagine for power and control," Ellyn replied.

Chapter 2 - Battle in the Village

The sound of clanking armor and swords battering against shields reached King Wulfred's ears as he stood in the middle of the battle fray. The king pulled his horse to a halt to survey the scene and several soldiers closed in around him and his son, who was mounted just behind him. They had formed a protective band around their current and future kings. In the middle of the village square, hundreds of men battled feverishly against the Northmen. The fighting had been underway for nearly an hour, and many lives from both sides had already been lost. Bodies of both Eurasians and Northmen were being trampled and the foul stench of death filled the air. Several peasants were fighting alongside the king and his soldiers. They were men from the village who did not want to stand back and watch their homes and families destroyed and took a stand, some armed with only makeshift clubs. Some women brave or frantic enough to come out of hiding stood on the doorstep of their homes, searching for their husbands and fathers, some weeping and screaming.

King Wulfred watched as a young child wandered out of her home past the gaze of her unaware mother. It was only when a horse of one of the Northmen nearly trampled the young girl that her mother realized the child had escaped and swept her into the house, slamming the door shut as if it would somehow erase the chaos beyond it.

"We seem to have arrived just in time, Your Majesty," a messenger rode up next to him and shouted above the noise. "This is a somewhat smaller attack than they have waged in the past and the ships brought only five hundred men or so. The reports I have indicate that none have made it beyond this village and into the countryside."

"Thank you, Dexter."

"Only five hundred?" Ivor asked.

King Wulfred nodded grimly. "I foresee that they are going to surrender soon and retreat, giving us a false sense of confidence in our victory through this small attack, and return with heavier forces. It is unlike the Northmen to wage attacks with such small numbers."

His horse whinnied, eager to return to the battlefield. The king looked up to the sky and saw a swarm of vultures circling overhead.

"Smoke!" one of King Wulfred's bodyguards shouted. A black cloud was rising from one of the wooden structures along the cobblestone road. The king furrowed his brow. "Come, let's put an end to this. Keep together, men."

King Wulfred drew his sword and the band of men pushed forward into the fighting. He heaved his sword up, down, left and right. The sun glared down and reflected off the steel armor and weapons. The king squinted his eyes and sweat dripped down his face as he pushed into the heart of the fighting, trying to break up the unity of the enemy forces. The sun rose past its peak and began its descent towards the horizon. But the men were unaware of the passage of time.

"They are beginning to retreat," a voice yelled to King Wulfred after almost an hour of the intense struggle. The king could barely discern his words above the sound of clanging weapons.

"Very good, press on," he replied. But he had barely uttered these words when a sharp exclamation grabbed his attention.

"Beware!" a bodyguard shouted. King Wulfred snapped his head up to the sight of a band of enemies surging toward him. The remaining band of the Northmen had united and were pressing forward in an attempt to cut down the king. With determination, they pressed into the heart of his men, shouting battle-cries at the top of their lungs.

King Wulfred braced himself and pulled up his shield, wielding his sword with his other hand. A shower of arrows struck the advancing Northmen, pelting against their shields and armor. Some fell. Others pressed on. The next moment, King Wulfred was in the middle of a frantic fight. His shield was the victim of many sword and dagger thrusts. His ears were filled with shouts, many the final cry of death as the Northmen were struck down one by one. All at once, the remaining warriors dispersed and what had moments before been a scene of fighting became one of desperately fleeing Northmen.

"Stand back!" yelled King Wulfred. "Do not pursue them! Hold back, men!"

He watched as the remaining Northmen darted or hobbled away from the village streets and toward the shore from where they had come. The Eurasian soldiers stood panting and wiping sweat and blood from their faces. Finally, the streets were utterly silent. No one spoke as they watched the prows of the enemy ships depart.

"Do not be caught in false confidence, men," King Wulfred said, breaking the silence. "We have killed many of our enemies, but I believe that was what they planned for this attack. The few hundred men we fought today are but a minority of the vast armies these men have come from. They will return, and with more strength than we have witnessed today. But we will not stand by and let them take over our kingdom, and this country. Take heart, and do not lose all hope, but don't celebrate a victory yet. This conflict is not over."

A trumpet was blown, summoning the soldiers back to the castle. King Wulfred turned to his messengers and said, "Assign guards to the coast to ensure they won't return unexpectedly. The council will still be held tonight as planned, but we must call for more to join us than were initially asked to come. Deliver messages to King Vortigern, King Armos and King Evander. Make it clear that this is a very urgent situation and that I request their immediate presence."

The three messengers bowed and departed.

"Your Highness," a voice spoke from behind the king. He turned his head and saw one of his soldiers standing with a young man, covered in blood and dirt. His peasant's clothes were tattered and torn.

"Who is this, Wallis?" the king asked, turning his horse to face them.

"I want to bring this young man to your attention, Your Highness. During the course of the battle, he joined our ranks and fought alongside us. He has just told me he was on his way to the castle for tonight's council when the Northmen attacked."

"Forgive me, but I do not recognize you as one of the kings I asked to come to the council tonight. Which kingdom have you travelled from? Are you in disguise in these peasant's clothes?" King Wulfred had climbed down from his horse and approached the young man, who was on foot. The young man bowed as he approached and straightened his shoulders.

"My name is Prince Julius of Veridell, many leagues to the northwest of here. I was on my way to your castle for tonight's council when the Northmen attacked. You are correct, it was my father, King Rowan of Veridell, to whom you sent a message bidding him to come to the council tonight. However, he fell ill today and could not come himself and sent me to attend in his stead. Because the threat of Northmen is well known to be a danger in your kingdom and ready to target especially those who bear any mark of royalty, he advised I dress as a peasant for more of a chance that I would be spared if I encountered any on my way."

The king nodded. "It is true the Northmen have been known to seek out the rulers of kingdoms along this shore in an attempt to take their lives and their place as ruler over the land. However, now it is not only royal families who are being targeted, but peasants and common folk as well. I am not sure your disguise would have done anything to save you in such an encounter, but I understand King Rowan's reasoning. I would like to extend my gratitude for your help today, and you're coming for the council in your father's place. I hope seeing and experiencing this firsthand will give you more of an understanding and willingness to convince your father that we are in need of help from whomever and wherever it comes. Follow us to the castle; the council will begin as soon as everyone has arrived."

Julius bowed and sheathed his sword.

Ellyn stood at the window of the sitting room, looking for any sign of a messenger bringing word from the battlefield. It had been hours since the soldiers had left to fight the Northmen and no news had reached them yet.

"I want my Mama," a small voice said behind her. "I want my Mama and Papa. I am scared that I will never see them again."

Ellyn turned from the window and sat on the couch next to Leela. The girl had revived after the physician had set and bandaged her broken bones. He had given her a hopeful prognosis, but she still did not have the stamina to even sit up on her own.

"We have already sent someone to look for them," Ellyn said, gently squeezing Leela's uninjured arm. Lucan sat silently in a chair nearby where he had barely uttered a sound since they arrived.

The door opened and Ellyn's youngest sister Gwendolyn entered the room. "How is Leela, Ellyn? Is she going to be alright?" She peered over Ellyn's shoulder at the little girl. Although her head was bandaged and her face was covered with scratches, Leela managed a weak smile.

"Do you think I can be friends with her, Ellyn?" Gwendolyn asked.

"I don't know, Gwennie; she is going back to her family when we find them. But you can certainly be her friend while she is here."

Following a knock at the door, a servant entered and said, "Princess Ellyn, I have been sent to inform you that your father and brother have just arrived from the battlefield."

"Where are they?" she asked, quickly rising from the couch. "They will be joining your mother in the drawing room soon."

Ellyn turned to her sister and said, "I'm going to find Mother, Gwennie. You can stay here and keep Leela company if you'd like."

Ellyn went to the drawing room where she found her mother wringing her hands anxiously. "Have you heard any news other than that Father and Ivor are on their way here?" Ellyn asked as she entered.

Queen Cordelia shook her head. "No, and I worry that the outcome will not be as he hoped.

He has been so worried because the Northmen have been growing in strength."

"Why won't the kings of nearby kingdoms simply make an alliance, as he has proposed? It seems to be an easy solution to our problem."

"I don't understand everything," she sighed. "But we are a larger kingdom than those we would be allied with, so they probably do not want to be at the mercy of another king. There is a very individualistic mindset in this country where kingdoms are very unlikely to put their own people and armies at risk to help another. The kingdoms of Eurasia have been self-reliant for generations and don't see the reason to live otherwise. But, for the sake of many lives, we can only hope they agree to take risks and change their ways."

At that moment, there was a knock at the door, and a servant announced the entrance of the king. He strode into the room, Ivor following just behind.

"Is all well?" Queen Cordelia asked.

"No, far from it. Their forces today were small and we easily conquered them, but this is only a small skirmish compared to what I believe is to come. I am beginning to fear for the future of our kingdom."

Ellyn looked at Ivor. He was standing with his arms crossed, listening to King Wulfred with a furrowed brow. It was strange to see his usual boyish grin replaced with the weight of responsibility to protect the kingdom he would one day rule.

"I have summoned kings of all the surrounding kingdoms for tonight's council and they will be arriving soon," King Wulfred continued. "It is urgent that we meet as soon as possible. Unless we can agree to combine our forces and fight the invaders together, they will outnumber us and conquer this land. It will be no easy task to unite them, though. King Evander of Lyntirith has been particularly against joining forces as he has no interest in protecting any kingdom but his own. He and I have never had diplomatic relations, as you know."

"How much destruction did the Northman bring to our villages?" Ellyn asked.

"Many lives were lost. When we arrived, dozens of inhabitants had been slain and it took the combined forces of all of my men to subdue them. This is not the last we will see of them, and I worry that we will not have enough strength and help of others to conquer them next time."

"Will we need to arrange accommodations for the kings to stay overnight, or will they be here for merely a day?" Queen Cordelia asked.

"They will likely stay until tomorrow. The council is sure to be lengthy, and it will probably be very late when we conclude. We may even need to assemble again tomorrow morning."

"I will go and speak to some of the servants about preparations," the queen said, rising.

Ellyn left the drawing room and went out to the garden to clear her mind. She sat down on a bench and put her head in her hands. Usually she was eager for the future and ready to take on any challenge, but for the first time she wished time would stop so she could avoid whatever problems lay ahead.

Chapter 3 - The Kings' Council

"Your Highness."

Ellyn stood up from the garden bench as Alys approached. "What is it?"

"There is a man in the drawing room. The council has almost begun and your mother isn't able to take time away from her preparations and requested you greet him instead."

"Do you know who he is?"

"Yes, he says he is Leela and Lucan's father. Queen Cordelia thought you would want to see the children off."

"Yes, I would."

Entering the drawing room, Ellyn found a man pacing and wringing his hands as he waited. She knew immediately that he was the father of Leela and Lucan, with dark features that resembled the two children she had helped earlier that day. When he saw Ellyn, he bowed. "Your Highness," he said respectfully.

"You have come for your children, I presume," said Ellyn.

He nodded. "Yes; Leela and Lucan. Our home is close to the shoreline and I didn't want them around if those men came anywhere near us."

Ellyn nodded to a servant in the doorway, who stepped from the room.

"I am sorry for all your family has been through and hope the rest of your family is safe. My father is doing all in his power to protect Eurasia and I pray the Northmen will be defeated soon," Ellyn said.

"So do I."

Before another word was spoken, the door opened.

"Papa!" Lucan ran to his father, who knelt and caught his son in a tight embrace. The man clung to his child and Ellyn thought saw his weary eyes glistening with tears. The servant approached carrying Leela, who reached for her father and was soon wrapped protectively in his arms.

Ellyn smiled as she watched the reunion between the small family.

"We'll be going now, Your Highness," the father said with Leela in one arm and Lucan in the other.

Ellyn nodded. "Take care of Leela. She has already seen a physician, and he said she has no serious injuries, but she should be treated with care for a few weeks. He said to leave the bandages on her arms for four weeks."

Ellyn watched from the window as Leela and Lucan left in their father's arms. She felt overwhelmed from the many emotions she had experienced that day and her eyes began to fill with tears. She heard movement from the doorway and turned around to see Ivor leaning against the frame. He walked toward her and rested a hand on her shoulder. "I know how you feel."

"I feel a lot of things. Anger, fear, dread of what's to come."

Ivor nodded. "It's too early to lose hope. Father will never rest until he knows his family and kingdom are safe. Surrendering is not an option for him."

Ellyn sighed and wiped her eyes. "Hasn't the council started already?"

"Not yet. I came to ask you about someone I just spoke to who came to attend it. His name is Prince Julius from Veridell. He said he met you in an unusual situation but didn't give any details. I've never heard the name and wonder if you remember him."

"Prince Julius? No, that doesn't sound familiar, but perhaps I'd recognize him if I saw him. Is there time before the council starts?"

"I think so. Follow me."

Ivor and Ellyn walked down hallways and corridors that led to the opposite side of the castle where the visitors of the kingdom stayed on overnight visits. Reaching the end of a hall, Ivor knocked on a door and it was opened by a servant.

"Is Prince Julius still here?" Ivor asked.

"Yes, Your Highness." the servant said, stepping aside. A tall young man appeared in the doorway.

"Prince Julius, my sister Princess Ellyn. Ellyn, this is Prince Julius," Ivor said.

Ellyn curtsied and, when her eyes met his, she was struck with a strange feeling of recognition. He bowed and said, "Hello, Princess Ellyn."

"It's you!" she exclaimed, forgetting to return the greeting. "We did meet, Ivor, earlier today. Aren't you the peasant from this morning? I didn't think I'd see you again and be able to thank you. But I don't understand. You look so… different."

He laughed. "I wondered if you would recognize me."

"What are you talking about?" Ivor asked.

"He's the one who saved us today," Ellyn said. "If it weren't for Prince Julius I would not be standing here. But I don't understand; were you in disguise?"

"Yes, I've explained the whole situation to your father. I would be happy to tell you as well, but I'm not sure I have time at the moment."

"You're right, the council should be starting now," Ivor said.

"Do you think we could meet later this evening? I'm intrigued," Ellyn said.

"As long as it is not too late when the council ends, come and find us in the visitor's parlor," Ivor said. Then the two young men turned and went down the hall.

Ellyn knew her younger sister would be interested to hear this development and went upstairs to her sister's room.

"Regan, listen to what just happened, you won't believe it!" she said entering her sister's room. Regan rose from her dressing table. "Good news is just what I need."

"I just spoke with the young man who came to my rescue earlier today! Apparently he is a prince here for the council but I don't understand why he was dressed as a peasant earlier today. I may be able to meet with him later so he can tell his story. Ivor said he is from Veridell; do you know where that is? I think I have heard of it, but I do not know how far away they are from us."

"No, I have never heard of Veridell. But this is so perfect!" Regan exclaimed. "You will be able to thank him. You must remember to tell Father and Mother; they will want to thank him, too."

"I'm not sure I'll tell Father yet; he has much more important issues occupying him right now.

But Mother will want to know and thank him."

"Now that you know he's a prince, have you changed your opinions on marriage?"

"No, I really don't think I will ever meet someone I will want to marry; all the princes I have met are snobbish and pretentious. They only pay attention to me because of my position or my looks, or perhaps for something else. If that were true, I would have no reason to love them in return and such a marriage would end unhappily, because it must be built on more than good looks. I want to stay and live with our parents here in the castle until the end of my days and not have to worry about marriage. I know it is expected of me to marry, but I would much rather live on as I am now."

"Not all princes are snobbish and pretentious; not Julius!" Ellyn rolled her eyes.

"Well, perhaps you'll change your mind someday. Anyway, if there is ever a prince interested whom you do not care for, you can send him to me. I may not be a sorry substitute."

Ellyn laughed. "You will make some prince very happy someday, Regan."

"I wondered if you would still be awake and come to join us," Ivor said as Ellyn entered the drawing room where he was sitting and speaking with Julius. They both stood as she approached them.

"Did the council just now finish?" Ellyn asked, taking the seat Ivor offered her on the couch.

She glanced at Julius sitting across from them and their eyes met briefly.

"Yes, it was dismissed for the night," Ivor replied. "Nothing has been resolved and we'll reconvene tomorrow. But enough about the council for now," Ivor said, turning to Julius. "I know Ellyn has been waiting to hear the story you have to tell."

"It really isn't a long or interesting story. I am from Veridell," Julius said. "You may or may not be familiar with my kingdom, as it is very far from here and we have no connection with yours that I know of. Your father asked mine to come to the council, but he fell ill today and sent me since he couldn't come himself. We had heard rumors in our kingdom that it was only members of royal families that the Northmen were attacking in their attempts to seize land and overthrow as many kingdoms as possible. My father wanted me to wear peasants' clothing for my safety in case I encountered any on the way. I thought he was being overly protective as usual and that the rumors we heard of the Northmen were exaggerated. I had no idea that I would find myself in the middle of the battle against them as soon as I arrived. It was only good fortune that I found you and your servant at just the right time today and was able to help."

"Your timing was providential; we were so close to losing our lives today," Ellyn said. "Did you know who I was when you found us? You seemed to know the way to the castle."

"I guessed by your attire that you were the daughter of a king and knew I was approaching the castle. I could hear the soldiers departing to fight the Northmen so I continued in the direction you were going when I found you. I'd decided to leave Veridell early this morning because it's a long journey and wanted to be sure I wasn't late to the council and I'm thankful I did."

"How was the council? Have you almost reached an agreement with any of the other rulers?" Ellyn asked.

"It isn't easy uniting people who have been living separately for so long," Ivor replied. "They believe they have nothing to gain by helping us, but Father has been arguing against this idea, insisting that if the Northmen are victorious against Eurasia, they will only move onto other nearby kingdoms, jeopardizing their families and people once they have defeated ours."

"That seems sensible to me; what is keeping them from changing their minds?"

"I think Father has persuaded some to his side, but they are all rulers of smaller kingdoms who would have more to lose if the Northmen did target their kingdoms. He wants to convince everyone to sign an agreement that would only be in effect until the Northmen are defeated. It is of course the rulers with larger kingdoms and armies who would probably be able to protect their own in an attack by the Northmen without help from others. King Evander from Lyntirith is the one Father is most hoping to convince because his army is several times as large as ours and, if he joined the agreement to help, the conflict would likely be shortened and the Northmen easily conquered."

"King Evander is not someone who easily agrees to be involved in the affairs of other kingdoms no matter how grave the danger is," Prince Julius added. "He really is only concerned with his own kingdom, which is large and powerful enough for him to protect with his own army."

"It's a shame he doesn't have the sympathy for the lives of other humans to do something as simple as fight off foreign invaders," Ellyn said. "It's not as if we are another species; we're not even from a different country. You would think King Evander considers us enemies that he wouldn't mind seeing defeated. Do you think he wants the Northmen to defeat us so he can take Eurasia from them?"

"I've thought of that, but I doubt it," Ivor said. "He's never been interested in taking more land for himself and I think, if he wanted to do so, he would be able to achieve that goal on his own. I think he just wants to protect his own people and soldiers, and doesn't want to endanger them regardless of the harm it could put others in."

"Do you think Father has a chance of convincing him?"

"He hasn't given up yet, and you know how persuasive and determined Father is. I'm confident he and King Evander will agree to terms of some sort before this council ends. He's not giving up without a fight."

Chapter 4 - Attack on the Castle

"What is that noise?" Ellyn looked up at Alys from the book she was reading. "I hear it too."

A voice was shouting something indistinguishable from outside with a sense of urgency. Ellyn went to the window and peered out. The sun was setting and the dusky lighting prevented her from seeing clearly, but she saw nothing unusual. Her bedroom window looked south over the castle grounds and rolling hills beyond the castle wall.

Only a day after the Northmen had attacked Eurasia, the kingdom had been tense and alert, waiting for another attack that they expected would come. Many families had packed their belongings and left their homes to travel inland to the other end of the kingdom away from the vulnerability of living near the shore. King Wulfred's council had concluded and the attendants were staying the night to rest before making the journey home in the morning. He had convinced three of the six kings to join their forces with his to fight the Northmen, increasing the Eurasians' numbers and chances of putting an end to the attacks. King Wulfred had still not convinced King Evander of Lyntirith to send soldiers to fight. King Wulfred knew Lyntirith's army with its size and skill on the battlefield would crush the Northmen. King Evander had agreed to meet King Wulfred in a private meeting in the following days, and King Wulfred was still determined to negotiate and convince the king to join the fight against the Northmen.

"Now it sounds as if there are two voices shouting," Alys said, joining Ellyn at the window. "Yes, but I still can't understand what they're saying."

Before she could say more, there was a frantic knock at the door. Alys opened it to a servant who looked past her at Ellyn and said, "Your Highness, you need to leave. We are being attacked."

"Right now? Where are my mother and sisters?"

"To the underground safe rooms, come with me."

Ellyn followed the servant, walking quickly down the hall and to the main staircase. "Are they coming here?"

"This is precautionary. They are attacking with more soldiers than yesterday, and King Wulfred wants his family safe before just in case they come this far inland."

Queen Cordelia met Ellyn when she reached the bottom of the staircase and placed a hand on her daughter's shoulder.

"Ellyn, I don't know where Gwennie is."

"What do you mean? She has to be inside somewhere."

"I hope so. I thought she was in her room, but her nursemaid said she came to find me over half an hour ago but I never saw her. I'm afraid she may have gone out to the stables to look for me; I was there earlier. I don't know why I wasn't more careful."

"I want to go and find her."

"No, Ellyn, it's too dangerous. We will ask one of the guards to search for her."

"I can't sit downstairs waiting around doing nothing while Gwennie is missing. I'll be back soon, I promise."

Before Queen Cordelia could respond, Ellyn turned and ran down the hall.

The whole castle seemed to be in hiding as Ellyn flitted through hallway after hallway, not meeting one person. All the while, she heard the sounds of intense fighting just outside the castle and wondered what her father and brother were doing at that moment.

Ellyn had almost reached the exit door to the courtyard when she heard several voices. She slowed her steps and tried to slow her breathing. She heard the sound of a sword being sheathed and she halted in the hallway, just around the corner.

"Yes, I am sure I want to go out and fight," a voice was saying. "Yes, I understand I will be in great danger, but I cannot sit inside and wait while a force of vile, unjust enemies tries to tear apart the lives of an innocent people. I cannot stand it. I must go out and help."

"The king ordered me not to let you go," another voice insisted. "He said you have a duty to your own country."

"Julius, is that you?" Ellyn stepped around the corner. The prince of Veridell was standing in front of the door, which was being barred by a desperate-looking guard.

"Ellyn, why are you here?" Julius asked, turning to face her, a look of puzzlement on his face. "Listen, it's very urgent. My sister is in danger."

"If your sister is in danger, I will send someone to find her," the guard said. "Tell me quickly where she is."

"No, please let me go," Ellyn begged. "I can't stay waiting inside, wondering if she is safe when I could be helping. Let me go out."

"Your highness, you don't seem to understand. The Northmen are attacking."

"I know they are," Ellyn said. "I must go to my sister. I can't stand staying inside. It is too overwhelming. I must go find Gwennie."

"Ellyn, don't you think you should go downstairs again? You are the princess of Eurasia after all," Julius said.

"I know who I am," said Ellyn indignantly. "And I know you understand how I feel. I can't sit around, in the safety of the castle, when my little sister is in danger. I have to find her. Please!"

"Where is she?" Julius asked quickly.

"Mother thinks she may have gone to the stables. Please, we have to go to her."

"I will go," the guard said firmly. "There is a battle taking place outside. Both of you seem either too immature or rash to understand the severity of this situation. I cannot risk putting your lives in danger."

A wave of adrenaline rushed through Ellyn's body, and it was suddenly as if she was not in control of her actions. She ran past Julius and pushed the guard aside, throwing the door open. At first, the guard was frozen in surprise, and stood in a state of disbelief as Ellyn dashed out the door past him. Without hesitating, Julius ran after her, and the guard was left in the rear, running after the two youths.

The courtyard was silent and empty, and darkness had now taken over. The moon was high and bright, and Ellyn darted under the white light across to the other side of the courtyard.

"What are you thinking?" Julius demanded, catching up with her.

"I don't know," Ellyn said, realizing tears were streaming down her face. "I don't know, but I need to find Gwennie. I would go mad if I had to stay inside, wondering if several members of my family are still alive. I have to do something."

The shouts of the guard were growing more and more faint and Ellyn and Julius ran out of the courtyard, and he watched them disappear with fear plastered on his face.

"Alright, wait," Julius said, pulling Ellyn to a stop as soon as they had left the courtyard. "We can't just run into this without thinking.

Tell me where the stables are and we'll get there the safest way possible."

"It's on the east side of the castle and we are on the south side right now. After we go around this corner, it will be just beyond the line of trees," Ellyn said breathlessly.

"Alright, stay right behind me and stay in the shadows," Julius said. As they got closer, the sounds from the battle grew louder, and Julius slowed his steps. Ellyn walked on her toes, trying to see over his shoulders. When they got near the end of the palace wall, Julius raised a hand for Ellyn to wait, then advanced, peering around the corner. Ellyn waited anxiously, waiting for him to make another move. Finally he turned around and motioned her forward. She gasped at the sight that met her eyes. It was a battle taking place right in the front of her castle. It was not close enough for her to see the details of what was taking place clearly, but the sight of it made her cringe.

"The moon is behind the clouds right now. If we run, I don't think we will be seen," Julius muttered.

"Let's go then," Ellyn said, darting around the corner. Without thinking of the danger she was in, she darted from behind the wall and ran as fast as she could into the concealing trees. Once past the line of trees, she ran across a small path and reached the stables.

"Let me go in first," Julius said urgently. Ellyn stopped and waited while he cautiously opened the side door and looked inside. It was dark and Ellyn could not see inside. She watched as he slipped inside and disappeared into the darkness. Ellyn looked around, then slipped in after him.

The darkness shrouded every possibility of seeing anything, and Ellyn strained for the sound of Julius's voice or footsteps. She took small, quiet steps across the stone floor, holding her breath, alert for any movement around her.

"Are you there?" Julius's voice startled Ellyn, as she realized he was standing right next to her.

She reached out and grabbed his arm. "Yes, is it safe?"

"I think so. So are you sure Gwendolyn is here?"

"I think so." Ellyn felt around until her hand reached the stable doors. The only sound that reached her ears was the horses in their stalls, neighing softly and breathing deeply, sensing things were not as they should be. At last, she reached the end of the line of stalls.

"Are you here, Gwennie?" she said in a loud whisper. Silence. A horse neighed in a nearby stall, causing Ellyn to start. A feeling of dread began to rush over her. "Gwennie, please answer if you can hear me."

There was a small shuffling. Ellyn's grip around Julius's arm tightened and she felt his muscles tense.

"Ellyn?" a small voice squeaked, sounding nearby, but very muffled.

"Yes, it's me, Gwennie, where are you? Come out; it's alright," Ellyn said, sighing with relief.

There was a shuffling nearby and small footsteps approached Ellyn and Julius.

"Gwennie, there you are," Ellyn said, enfolding her sister tightly in her arms. "It's alright."

"I was afraid," Gwendolyn said, her voice shaking.

"I know," Ellyn said, holding her sister tightly. "We need to go inside now where it's safe."

But a loud crash broke her words. Moonlight flooded through the door as it was pushed open, and a shadow filled the doorway. Ellyn gasped and Julius grabbed her and Gwendolyn and opened a stall door, pushing both of them inside as he followed close behind. He pushed them to the ground and closed the door, standing behind it with his hand on the hilt of his sword. Ellyn squeezed Gwendolyn in her arms, shaking with terror.

"Are we going to die?" Gwendolyn whispered into Ellyn's ear, her voice trembling in fear. "Hush, don't make any noise," Ellyn murmured in her ear, leaning close to her. She was trying to remain calm in order to keep her sister at ease, but her hands were shaking uncontrollably and she bit her lip, trying to keep from screaming. Glancing up at Julius's face, she was barely able to make out his features in the dim light. His jaw was clenched, and his tense features were frozen into an intense expression as he peered through the wooden frames of the stable door. Ellyn heard slow, steady footsteps walking towards them across the hard floor. She winced as each step brought the potential enemy closer to their hiding place. Her whole body began to shake involuntarily, and she held Gwendolyn tighter, squeezing her eyes shut.

"Why did I do this?" she thought restlessly. "Why didn't I stay in the safety of the castle? Poor Mother must be so worried. If only I had thought first. I am to be fully blamed for this whole ordeal." She bit her lip and her heart lurched as the footsteps stopped and the silence throbbed in her ears.

It did not last long, though. The frighteningly still air was soon interrupted by the sound of more voices echoing from beyond the stables. She began to smell the distinct aroma of smoke filtering through the walls of the barn and she buried her face in her arm, trying not to cough.

"We need to escape while we can," she thought frantically. Visions of the building burning down around them filled her mind and she cringed at the thought.

A sudden movement caused Ellyn to start, and her head whirled towards Julius. With one powerful move, he threw open the stable door and unsheathed his sword. The stable door slammed open against the wall and the horse inside screamed in surprise. Ellyn heard an exclamation of surprise and Julius shouted, "The back entrance!"

She was so startled that, for a moment, she could not move. Fear had taken hold of her, and made her unable to speak or move. But the sound of a sword crashing against a metal shield brought her back to her senses and she scrambled up, pulling Gwendolyn to her feet. Ellyn did not even take the time to turn her head toward the sounds of an intense struggle taking place only a few strides away. She pulled Gwendolyn out towards the back entrance, and through the door into the dark night. As she stumbled into the chill air, the sounds from the battle rang clearly over the grounds, and Ellyn almost expected to find herself in the middle of the fighting. The sounds of thundering hooves, men yelling and arrows twanging off the bow strings caused the ground under her feet to tremble and shake. Ellyn pulled Gwendolyn beyond into the first few rows of trees situated just beyond the stable walls until they were concealed by the thick, leafy branches.

"I want Mother," Gwendolyn whispered, looking at Ellyn with a tear-streaked face when they finally slowed their steps. Ellyn was scrutinizing their surroundings, looking for any possible signs of danger.

"So do I," Ellyn said in a low voice. "But we'll have to be careful going back to the castle so that we aren't seen." She peered through the trees and could barely see the door of the stables from which they had escaped, looking for any signs of movement. Where was Julius?

"Can we go now?" Gwendolyn begged, bouncing nervously on her toes. "It's getting cold and I don't want to be outside any longer. I'm afraid."

Ellyn took a deep breath and squared her shoulders. "Follow right behind me," she instructed. "And tell me if you see anything unusual. We're going to go around to the back of the castle, staying concealed in the trees, and if no one is in sight, we should be able to run across to the south side and enter there. But we'll have to hurry and stay under the shadows. Hurry, now."

The two girls hurried through the trees, doing their best to avoid colliding into anything or tripping over roots or brambles in the dark. The shouts of the men grew quieter and Ellyn's hopes began to rise as the distance from the tumult grew. She began to wonder how Julius was faring, and if he had safely managed to overcome his opponent.

"I have put Julius in so much danger," Ellyn thought dejectedly. "It would mean calamity to his country if he were to suffer harm, and I may have been the cause of a great tragedy." Ellyn shuddered and pressed on through the trees determinedly.

When they had run along the edge of the trees until they had reached the back of the castle, Ellyn cautiously advanced past the line of trees and scanned her eyes left and right for several minutes. Smoke was rising from behind the castle, forming a black cloud that blocked the light of the moon. Even though shouts were echoing through the air, not a soul was in sight, and Ellyn took a deep breath, clasping Gwendolyn's hand tightly. Then both girls streaked across the grass and all the way up to the castle entrance.

"Who's there?" A sharp voice caused Ellyn to stop in her tracks. She took a step back and looked up with alarm. One of the guards was standing menacingly next to the castle entrance holding his spear tightly at the ready.

"It's Princess Ellyn with my younger sister," Ellyn replied, her voice shaking as she tried to catch her breath from the desperate run. She stepped forward and the guard stared at her with disbelief.

"So it is," he said breathlessly. "Come inside and I will bring you to safety. Make haste. We are in great danger here."

Ellyn followed the guard back inside and all the way to the steps leading downward where her family was waiting. As she walked down the steep steps, led by the light of the torch in the guard's hand, the strain of all that had taken hold of her over the last hour suddenly came pouring down over her like a torrent. She began struggling to hold back her tears and her legs started to feel weak as the gravity of the situation finally began to sink in.

"Ellyn!" Queen Cordelia exclaimed passionately when her daughter entered the back room where her family was still waiting. She stood up from the chair in which she had been sitting and took a step forward, staring at Ellyn in disbelief.

"I'm sorry, Mother!" Ellyn declared, covering her mouth with her hand, trying to contain her tears. The expression of fear and displeasure on her mother's face made her feel miserable, and she took deep breaths, trying to control herself. Gwendolyn ran to her mother, who knelt and wrapped the trembling girl in her arms.

"How could you have been so foolish?" her mother asked, comforting Gwendolyn. "One of the guards should have gone out to find Gwennie. It is much too dangerous for you."

"I know now, I'm sorry," Ellyn sighed, sitting in a chair next to Regan and pulling her knees up, resting her chin on her knees.

"What is it like out there, Ellyn?" Regan whispered fearfully.

"It's horrible," Ellyn said grimly. "I didn't really see anything, but the castle grounds are teeming with enemies. I think they are really trying to overrun the kingdom this time. When Julius and I…" Suddenly she stopped. She thought back to when she had left Julius fighting against the armed figure in the dark stable. Where was he now? She shuddered and squeezed her eyes shut.

"I wish this was just a horrible dream," she said to Regan.

"I think it is a horrible dream," her sister replied. "But we are unable to wake up from it."

Hours passed, each moment spent in dreaded silence, hoping for, yet fearing the sound of footsteps in the passage, bringing news from the battlefield. Gwendolyn fell asleep on her mother's lap, but even though the night progressed into the early hours of the morning, none of the others could find enough comfort, in either mind or body, to relax enough to fall asleep.

Ellyn spent those long, dragging hours disparaging and reproaching herself for her rash act that could very well have cost her a great deal of pain. She thought over those moments in the stable over and over, so that it was almost as if she had been taken back a few hours and was reliving the frightening moments again. And the whole time, she was wondering what the outcome of the struggle in the barn had been. Had Julius escaped?

Ellyn's eyes began to sting and grow heavy, but the cold, hard floor provided no comfort. Every minute seemed like an eternity, and all she could do was wait and think.

At last, footsteps echoed through the passageway. Ellyn looked up and held her breath, staring at the closed door. A key rattled in the lock of the door, fastened from the inside. A guard opened the door and said, "The danger has passed, and King Wulfred is waiting in the drawing room."

Queen Cordelia breathed a sigh of relief and stood, holding Gwendolyn asleep in her arms. Ellyn stood and groaned, every muscle in her body complaining. She stretched and rubbed her sore eyes. Though her muscles were throbbing, her suspense to see how her father and brother had fared took precedence over her exhaustion.

When she reached the top of the stairs and stepped into the hallway, she saw sunlight streaming through the windows. It was morning. She looked at Regan in astonishment. Her sister's hair was hanging in strings down her back and her dark eyes were half-closed.

"Cordelia!" King Wulfred's voice echoed through the hallway and Ellyn's heart leaped with joy. Her mother was soon wrapped in his arms, leaning her head against his shoulder. The king was covered in dirt and grime, and his face was grey with weariness. He looked sorrowful, and Ellyn looked around, searching for her brother.

"Father, where is Ivor?" she asked quickly.

"Ivor is safe. He did suffer some injuries and is being treated, but he is safe," he replied slowly.

Ellyn wanted to ask about Julius, but her father's countenance was so downcast that she did not want to press him with another question. So she gave her father a tight embrace and trudged wearily upstairs to her room to wash her face and relax after the night's events.

Alys was already in her room, filling a basin with water. She looked up as Ellyn entered her room and closed the door dejectedly.

"Oh, Ellyn, you look exhausted; how awful the night must have been," Alys said with sympathy. Ellyn nodded slightly and sat down, exhaling and closing her eyes while Alys undid her hair and began washing her face. The cool water refreshed her and felt soothing against her soreness. Her muscles finally began to relax and the tension in her body began to ease.

"I suppose you will want to sleep for a while?" Alys asked.

"I think I will collapse if I don't," Ellyn replied. "But I want to see Ivor first and be sure that he is unharmed. And also, I have not heard any news about Julius. I want to see if he is safe."

"Prince Julius was fighting?" Alys asked in disbelief. "I thought he would be taking safety somewhere, considering his circumstances."

"So did I," Ellyn responded, not wanting to engage in the details from the night before. "Do you want me to find out for you so that you can rest?" Alys asked.

Ellyn thought for a moment, then said, "If you could find out where they are, that would be helpful, but I still hope to talk to them before I sleep. I don't think I could rest before I see them."

"Very well, then," Alys said.

Once Ellyn was alone in her room, she stood up from the chair in front of her dresser and walked slowly to the window. It was a beautiful morning. Rays of sunlight streamed from the sky, causing the wet grass to sparkle. The trees looked lush and fresh, and Ellyn could hear birds singing from her closed window. But the new, fresh morning did little to calm Ellyn's spirits. Visions and sounds from the night before continued to flash through her mind.

"How can there be beauty and life in the world when there is also so much despair and hopelessness?" Ellyn murmured to herself. She sighed and leaned against the window frame, resting her head against the wall. Every part of her body was begging for her to lie down and rest, but her mind urged her to stay awake until she could find out whether or not Julius was safe.

At last, Alys returned. "Your brother is in the sitting room down the hall with the physician," she told Ellyn. "I did not see, nor ask about Prince Julius, but perhaps your brother will know."

"Thank you, Alys," Ellyn said. "I'll be back soon."

She left her room and trudged down the hall to the room Alys had directed her to. She heard voices inside the room and paused before she knocked on the door. A servant opened it and let her inside.

Ivor was sitting on a couch, leaning his head against the back of the couch and staring at the ceiling. The physician was standing over him, wrapping his arm in a thick cloth. Ellyn saw bloodstained linens nearby and approached her brother nervously.

"I'm alright, Ellyn," Ivor said wearily, lifting his head and looking into his sister's face. "Only a few injuries. It could have been much worse."

"Was it really that bad?" Ellyn asked.

He nodded. "Very bad. The only reason they were not able to overcome us was because a violent storm struck in the middle of the battle, and the rain was so blinding that we could barely see one another, and hardly knew if we were fighting friend or foe. Then the hail came, so large that it struck down several men. The Northmen left, but I know it will not be for long. They know they have the strength to overcome us and they will, unless we do something to strengthen our forces. It is our only option."

Ellyn shuddered. She watched in silence as the physician finished his work, then left the room to see to other injured victims.

"Ivor." Ellyn sat beside him once he had left. "Did you see Julius? Is he alright?"

"What do you mean?" Ivor asked. "Father ordered him not to join the battle last night."

"Yes, I know," Ellyn said, her hope beginning to dwindle. "But something happened last night. I, well, I made a mistake and I think I might have caused Julius harm." She paused as she felt her shoulders sinking under the weight of her guilt.

"What are you talking about, Ellyn?"

Ellyn opened her mouth to speak, but there was a knock at the door. A servant opened it and Prince Julius entered the room.

"Julius!" Ellyn gasped and stood up, tears filling her eyes. "I was afraid that…"

"Yes, I know," Julius said calmly. He walked expressionlessly across the room and sat down across from Ivor, leaning back in the chair. Ellyn noticed streaks of dried blood on his arm and his left eye was a frightening shade of black.

"Julius, I apologize for the situation I placed you in last night," Ellyn said, her voice shaking. "I wasn't thinking, I…"

"You're sorry?" Julius asked, looking up earnestly. "No, you shouldn't be. I thought you would be bitter toward me because of my impetuousness. I was to blame; it was not your doing. I am the one who needs to apologize."

"But…"

Julius held up his hand to stop her. "It was thoughtless of me to allow you to be in such danger last night, Ellyn," he insisted. "It was wrong of me. I should have thought first."

"I should have as well," Ellyn replied. Then their eyes met and Ellyn saw his expression soften. She had the sudden urge to run and throw her arms around him, but then turned and saw her brother, staring from one to the other with bewilderment.

"I'll let you tell the tale if you wish," Ellyn said. "I am so exhausted; I need to go rest now. I'm glad both of you are safe and well."

Ellyn stepped out into the fresh afternoon air. After several hours of sleep, she felt more refreshed and revived. Scanning the castle grounds as she stepped out, Ellyn noticed guards standing at every corner, keeping a keen watch in every direction. Soldiers were standing up on the castle wall which encircled the castle and the heavy wooden door was fastened shut.

"How did they get past the wall last night?" Ellyn asked, turning to Alys who had accompanied her outside.

"I heard that only a percentage of them got past the wall by floating through the water in the moat, and they were easily overcome. But most of the battle took place outside the castle wall."

Ellyn scanned the scene that met her eyes with amazement. "This was where only a percentage of the fighting took place? It looks like an entire war was fought here."

On the east side of the castle, the grass had been trampled underfoot so that the ground was entirely covered with mud, which showed the aftermath of the battle. Horse hooves and footsteps were imprinted in the mire. One of the outbuildings that was located only a few hundred meters from the castle had been partially burnt, and the ground around it was black and lifeless. The trees that had been full and green the day before were now withered, and the bark was grazed with deep spear marks. The bushes and flowers that had been planted along the castle wall were now broken and trampled. Ellyn took slow, dejected steps along the stones that led from the cobblestone path in front of the grand castle. She knelt and picked up a flower, which was flat and torn at the edges. Most of its petals had fallen off.

"This is how I feel right now," Ellyn said, turning to Alys. Her servant smiled grimly and took the flower.

"Maybe it is, but the flower came from a small seed that was nurtured into a small bud and into the beautiful flower it once was. But even though it's wilted and harmed, it's not dead." Then Alys reached between the petals of the flower and pulled out a small seed. "See?" she said. "Another beautiful flower, new and beautiful, can still sprout from this one, even though it is wilted and dying." Ellyn watched as Alys knelt and pressed the seed into the earth, and covered it with dirt.

"There!" she said, standing up with a hopeful smile. Ellyn managed a small smile back and turned to continue walking. Every time she saw a new mark of damage, or sign of the presence of their foes, she felt more and more discouraged. This place had been her home ever since she was born, and every part of it was so familiar to her that she felt a sense of loss at seeing it so destroyed. Her life was being torn apart, and she had no way to bring it back. She took slow, steady steps over the wreckage, staring in disbelief at the destruction and waste that she had always called her home. She turned and looked up at the castle. It stood proud and tall in the middle of the damage. Not one of its bricks had been marred, but Ellyn thought it looked so vulnerable, standing in the middle of the wasting grounds.

"Excuse me, Princess Ellyn."

She turned, facing a servant who curtsied and said, "Your presence is requested in your Father's library."

Ellyn nodded and cast one more lingering look around the cluttered aftermath of the battle. Then she turned and walked through the side door through which she had come. She stepped inside and walked upstairs and down the hall to her father's personal library. Entering the room, she found both her father and mother in earnest conversation with Ivor also sitting nearby. All three of them looked up as she entered.

"Sit down Ellyn," Queen Cordelia said calmly.

Ellyn closed the door and looked into her mother's face, and then her father, and Ivor's, trying to determine the meaning of their expressions. But all she saw was weariness and worry.

"What is it?" she asked with concern as she sat down.

"Well." Her father cleared his throat. "I have decided that I must send all of you away… for a while."

"What?" Ellyn cried, standing up quickly and staring at her father. "I don't want to leave!" she insisted. "I could never leave my home."

"I know it will be hard for you," he replied. "But sit down and let me explain."

Ellyn took a deep breath and slowly lowered herself onto the couch again, glancing at Ivor. He was watching her gravely. Ellyn's head was throbbing, but she looked at her father, waiting for him to continue.

"I have decided to send you away," he continued, "because it is very, very dangerous for you to remain here. I will stay with Ivor and we will devote ourselves to trying to save our kingdom and its people. But it is adamant that the rest of you leave to escape harm. I cannot allow you to stay when we are in such jeopardy here."

Ellyn felt her eyes brimming with tears. There was so little hope left. Leaving Eurasia would probably mean leaving her father and brother forever.

"But there is no place for us to go," Ellyn said, trying to keep her voice from shaking.

"As a matter of fact, there is," the king said. "Julius's advisor arrived today, having received the message from Julius. It is a rather long story that I will try to condense as much as possible. Do you remember that Julius was travelling on the way to Brystol, the kingdom of his father's brother, King Walter, so that he would be safe from his other uncle?"

Ellyn nodded.

"Well, Julius's advisor, Quinn, arrived just a few hours ago and is going to see that Julius is transported safely past the borders of our kingdom and into Brystol. When Julius was explaining his plans to me, I devised the idea that the walls of Brystol might prove to be a safe haven for my wife and children as well. I spoke to Julius and Quinn and both seemed to approve of the idea. I have already sent a message to King Walter of Brystol, asking his permission to send you there for as long as need be. Julius also sent a letter along, explaining the situation in more detail. I hope to receive a message from him later today."

"What if he declines your request?" Ellyn asked.

"Then I will find another location for you to go to. I will not allow for you to stay much longer. It is much too dangerous for you."

Ellyn's brow furrowed and she felt a sinking feeling inside of her. Leaving her home could mean leaving it forever. And what about her father and brother? How long would it be before she saw them again, if ever?

"Why won't the other kingdoms ally with you as you have been proposing?" Ellyn asked angrily. "Are they too selfish to care about us?"

"It is not as simple as it sounds," her father said gently. "Although I wish it were. The kingdoms of our country have very separate cultures and have the mindset of living as individual kingdoms instead of uniting together. I have not given up in my negotiations with King Evander. He rules one of the largest kingdoms in the country and if I can form an alliance with him it would be a great advantage for us. But it has not been easy trying to convince him to form an alliance with Eurasia."

"Must we leave though?" Ellyn asked.

"Yes," he replied. "You must. Julius will be leaving tomorrow and if we receive a message from King Walter, agreeing to my request, you will all be leaving with him."

Chapter 6 - Welcome to Brystol

Ellyn threw her arms around her father's neck and clung to him, burying her face in his shoulders. He wrapped his strong, protective arms around her and squeezed her tightly, then pulled away, holding her face in his hands.

"Don't cry, Ellyn," he said gently. He looked into her eyes and brushed a wisp of blonde hair from her forehead. Ellyn took a deep breath and pressed her lips together, unable to speak.

The king then turned to his other children, tenderly bidding each of them farewell. Ellyn's heart felt heavy, and she detected a hidden hopelessness in her father's countenance as he said good-bye to his family, perhaps for the last time. Looking at her mother, she saw tears in her eyes and looked away, trying to hide the tears gathering in her own. She knelt and picked up a withered leaf from the ground. She twisted the stem between her thumb and forefinger a few times before crushing it in her hand. Small flakes from the dead leaf swirled away into the breeze and Ellyn brushed her hands together, watching the remains of the leaf scatter and disappear. A single raindrop fell into Ellyn's cheek and she looked up at the sky. Grey clouds were rolling slowly overhead.

"Are you sure you don't want to ride in the carriage with us, Ellyn?" Queen Cordelia asked, approaching her daughter. "It looks like it may rain soon and you don't want to become ill." Her voice was quiet and hoarse, and she cleared her throat gently after she spoke.

"I'd rather ride on horseback," Ellyn replied. "If it begins to rain steadily, I will come in out of the cold. But I would rather ride out in the fresh air if I may."

Julius was already sitting astride one of the steeds, watching the farewells of the royal family gravely. Just ahead of him, several guards occupied a procession of horses, who were stamping at the ground, eager to move onward. Three carts, full of chests and boxes followed in the procession and the royal carriage stood in the center of the procession, both doors open. Several more armed guards on horses trailed just behind.

"Are you alright?" Julius asked as Ellyn pulled herself into the saddle and fumbled with the

reins.

"No," she replied, staring at the ground. A tight knot in her throat kept her from saying

another word and Julius fell silent.

Ellyn looked up and saw Ivor looking through one of the upstairs windows of the castle. He had already said his farewells and now watched solemnly from inside. Ellyn bit her lip as he turned from the window and she lost sight of him.

A shout from the leading guard rang out and the horses bobbed their heads up and down as the procession began to move. The wheels squeaked and creaked as they began to rumble over the cobblestone path. A sharp breeze caused Ellyn to shiver and she tightened her hands around the reins.

She trained her eyes straight ahead, focusing on the path in front of her rather than what lay behind. The cobblestone path turned to a dirt road as it led from the castle grounds.

After they had passed through the castle wall and down the forest path, Ellyn turned and glanced behind her. She saw the castle peaks standing over the crenellations. She saw vines twisting up the wall and a guard locking the gate. She saw the tops of trees over the wall, swaying in the wind. In only one glance, she saw a glimpse of the childhood she was leaving behind, perhaps forever.

She twisted her fingers through the reins and her eyes darted toward Julius. He was watching her. Ellyn straightened her shoulders and looked straight ahead, ignoring the urge to turn back again for a last glance at her home.

A raindrop fell on her nose, and directly afterwards, another splattered on her arm. And then a deluge of rain began to pour from the heavens. Ellyn hunched her shoulders together and shivered.

"I see it, Ellyn," Gwendolyn said, pulling aside the curtain that covered the carriage windows. "I see Brystol. Do you see it?"

"Yes, I see it," Ellyn said, with none of the eagerness her sister showed. After hours of being rattled around in the tight quarters of the carriage with hardly enough room to breathe, her legs were feeling numb and she felt like a butterfly stuck in its cocoon.

Raindrops fell steadily on the roof of the carriage, where Ellyn had moved to at her mother's insistence. She pulled aside the corner of the curtain and gazed out of the rain-streaked window. Julius was riding steadily alongside the cart, rain streaming down his face and soaking his clothes. His hair was a darker blonde than usual and was dripping with rain. He was moving rhythmically with the strides of his horse. With every step the horse took, water splashed from the dirt road under its feet, and a shower of water droplets fell from his mane and tail. Ellyn looked past the road and out into the grey beyond. The trees lining the road drooped and swayed in the rain, and a low rumble of thunder echoed in the distance.

At last, the procession ground to a halt inside the palace courtyard. The doors of the iron gilded carriage opened, and the weary travellers eagerly stepped out of the carriage into the fresh, crisp air.

"We must hurry inside, the rain is not good for our health," Queen Cordelia said nervously. A flurry of servants had already begun busying themselves with carrying bundles and chests through a side door in the castle.

They were escorted from the damp courtyard into a roomy entryway, leading into a wide hall, lined with doors on every side. Small statues stood on pedestals between each door and ornate paintings lined the walls.

Ellyn trailed behind everyone else, taking slow, even steps down the corridor.

"Ellyn," she heard Julius's voice beside her but kept walking, keeping her eyes trained downwards. "Ellyn, I don't want to presume that you feel like the company of another person," he pressed on, despite her silence. "But I don't like seeing you so downcast and I want you to know that if you want someone to talk to, I am here."

"So are my mother and sisters," Ellyn replied shortly. "Yes, I know," he said, his words trailing off.

"I'm sorry," Ellyn said, halting in the middle of the hall. She started to go on, but he broke her off.

"I understand why you are upset; that is why I am offering to talk, if you would like. However, solitude can be comforting as well, if that is what you prefer."

She looked up into his eyes. He was watching her with a concerned expression.

"I would like to talk later," she said after a moment of silence. "After we are somewhat settled.

But where could we meet?"

"I'm sure there is a guest sitting room somewhere, we will have to see. But you should go up to your room with your family and refresh yourself. We will meet somewhere later."

Ellyn nodded and looked ahead. Her mother and sisters were climbing a wide galley of stairs, and Regan had turned and was beckoning Ellyn to follow.

"When will we meet King Walter and his family?" Ellyn asked. She was seated on a settee in her mother's room, resting her chin on her knees. Alys had helped her change from her damp clothes into a fresh afternoon gown. Her hair had been braided into a wreath around head with a ribbon threaded between the strands of the braid.

"We will meet him during the evening meal tonight," her mother replied. She was sitting in front of a mirror, her maidservant brushing her long, golden hair. "He was called away early this morning and will not be back until tonight, I was told. Since it is already late afternoon, we will not have to wait much longer for the meal."

"I am so exhausted. I hope it does not last very long," Ellyn sighed.

"I am sure our long journey will be taken into consideration and they will not keep us very long," her mother replied.

Ellyn gazed out the window, looking out over rolling hills and meadows. The sun had at last found an opening in the cloudy sky and was already on its downward descent.

"I am going to inquire whether or not there is a sitting room to which we have access," Ellyn said, standing.

"I was told there is one just down the hall," her mother's maidservant said.

"I will go visit it, then," Ellyn said, standing on her toes to stretch her feet. She opened the door and stepped out into the hall. Her footsteps echoed in the empty hall with a hollow and lonely sound.

She saw a glass door, through which she could see a wall lined with intricate paintings. As she approached the door, she saw Julius sitting in a chair facing the door, looking down at a book which was placed on the table in front of him, toward which his attention was directed. As soon as her hand touched the doorknob, he looked up quickly and stood as she entered.

"I wondered if you would find your way here," he said as she gently closed the door.

Ellyn scanned the small room and looked down at the book which he had been reading. The pages were filled with small, delicate characters and Ellyn scanned the pages quickly, recognizing the words from the Bible, one of the only books that was in print.

"I remember I used to find my reading lessons such a chore," she said thoughtfully. "I didn't think it fair that I had to learn to read and write even though other children didn't." She thought back to those days many years ago, struggling over her page of letters, with her impatient tutor giving her instructions.

"If you had lived even half a century before, there would have been no books, and no reason for you to read," Julius said.

She tilted her head, but said nothing.

"Why don't you sit down?" Julius suggested after a brief silence, indicating a small couch. She sat down and rested her back against the couch, relaxing her aching body, which had been knocked around in the carriage for many hours. Julius sat down across from her and both sat silently for a few moments.

"Do you have any cousins who live here?" Ellyn asked.

"King Walter has one son who is very near my age. But I have never met him and know nothing about him except that his name is Prince Edwin and that his mother died many years ago so he has lived alone with his father since childhood."

Ellyn nodded, staring vacantly into the distance. "Our country's system of authority is strange," she said thoughtfully. "Even though your uncle is the king of a state, you have never met him and know very little about his family. The kingdoms are so separate and uninvolved in the affairs of other kingdoms, few of the other kingdoms have any interest in the affairs in Eurasia with the Northmen. They will only begin to care if their own countries are afflicted."

"The independence of the kingdoms of which you speak can be both a blessing and a curse," Julius commented. "In other countries, sometimes the kingdoms are too involved in the affairs of another kingdom, and there is constant rivalry for a throne, resulting in general upheaval in the kingdoms. We have not had such problems, however. But we are too far the other direction. Some interest and care in other kingdoms can be beneficial, such as in the case that Eurasia is enduring with the attacks from the Northmen. And other smaller kingdoms might do well to receive protection from surrounding kingdoms. But that is not the way we think. My father believed that, someday, the kingdoms would decide to unite into one large country with smaller kingdoms that work together, rather than the system we have now. But if that is the case, it will probably be many years from now." Julius paused and said, "I am probably boring you. I know you must be somewhat involved in politics, but that does not mean you appreciate political discussions."

"I was the one who initiated the discussion," Ellyn said. "And there is hardly a way to avoid the political aspects of my own land right now. It is all my father and brother have been talking or thinking about for many months now. Father is desperate to save Eurasia. Our family has been rulers of the kingdom for over a century, almost since it was founded. And the people under his rule are not merely people to him. They are families with fathers and mothers and children. He is so concerned about them, he will do almost anything to save them. The havoc on our land that was caused by the Northmen has been such a devastation to him. Every time I saw him for many months past, he looked anxious or exhausted or upset. It has been such a long time since I have seen him as the easy, content father who used to help me in my archery or play with the little ones in the evening. And poor Ivor, knowing that his future as king of Eurasia is in such jeopardy and…" Tears were now streaming freely down her face, and she was wringing her hands together. She couldn't remember when the tears had begun to fall and covered her mouth to hold back her sobs. And then Julius was sitting by her side, resting his hand on her shoulder. Without looking up, she leaned over and rested her head on his shoulder, her body shaking with controlled sobs. He wrapped his arms around her and held her tightly.

"Welcome to Brystol," King Walter said in a deep gravelly voice from the head of the table. "Thank you for your hospitality in allowing us to stay here," Queen Cordelia replied, bowing her head.

"It will be my pleasure to allow you to remain here as long as necessary," the king replied. "And may I introduce you to my son, Prince Edwin."

A rather short, dark haired young man bowed solemnly and looked into Ellyn's eyes as he straightened. Ellyn flinched and looked away quickly. It was not the first time their eyes had met and she felt uncomfortable that he seemed to be watching her whenever she looked towards him.

Chairs scraped against the floor as the king gestured for everyone to be seated and Ellyn looked purposefully at her plate, feeling Edwin's eyes following her every move.

The room was silent for several minutes, except for the sounds of silverware against dishes as the servings of mutton and bread slowly began to diminish. Reaching for her spoon and bowl of stew, Ellyn could not help casting her eyes toward Edwin. At last, he was looking at his meal instead of towards her and she had the chance, for the first time, to briefly study his features. His light skin contrasted the dark hair and his thick eyebrows were furrowed so that they almost seemed to touch his dark eyelashes. A light dusting of facial hair spread from his ears down to his chin. Just as she looked away, she saw his head turn toward her again in her peripheral vision. Looking across the table at Julius, Ellyn noticed his eyes dart momentarily toward the end of the table where Edwin was sitting. Although the room was silent, Ellyn felt that someone had said something that made everyone uncomfortable. She was relieved when the king spoke at last.

"Have all of you settled in, or is there anything else you would like me to make sure is taken care of before the day ends?"

"We are comfortably settled, thank you, although I would like to dispatch a letter to my husband if possible," Queen Cordelia said.

"Certainly, it will be sent as soon as possible."

Silence reigned again, and when Ellyn looked up, she saw King Walter scanning the faces of the group around the table. When his eyes met hers, they stopped, resting on her, and then he said, "You are not the eldest child are you, Princess Ellyn? Or are you indeed the heir to your father's throne?"

"No, my elder brother, Prince Ivor, is the successor," Ellyn replied. "I am the second child." The king nodded thoughtfully, still looking at her. Ellyn shifted uncomfortably in her chair, feeling it would be discourteous to look away.

"You must be past fifteen now, I would presume, but yet you have not married. Forgive me for asking, but is there a reason why? I know it is the custom for young ladies of royalty to marry at fourteen or fifteen, perhaps younger on occasion."

Ellyn was taken aback at the bluntness of the question, asked by a man she barely knew. She hesitated, trying to think of what to say. But Julius broke in before she could speak.

"It is not always customary for princesses to marry at the young age you suggest, Uncle. There have been many royal families that do not give their daughters in marriage until they are almost nineteen. It depends on the kingdom, or the situation the family is in. Moreover, matrimony has not been forefront in the mind of King Wulfred lately."

"That is true," Queen Cordelia said quietly.

"Indeed, I find it perfectly ordinary, if not in fact gratifying that Princess Ellyn is not yet married," Prince Edwin said. Ellyn saw Julius's fork freeze on the way to his mouth at these words. "It conveys an understanding of the gravity and significance of what marriage is, and the political aspects it entails, both domestically and nationally."

Ellyn tried to unconcernedly return to her meal, although she felt several pairs of eyes on her while she did so. She thought of the solitude of her bedroom and wished she were alone in the privacy of her room where no direct questions would be asked of her. Lifting her eyes, she saw that Prince Edwin was gazing at her, and the corners of his mouth curved up when their eyes met. She looked quickly away.

Chapter 7 - The Alliance

Ellyn closed her eyes and inhaled deeply as a crisp wave of air blew through her hair, twisting and weaving the strands together. The light of the sun warmed her so that, even though the breeze had a chill edge, it did not bother her.

"The air here in Brystol feels different than in Eurasia," she said, opening her eyes and turning to Julius, who trailed just behind her on the dirt pathway. "There is less moisture in the air, since it is not along the shoreline, and it's not as warm. It's refreshing."

She glanced back at the castle, now nearly a quarter of a mile away. It felt strange being so far from the walls of a castle, after such a long time of being kept inside. She felt a sense of insecurity, but at the same time, a vibrant freedom that she had not felt for a long time.

"What do you think of Brystol and its inhabitants, after nearly a week here?" Julius asked as they continued their leisurely walk down the path.

"Well, I miss home, of course, and I wonder nearly every moment about Father and Ivor. However, it is comfortable here and I do feel much safer. And it is not as though I have come here alone. My mother and sisters are here, and you as well. If I was here alone, I would be much more lonely. I am glad we are only here temporarily, though."

"And my uncle and cousin? What are your opinions towards them?"

"Your uncle is very friendly, almost too friendly," Ellyn said, smiling. "He has not had the gentle presence of a wife for many years, and perhaps that is one of the reasons he sometimes lacks tact. But, despite that, he is very kind, and generous to allow strangers to abide in his home for an unknown amount of time."

"And my cousin?" Julius pressed.

Ellyn stopped and turned toward him, smiling understandingly. "I know what you are thinking," she said, "and don't worry. His attempts to charm me have not been successful."

Julius's face relaxed into an expression of relief, and he returned her smile. Then he looked past her, and Ellyn saw his brow furrow. She turned and looked where his gaze was directed and saw a figure riding a swift, black horse, galloping towards them. She squinted her eyes, trying to identify the rider.

"It's him, isn't it?" she asked.

"I did not think he would be back so soon," Julius sighed. "He has the uncanny ability to interrupt us wherever we happen to be. But, it is his home, I suppose."

Before long, Edwin overtook Julius and Ellyn, greeting them jovially as he leaped from his horse's saddle and took her by the reins.

"It's a lovely day for walking, as I see you have discovered," he said, falling into stride with them next to Ellyn.

Ellyn smiled and nodded.

"We were just discussing turning back before you reached us," Julius commented. His tone was genial, but Ellyn knew that it was difficult for him not to allow annoyance to creep into his voice. Edwin's interruptions during their conversations had become a frequency, but Julius had not yet shown any signs of irritation in his presence.

"Yes, you've walked a long way," Edwin replied, looking back at the castle. "I need to return as well. It has been too long since I've had a full meal. Perhaps we can walk back together."

"Certainly," Ellyn said, her heart sinking slightly.

The trio began walking back in silence. Their steps were more brisk and steady than the leisurely pace Ellyn and Julius had been walking in before.

"Are the sights and views as breathtaking in Eurasia as there are here in Brystol?" Edwin asked, breaking a somewhat lengthy silence.

"Eurasia is very beautiful," Ellyn replied, "but in a different way than Brystol. We do not have mountains, and very few hills as you have here. And being a kingdom along the Flegian Sea, the smells and sounds are different. There are lots of trees around the castle, so the autumn colors are wonderfully vibrant. But once you are past the limits of the castle grounds, the trees diminish, and you reach the village, and, just beyond, the shoreline. I have been there before, but it was once many years ago. We do not travel beyond our castle walls very often."

"But how can you be always inside without the pleasures of nature to please you?" Edwin asked.

"Our grounds are very extensive, and I often went riding in the forest, or in the meadow just north of the castle. But I was unable to do so for several weeks when the Northman began attacking. It is comforting to be outside once again."

"Well, if you ever feel so inclined, we have several horses, and you are most welcome to ride if you wish."

"Thank you. I hope I will be able to soon."

"And, unless you prefer otherwise, I would be honored to join you," he added. Then he tilted his head to look past Ellyn at Julius. "And you as well, cousin, if you wish."

"Thank you," Julius responded.

"Well, here we are. I will depart now," he said as they approached the castle. "Thank you for allowing me to intrude on your company. I look forward to our next discussion."

Edwin led his horse off of the path toward the stable, where a stable boy was striding out to meet him.

"Maybe he has been lonely," Ellyn suggested when he was out of hearing range. "He has no brothers or sisters and no one of his age to associate with."

"Perhaps so," Julius said, but he did not sound convinced.

As they stepped through the door, a servant immediately approached them and said, "Princess Ellyn, your mother is very anxious for your presence in her room."

Ellyn felt a pang of worry, thinking of her father and brother at home. "I should hurry, then," she said, turning to Julius.

"Of course," he replied.

Dreading that her mother had some terrible news to convey, she nervously hurried up the stairs and down a hallway until she reached her mother's door. As she entered, Queen Cordelia jumped up from her chair and beckoned her daughter into the room.

"What is it, Mother?" Ellyn asked breathlessly.

"Don't worry dear," her mother replied, although the worried look on her own face was less than comforting.

"We have received word from Father."

"What is it?" Ellyn asked anxiously.

"Well," the queen hesitated, then looked at a folded piece of paper in her hand. "I don't know.

He only sends for you."

"He is sending for me?" Ellyn asked, bewildered.

"Yes, although he does not say why or give any indication why you are needed back at home. But it is apparently urgent, for he has sent the carriage with this letter and you are to leave immediately.

"Immediately?"

"Yes, almost at this very moment."

Ellyn was spellbound for a moment, wondering what her father's urgency meant, and why he had not explained anything in the letter.

"What about my belongings?" she stammered, trying to gather her thoughts.

"They have already been collected and are waiting with the carriage. We were just waiting for you to return for the carriage to depart. They are very anxious to leave, and hope to arrive in Eurasia before sundown. You must hurry. Come with me, I will walk down with you."

"Wait," Ellyn said, placing her hand over the door before her mother could open it. "Are you sure about all of this? I don't understand any of this."

"Nor do I," her mother replied. "But here is the letter from your father."

Ellyn took the paper and read these words: "Send Ellyn to Eurasia immediately. There is no time to lose. Do not let a minute pass once the carriage has arrived, but let her be on her way the moment this note reaches you." He had signed the paper, and there was a smear of wax below his name, from the seal that had secured the letter closed.

"So you see, you must hurry," her mother said when Ellyn had scanned the words. She opened the door and stepped into the hall. Ellyn followed her mother, her head whirling. When they reached the top of the stairwell, Julius appeared, coming from downstairs. Ellyn grabbed his arm as he was about to pass her.

"Julius, I'm leaving," she said, looking frantically into his eyes. "What?" he exclaimed. "What are you talking about? When?"

"This very moment. My father has sent for me, but I do not know why, nor when I will return. Good-bye." Feeling tears come into her eyes for a reason she did not know, Ellyn turned away to go down the stairs.

"Wait," Julius said urgently. "Let me at least accompany you to the carriage." He followed Ellyn and her mother downstairs and out to the courtyard. The royal carriage of Eurasia, which had transported

Ellyn and her family to Brystol only a few days before, was waiting, with two servants standing on the back.

"At last." One of her father's most trusted advisors stepped forward when she appeared. "Time is of the essence," he said, opening the door for Ellyn to enter the carriage." She stepped inside and sat down, leaning forward to look out the window. Julius grabbed the frame and looked back at her, but both were at a loss for words, and not a word was spoken. The next moment, the carriage lurched forward and Julius's face disappeared from the window. She turned and looked through the back window. He was frozen in place, his hand still raised from where it had grasped the window frame, and he was staring after the carriage.

"Please explain to me what is happening," she said, turning to the advisor. He shook his head decisively. "You will find out when you arrive."

The wheels of the carriage ground to a halt in the courtyard of Eurasia's castle. The door was opened and Ellyn stepped out into the dark night. It was calm, and crickets chirped melodiously, but Ellyn felt anything but calm as she was led inside, surrounded by a flurry of activity. She was rushed into the closest parlor. Several candles cast long shadows along the walls and King Wulfred stepped forward as she entered the room.

"Father!" Ellyn gasped, clinging to him, her body shaking. "What is wrong, Father? I'm so confused."

He wrapped his strong arms around her and ran his fingers through her hair. "Relax, Ellyn," he said. "You are shaken, and I want you to sit down and catch your breath before I tell you what I must say."

Ellyn allowed him to lead her to a small couch and they both sat down. Ellyn felt safe at last, sitting next to her father. But his face looked weary and sad, and he was looking at Ellyn with concern etched on his face.

"Please, tell me what I have come here for," Ellyn said, taking deep breaths to calm herself.

"Well, dear," King Wulfred began, and then paused, searching for words. He was looking directly into Ellyn's eyes and his hands rested on her shoulders. Ellyn bit her lip nervously. Finally, he spoke again,

"I know this will be a shock to you, but within this very hour, you will have to leave Eurasia again."

Ellyn's face clouded, and she waited for him to continue, a feeling of dread rushing through her.

"You will be taken out to shore and will board a ship, where you will be taken to King Evander's kingdom in Lyntirith."

"Why? I don't understand," Ellyn said, wringing her hands together.

"King Evander has finally agreed to ally with Eurasia to fight off the Northmen, but there are terms that I had to agree to. In short, you are being sent to marry his son, Prince Corbin."

Ellyn was speechless. She stared at her father, stunned. He looked back, waiting for her reaction. She felt as though she was going numb and gasped for a breath of air. Still, she could think of nothing to say; her voice was caught in her throat. She was about to faint and get sick all at once. There was a horrible pain in her stomach as she tried to let the information sink in. Then all at once, she burst into tears, and her father enfolded her in his arms, letting her cry.

Ellyn's despair soon turned to anger and she pulled away from her father, looking at him through her tear-filled eyes. "Why, Father? Isn't there any other way? I don't want to leave, I can't leave."

"I'm sorry, Ellyn, but no, there is no other way. You must go. If you do not marry Prince Corbin, King Evander will not join his forces with mine. Without his army, I believe our country is doomed, but with Lyntirith, we will almost positively be able to fight off the Northmen permanently."

"But, Father, I don't want to marry a stranger I have never met. I don't think I could bear it!"

She began to shake with sobs, and covered her mouth with her hands as tears fell rapidly down her face. King Wulfred tenderly stroked the side of her face with the back of his hand. "I know, Ellyn," he said. "But it is not a question of choice. This marriage is not being arranged for your happiness. It is for the welfare of not only our family, or our kingdom, or even the surrounding kingdoms. The sacrifice you are making is for your entire country. I know this is very hard for you, especially since your acquaintance with Prince Julius has been deepening since you met. But King Evander would not negotiate with me. I attempted all I could think of for hours and hours last night, but this was his final option. I am truly sorry, my daughter."

All the time he was talking, Ellyn had been making a valiant effort to calm herself. But she could not stop thinking about Julius.

"How will I tell Julius, Father? He will be heartbroken."

"He will find out soon enough. I will write to your mother in Brystol and he will know then."

"But I will not be able to see him before I go," she said, struggling to speak through her weeping.

"I know," he said tenderly.

Ellyn lowered her head, remembering their hurried farewell. It was probably the last time she would ever see him again.

"Alys will be accompanying you, and everything is ready for you to depart. King Evander was insistent that you be en route by tomorrow morning. Our carriage will take you to the eastern shore where a ship from Lyntirith will be waiting once you arrive. Your voyage will only last a day at the most, and you will arrive the day after tomorrow. The plans to transport you by sea are for your safety, and speed as well, so that you will not have to be driven over uninhabited land, or through unknown kingdoms. The parts of the ocean you will sail through are very safe, and you have no need to fear for your safety."

"It is not for my safety I fear," Ellyn sobbed.

At that moment the door opened, and Ellyn looked up as Ivor entered. His face was somber and grave, and he looked down at his sister with compassion. She turned her head and buried her face in her hands.

"I'm sorry, Ellyn, but I must insist that you go out to the carriage now," King Wulfred said gently. "If I do not meet all of King Evander's terms, he will not stand to them. You must go."

Ellyn nodded and reached for the side of the couch to stand. She wiped her wet cheeks, and looked up at Ivor as she stood. He approached her and pulled her into a tight embrace. She leaned her head against his shoulder, pressing her lips shut tightly

"I know this is the hardest thing you have ever done," he said softly. "but you are brave, and this is for a very valiant cause."

Ellyn squeezed him tightly, unable to speak.

"Come, daughter," King Wulfred said, gently, resting a hand on her back. She followed him out the door into the hallway and back out to the carriage which she had just spent several hours in. She climbed inside and looked out the windows, taking in every detail before she left her home for the last time. Then the coachman spurred the horses into a quick walk.

Once they had passed through the castle gates, Ellyn turned and watched the castle until it had disappeared from view.

Alone in the carriage, she was at last able to cry freely, which she did until her eyes wouldn't let any more tears fall. She sat in emotionless silence, staring out into the darkness, pondering everything that had happened to her that day.

She was so lost in her misery that she was hardly aware when the carriage stopped and the door opened.

"The ship is waiting, your highness," a gruff voice said.

Ellyn stepped out of the carriage and was led toward the shore where a small boat was waiting. The water glittered in the moonlight and a white sails of the ship were tied. Night shrouded the details around her, and a line of lanterns lit the pathway leading to the shoreline. She saw the lights of a great ship, waiting out in the black waters of the ocean. Waves splashed onto the sandy shore and a few crabs scuttled into hiding as Ellyn approached the boat.

She hardly even noticed the man guiding the boat, or the water lapping against the sides.

Staring down into the black water, she wrapped her shawl tightly around her shoulders and shivered.

As soon as she entered the ship, Ellyn was led below deck to a very small cabin that contained one bed and a few meager pieces of furniture. She was appalled by the simplicity and compactness of the room. It was hardly as big as her closet. She sunk down into the bed and was disappointed to feel the hard board below the thin mattress. She hoped that the ship was not any indication of what the palace at Lyntirith would be like.

Alys had already entered the room and was arranging her things in a very small wardrobe, which was set up against the wall. Neither of them spoke; each was lost in her own thoughts.

"You must be exhausted," Alys said at last, adjusting the pillows on the narrow bed. "Lie down and sleep. You may feel better in the morning."

Ellyn collapsed on the bed and buried her face in the pillow.

When she finally awoke, Ellyn sat up in bed and looked around, trying to remember where she was, and why she had such a terrible headache. It did not take long for the events of the night before to return, and she fell back onto her pillow and stared blankly at the ceiling.

"Would you like some food?" Alys asked, cautiously approaching the bed and looking down at Ellyn anxiously.

Ellyn shook her head.

"Please, you must eat. I insist. Otherwise you may become ill."

Sighing, Ellyn sat up and Alys propped up her pillow so that she could lean comfortably against the headboard. She gave Ellyn a tray of food and sat down in a chair next to the bed.

"You needn't tend to me like a nurse. I'm not ill," Ellyn said, pulling at the bread on her plate. "I know. But I thought you might want someone to talk to. I know I'm not a very good

conversationalist, but I can listen."

Ellyn lowered her eyes and pressed her lips together. "I still cannot believe this is happening to me," she said woefully. "One day I was content, living with those I know and love, and the next I am being taken to a place I know nothing about to live with people I know nothing about and marry someone I know nothing about." She shuddered and squeezed her eyes shut. "I know I am going to be desperately lonely and miserable there. This day is the beginning of a lifetime of grief and unhappiness."

"We don't know what Lyntirith has in store," Alys said.

"And I don't want to know," Ellyn replied. "I miss Julius already. If only we could have said good-bye. It is too late now, though. I will never be able to see him again."

A knock on the door interrupted her, and Alys stood and opened it. A man appeared in the doorway and bowed his head respectfully.

"I have been designated to assist you if you should need anything," he said, his mouth twitching sideways as he spoke. Something about his steady gaze made Ellyn uncomfortable. Even though he was speaking to Alys, his eyes bored into Ellyn's. His hair was thin and greying, even though he could not have been yet forty, and he had a scar along his face. Ellyn shuddered and looked away.

"Thank you," Alys said. "May we have your name in case we need you?"

"I am Cadwallo," he said. "If you need me, open the door and yell my name. Someone will be sure to hear you and tell me."

He coughed a thick, raspy cough and then turned and walked away.

"He's so coarse!" Ellyn said to Alys as she closed the door. "I hope we will never need him for anything."

"He has not been raised in the refinement of a castle as you have. He is a lowly sailor, and I have always heard the sailors tend to be uncivil. But we will not be here for very long; it is only one day."

The day slowly dragged on. Ellyn had nothing to do except to sit and wonder what would await her when the ship reached Lyntirith. She tried not to muse very long about what Prince Corbin might be like, because whenever the possibilities began to enter her thoughts, they made her dread her arrival even more. She wondered if any other members of the family resided there, and what they would be like. The more she thought and wondered, the more she fell into fear and trepidation.

She walked about the tiny confines of her room occasionally, but the constant movement of the ship, bobbing up and down with the waves, made her feel queasy, so she spent many hours staring at the bare wall. Alys tried a few times to converse, but soon realized that Ellyn did not feel inclined to speak, and fell silent, beginning many hours of silence.

After many, many hours, Ellyn's eyes had begun to grow heavy, and she wondered what time of the day it was. But with no windows or any way of telling what position the sun held in the sky, she did not know whether it was day or nighttime. Eventually, she drifted off to sleep, falling into a restless subconsciousness.

A knock at the door startled her from her sleep after a few hours, and she lifted her head, wiping her sore eyes as Alys went to the door. The darkness prevented her from seeing anything, but she saw a slight glow from a candle when the door opened, and Cadwallo's gruff voice said, "I have a message from the captain. We are within sight of Lyntirith. We will be arriving around daybreak."

"Only a few short hours and I will be arriving in the place that will now be my home," Ellyn thought dismally "When we step off the ship and onto land, the first part of my life will be ending, and a new one will be beginning."

Chapter 8 - A Royal Wedding

Ellyn stared blankly out of the carriage window which was transporting her from the shoreline to Lyntirith's castle. For many miles, all that had met her eyes were vast plains with long fields of grass and wildflowers waving in the breeze. The sky was grey and bleak and a chill breeze blew into the carriage. She coughed as dust from the road was blown through the window and tried to blink the gritty dirt from her eyes.

The landscape underwent a transformation so subtle that Ellyn hardly recalled the change in terrain from open plains to overgrown forest paths. She was soon breathing in the familiar woodland smell, which seemed to whisk her away to the forest in Eurasia where she had spent many hours on horseback in days past. Those formerly happy memories now caused her painful nostalgia. She tried not to think about everything she was leaving behind, but it was impossible not to. Every time she looked out of the carriage window, she expected to see Julius riding alongside it, as he had on their journey to Brystol. Every thought she dwelt on as an attempt at distraction reminded her of him.

As she pondered these memories with sadness, she noticed the grey peak of a building through the trees. More peaks came into view as they grew closer, and, all at once, the carriage emerged from the trees, and Ellyn found herself staring up in awe at a massive structure. The castle of Lyntirith looked dark and foreboding. The overcast skies provided an even more menacing appearance to the towering building. Staring in awe out the window, she gazed at the magnificent palace as they rolled into the courtyard. It was constructed of white-grey bricks and decorated with intricate architectural designs. She saw a watchtower on the roof and peaks surrounding it. At each corner of the castle was situated a cylinder-shaped cove with tall cone-shaped roofs.

Servants and horses moved in a small steady stream inside the courtyard and were bustling in and out through one of the entrances. Beautiful columns were spaced evenly around the circular area and many tall, rectangular windows offered a view from inside the castle to the courtyard. She was so captured by the splendor of her surroundings that she was startled by the halting of the carriage.

Numerous servants surrounded the carriage and began unloading all of the boxes and chests. Ellyn frowned and pressed her lips together as she stepped onto the pebble covered ground. Smoothing her dress, she looked at the doorway ahead through which she would be entering, wondering what would greet her on the other side. It stood open with a servant on either side, but the interior was so dark that she could not see beyond the doorway.

"Follow me," the servant to the left of the door said stiffly as Ellyn approached. He stepped inside and she followed. Ellyn blinked in the dim lighting. They were in a foyer, with a stairway in the corner and several entryways leading from it. Ellyn followed the servant out through a hallway and through several corridors until they came to a winding staircase. She was led up the stairs and down a hallway until the servant stopped and gestured toward a wooden door. Ellyn saw that it was one of only a few doors along that hallway, and that there was one just across from it. Before she could observe any other details, the servant said, "This is your room, Your Highness." He opened the door and stepped aside for her to enter. "If there is anything you need, please pull the rope next to your bed and we will attend to it immediately. Your belongings will be delivered shortly.

Ellyn nodded and stepped past him into the room.

Before closing the door, the servant added, "Someone will arrive shortly to escort you down to the grand parlor where you will meet the royal family."

Bowing, the servant left, and the sound of the door shutting echoed in the hollow room. Then there was silence. It was the first time Ellyn had experienced such utter silence for a long time. There was no sound of crashing waves and thumping sails. No rattling carriage or servants talking. No horses whinnying or rattling carriage wheels.

She took a deep breath and looked around. The walls were beautifully decorated with murals and paintings. An intricate gold molding travelled the perimeter of the room at the top of the wall. The floor was wooden strips, arranged in a zigzag pattern. A desk sat along one of the walls and in the far left corner of the room was a small cot for Alys. There was a fireplace along the right wall and her bed stood nearby. Curtains were attached to each of the four posters, and a teal- and gold-colored comforter was spread over the bed.

The door opened, and Alys stepped inside, holding a box.

"It is somewhat smaller than my room at home," Ellyn said, without turning to look at her.

Alys opened her mouth to speak, but Ellyn spoke before she had formed her words. "Why did I call that place home?" she asked with a hint of anger in her voice. "That place is not my home and never will be again. This drafty, dreary palace is my home now forever. I will never see my old home again."

With these words, she sank down onto a nearby chair and crossed her arms. "I hate this place," she said through clenched teeth. "And I hate everyone here."

Alys came to Ellyn's side and rested her hand on her shoulder, but Ellyn shook her head and shrugged Alys's hand away, standing up quickly. "Are these Northmen such a threat that my father would be forced to banish me from my home to this desolate wasteland? I still cannot fathom how he could do such a thing." She yanked the shawl from around her neck and threw it onto the floor, kicking it away from her.

"Don't just stand there; help me change so I don't meet my future family looking like a barbarian."

A quarter of an hour later, the door rattled as a knock was heard from the other side. Alys opened it to a servant standing stiffly in the doorway.

"The royal family of Lyntirith requests the presence of the princess Ellyn in the royal parlor," he said. "The wedding ceremony will commence in a very short time. I have been ordered to escort you to the parlor."

Ellyn rose from the chair in which she was seated. Alys had changed her from her traveling clothes into one of her most extravagant gowns. Her face had been washed and her hair neatly arranged in an elegant twist. She walked briskly to the door; her chin held high resolutely. The servant closed the door behind her and began striding down the hallway. Ellyn followed. Her heart began pounding in her chest, and her stomach felt queasy. But her face did not convey any of the uneasiness and fear she was feeling. It was set in an emotionless stare as she kept her eyes trained straight, following the servant downstairs and through hallways.

At last, they stopped in front of two tall, closed doors. The servant paused and turned to look at Ellyn before he opened it. She took a deep breath and tried to straighten her back and relax her shoulders. And then the door opened, and the servant was announcing, "Her Royal Highness, Princess Ellyn of Eurasia,"

The room which Ellyn entered was grand and magnificent. The golden, textured floor was so shiny it looked like glass, and there was intricate molding that lined the wall where it met the ceiling. Murals were etched on every square inch of wall. But Ellyn hardly noticed the lavishness of the room. She immediately looked straight ahead to the end of the room. A stiff, harsh man was sitting on a chair, his eyes piercing into Ellyn as she approached. Her eyes locked with his, and his stare was so intense that she could not remove her gaze as she walked towards him into the room. It was not until she stood in front of him and knelt, bowing her head, that she finally loosed him from her own icy stare.

When she stood and lifted her eyes, she observed at his right a dignified and beautiful woman, the queen of Lyntirith. Her dark hair framed her striking face and she sat with an air of dignity. Her eyebrows were arched and her thin lips pressed together, and she looked Ellyn up and down with condescension.

For a brief moment, Ellyn's eyes flitted towards the young man standing at the king's side. Though she had barely glanced at him, his image was imprinted in her mind. Prince Corbin of Lyntirith had dark hair, just like both of his parents, and very dark eyes. There were creases in his forehead from his furrowed brows. He had a light dusting of facial hair around his mouth and along the sides of his face and thick, knitted eyebrows. He was staring back at her expressionlessly, standing tall with his arms behind his back. His jaw was set firmly, outlining the sharp cheekbones. A sword was sheathed at his side, and a brass buckle fastened itself around his gold, embroidered tunic.

"Welcome to Lyntirith, Princess Ellyn," King Evander finally said in a tone that was far from welcoming. "Here you will forever find your home, and hopefully you will find it suitable."

"The ceremony will be held at a chapel north of the castle," the queen added coldly. "It will be a private ceremony, with only the royal family and a few others in attendance. We will send someone to escort you there very shortly."

Ellyn bowed her head in response.

"Do you have any inquiries for us before you are excused from this room?" the king asked.

Ellyn had many curt and ungracious replies that she would have liked to say, but refrained from shocking the king and queen with her vulgarity. "No, Your Majesty," she said, her voice sounding empty in the silent room. "I have found everything to be adequate for the time being."

"Then I hope you will find the time to change from these childish rags into proper attire before the ceremony," the queen said curtly.

Ellyn felt a rush of hot anger surge through her and she returned Queen Guinevere's glare. "My attire is no concern of yours, Your Majesty," she said shortly. "And if you make it yours, I will be glad to listen to your comments and choose my garments contrary to your advice."

The queen stood quickly, her tall frame towering above Ellyn, who gazed back with unperturbed boldness.

"Impudent girl! You will do well to recognize your place here as insignificant and of no consequence."

"And as someone, as you have not taken into account, who will one day replace you."

"Silence!" the king bellowed. "Do not let any other phrases of this sort fall from your lips, girl. Now leave this room immediately."

With arched eyebrows, Ellyn turned with her head held high and glided from the room. As she stepped out into the hallway, her hands were shaking, not from fear, but from rage. She wrapped her fingers around the necklace fastened around her neck and yanked it off, clenching it in her fist. The servant standing at the door blinked and took a step backwards.

"What is wrong?" Ellyn asked. "Take me to my room without further delay."

The servant flinched and began walking briskly down the hallway. Ellyn fell into step behind him, taking deep breaths and trying to calm the surge of exasperation coursing through her.

"The ceremony which has joined the hands of Prince Corbin Evander Terrowyn, future king of Veridell and Ellyn Cordelia Lorelle of Eurasia is now concluded," a solemn bishop said, his voice echoing in the chapel. "Please join as I pray a blessing on the wedded couple."

Ellyn was kneeling in front of the altar in the chapel, Prince Corbin next to her. Their eyes had never once met throughout the ceremony and the only words they had thus far spoken in one another's presence were the wedding vows. Ellyn had only a few times dared to glance at his face, and every time it was set in the same solemn, unwavering expression of cold distance.

The bishop approached them and, laying his hand on their heads, solemnly prayed, "May God bless, preserve, and keep you; the Lord mercifully show his favor whilst looking upon you; and so fill you with all spiritual benediction and grace, that ye may so live together in this life, that in the world to come ye may have life everlasting. Amen."

The few observers echoed "Amen" with repeated solemnity. The couple rose and turned. The ceremony had ended. They were husband and wife. Ellyn felt her hands begin to shake, and she fought to contain herself and hold back the tears that were trying to force themselves from her eyes. All she could imagine was a church full of hundreds of royal guests sitting in the wooden pews in front of her with Prince Julius at her side, and her family smiling radiantly from the front row. But, her eyes only met with the cold, piercing eyes of Prince Corbin's parents, and the indifferent faces of the others in attendance, none of whom Ellyn had seen or knew.

The only sounds in the chapel were the soft tapping of their shoes against the hard wooden floor as they walked slowly down the aisle. Ellyn glanced at the guests sitting in the pews as she passed, and her eyes met with a beautiful young woman, sitting very close to her at the end of the pew. Her dark eyes were piercing into Ellyn's and she was glaring at her with an expression of disdain. The unwavering expression of contempt stirred a feeling of uneasiness in Ellyn's stomach and she looked away quickly.

"How was the wedding ceremony?" Alys asked. Ellyn had just returned after a very long and substantial feast which had followed the wedding ceremony. She was leaning back against the pillows on her bed, staring up at the ceiling.

"It was adequate," she said. She turned her head and gazed out the window. The moon had already begun to shine in the sky, even though it was not completely dark outside. "The same moon Julius looks upon every night," she murmured to herself with despondence.

"I have met one of the servants while you were gone," Alys said. "She is going to help me become acquainted with the rituals here, and you as well, if you need her. Her name is Hildegard. She seems nice enough."

"That is more than one can say of the family who employs her," Ellyn muttered.

"Ellyn, won't you please tell me about them? I am so curious to know," Alys said. "If you would rather not speak though, do not feel obliged."

At the sound of a door closing somewhere beyond her room, Ellyn raised herself from the pillows and held up her hand for silence. She stared at the doorknob. After a prolonged silence, she breathed a sigh of relief and fell back on the pillows once again.

"Who was that?" Alys asked.

"Prince Corbin's room is just across from mine," Ellyn replied. "And I hope I don't have to see him anymore tonight. I can barely stand being in his presence, and am filled with a dread at the sight of him. He hardly speaks. In fact, we have never had one word of conversation, though we sat side-by-side at the wedding feast for hours. I have only heard his voice during our wedding vows, and when speaking to others. I know he dislikes me, for the only times our eyes meet, he looks away very quickly with an expression of displeasure. He is tall, as well. I only come to his shoulder, I would guess. And there are King Evander and his wife, Queen Guinevere. They are both severe and disapproving. He is always frowning, and his face always wears an expression of disapproval and harshness. Queen Guinevere is no less austere, and very distant. I can tell she loathes me by the way she looks at me and speaks to me. I wonder what they think when they look at me. There is such friendlessness and coldness in their gazes."

"Well," said Alys slowly. "At least you were not forced to marry an ugly wizened old man." Ellyn squinted. "That is hardly encouraging," she stated.

There was a knock at the door. Ellyn jumped and held her breath, watching Alys as she stood to answer the knock.

Alys unfastened the lock at the door upon reaching it, but she blocked the knocker from view, and Ellyn tilted her head slightly, trying to distinguish their visitor. She breathed a sigh of relief when she saw that Alys was conversing with a servant girl.

"That was Hildegard," Alys said, returning. "She was just giving me a few more bits of information she forgot to tell me earlier."

"What will our day consist of tomorrow? What daily customs does this family have?" Ellyn asked.

"Well, according to Hildegard, most of them arise somewhat late in the morning and eat in bed. So you will not need to concern yourself with waking early tomorrow. After that, I am not sure what the day will consist of for you. I will be very busy with various tasks, but I will always be available for you if you need me."

"Well, I suppose I shall have to wait to find what tomorrow will bring," Ellyn said. "I dread waking tomorrow and not finding myself in my own familiar room."

"This is a very nice room though," Alys said encouragingly.

"But it is not my own." She ran her fingers through her hair and said, "What a long and tiring day this has been. Only yesterday morning, I woke with most of my own family to greet me, and Julius, as well. Tomorrow I will wake up to a strange room in an unfamiliar place with a husband whom I hate."

"Do you really hate him? That is a bit harsh."

"Yes, I hate him," Ellyn said determinedly. "It is because of him that my happiness is shattered. He hates me as well; I made certain of that. If I am going to be miserable here, I don't want to be the only one of the two of us who is unhappy." And with these words, Ellyn buried her face in her hands and began to weep.

Chapter 9 - Ellyn's New Life

Ellyn was lying wrapped in a cocoon of blankets which were pulled over her head. She blinked and opened her eyes drowsily, stirring subconsciously. As she laid in the dark nest of blankets, she listened for the welcoming sounds of morning, but her room was strangely quiet. Instead of the singing of birds outside her window heralding a new day, a dull silence reverberated in her ears. Throwing her blankets aside, she sat up in bed and looked around. She expected to see the familiar, comfortable surroundings of her own room with her gown hanging on the peg by her bed. Instead, the room looked looming and empty. Heavy curtains covered the windows so that the morning light was unable to penetrate into the room. Ellyn's heart sank and she fell back onto the pillows as memories of the past few days flooded into her mind. She stared blankly at the ceiling.

The door opened, and Ellyn lifted her head as Alys entered.

"Oh, you're awake already," Alys said cheerfully. "I thought you would be exhausted from yesterday and would sleep longer. I will go down and bring your breakfast."

"I'm not hungry."

Alys stopped in her steps and turned. "But you must eat," she insisted. "You will feel better afterwards."

"I'm not hungry," Ellyn repeated. She sensed that Alys was about to speak again and said, "I'll eat later, but not now. Please go away." She turned her head away and stared at the floor. She tightened her hands into fists to keep them from trembling. The sound of the door opening and closing as Alys left echoed in the hollow room.

Ellyn took deep breaths and tried to swallow away the tightness in her throat. At last, she swung her legs over the side of the bed and shoved her blankets aside. Wrapping her robe around her small frame, she crossed her arms. Her body was stiff and sore from the many hours she had spent being jostled in the carriage the day before, and she winced as she slid to the floor. Her bare feet felt numb against the cold, hard boards, and she looked to the end of her bed for her slippers. But her trunk still sat partially unpacked in the corner of the room.

She walked on her toes over to the window, hunching her shoulders and hugging her arms around herself, trying to keep away the cold. Sunlight streamed into the room as she pulled aside the heavy curtain, and she squinted and blinked in the morning light. As her eyes grew accustomed to the brightness, she began to survey the landscape from her window. The grass and trees glistened with a thin layer of frost. A creek wound through the terrain, and large boulders and trees lined the creek bed. Just beyond, the stone wall surrounding the castle stood grey and foreboding. At her own home, the castle wall had made her feel safe and secure. Now, she felt imprisoned. Turning away from the window, she let the curtain fall back into place, and the room was once more dark and cold without the warm rays of sunlight shining through the glass panes.

Ellyn reached for the rope next to her bed and pulled, then slumped into a chair, pulling her legs up off the cold floor and hugging her knees.

Less than a minute later, the door opened and Alys entered, holding a tray of food with a bowl of hot porridge and other dishes. She set the tray on a small table next to Ellyn and partially opened the curtains to let in the sunlight that was trying to push its way through the thick cloth. The maidservant opened the truck and began unpacking the rest of its contents while Ellyn absentmindedly nibbled at her bread, staring off into nothingness. While her expression was somber and lifeless, her mind was alive with the thoughts of her family.

"Father has probably been busy for hours already," she thought reminiscently. "His nights were growing shorter and his days longer. He is probably writing at his desk, reviewing strategic plans with some of his advisors. Or maybe he has left on some important business. Ivor is no doubt with him. And Mother must have already risen as well. I wonder if Father has sent her the letter about my arrival here in Lyntirith? Perhaps she does not know yet and thinks I am in Eurasia with Father and Ivor. Whether she knows or not, she is surely worried. And I wonder if Julius knows yet."

Her thoughts froze and she stared into space. She could see his face as if he were standing in front of her. She squeezed her eyes shut, trying to capture his face in her memory. She wondered what his reaction would be when he discovered they would be forever separated. Pressing her lips together tightly, she sank deeper into melancholia.

"Is this all my life will consist of from this day onward?" Ellyn asked at last, breaking the tense silence. "Just sitting and staring?

"No, I'm sure you will be otherwise occupied," Alys said slowly. "Hildegard, the servant I told you about, gave a list of instructions that you should know."

Ellyn nodded, urging her to continue.

Alys took a deep breath. "First of all," she said, "your room is located on the western wing of Lyntirith. The hallway in which your bedroom lies mostly contains bedrooms, but there is a sitting at the end of the hall. As you probably already know, Prince Corbin's room is just across from yours, but the rest of the bedrooms along the hall are empty, and are only used for very important visitors. Down the hall and across the balcony, you will enter the eastern wing of the palace. If you turn right, you will be led to the sleeping quarters of the rest of the royal family, including the king and queen. However, if you cross the balcony and turn left, rather than right, you will enter the portion of the east wing which you may have access to. There are several other rooms as well, including a study. Previously, only Prince Corbin had access to these rooms, but now you may use them as well."

Ellyn stopped chewing and looked up for a moment at Alys, who continued talking. "You will probably spend most of your hours upstairs. The rooms downstairs are mainly used for entertaining, or are nearly always inhabited by members of the family. You will use them when you go down for feasts, or other such occasions. Does this all make sense?"

Ellyn nodded, swallowing. "What does... Corbin usually do during the day?" she asked, his name sounding strange coming from her own lips. "How often does he use the rooms you spoke of in the eastern wing?"

"Hildegard did not give me very much information on his daily schedule. She did say he was usually away in the morning for various reasons. In the afternoon, he sometimes goes riding or hunting, or to one of the rooms in the eastern wing. I can ask Hildegard more questions if you wish."

Ellyn nodded and returned to her meal.

"There is one more thing," Alys said, folding a piece of linen as she spoke. "Queen Guinevere has requested to speak with you when you are ready. She will meet you in the drawing room down the hall."

Ellyn sighed heavily.

"Thank you for taking time for this brief interview," Queen Guinevere said stiffly, gazing at Ellyn with an austere expression. Ellyn shifted in her chair, uncomfortable under the woman's steady, scrutinizing gaze. She opened her mouth to respond, but the queen spoke before any words could come from her mouth.

"I will make this as succinct as possible. In short, I want to understand the amount of education you have received, in order to determine whether or not you will need any further tutoring."

Ellyn was horrified. "She does not think I have been properly educated," she thought angrily. "I am a princess of Eurasia. Does she forget my title?" Then she said aloud, "I see, Your Majesty."

The queen continued, without taking her eyes away from Ellyn. "Have you been trained in any logical or philosophical works?"

"Yes," Ellyn replied confidently. "I was trained by a tutor for five years and studied the works of Plato, Aristotle, Epicurus, Cicero and Augustine, examining in depth their philosophical and rhetorical works."

"And did you study history, geography and economics?"

"Yes, Your Majesty."

"And did you study these subjects specific only to our country, or other lands as well?"

"My studyings were not limited only to Eurasia, but other nations as well," Ellyn replied. "How many languages are you fluent in?"

Ellyn paused and raised her eyebrows. She hesitated, then said, "I speak only my native tongue."

The queen looked appalled. "That is inconceivable," she declared.

"All of the kingdoms in Eurasia speak the same language," Ellyn said dryly. "It seems learning the languages of other peoples would be a waste of time, considering we would never use the knowledge."

"On the contrary," Queen Guinevere said sternly. "I will find a tutor who is fit to train you in the primary languages spoken in lands near and far. As the future queen of Lyntirith, it is vital you be able to communicate with those outside of our country."

Ellyn bit her lip to keep from speaking, and merely bowed her head respectfully.

"I am determined to ensure you are a well-educated, well-bred young woman. The queen of Lyntirith is not allowed to be a woman of low quality. Ever since my son was born, his father and I have had a very clear opinion on the character of his wife. But since we were not able to arrange a marriage as we otherwise would have, we will have to mould you into the young woman that you must be."

Ellyn clenched her teeth together but said nothing.

"Corbin has similar expectations, and it is your job to fill them. You must be faithful, trustworthy and truthful. Your future duty as queen of Lyntirith is not one of luxury and ease. You need to be dependable. You will need to sacrifice your wishes and desires. And if you are not fit to fulfill this position adequately, you will be taught to. I am understood?"

"Yes, Your Majesty," Ellyn said.

The queen nodded, staring into Ellyn's eyes uncompromisingly. Then she finally stood and turned to the door. "That is all for now," she said. "If I have any more questions or remarks, I'm sure you'll be willing to hear them. You may go back to your room now."

The tall woman turned and walked out of the room with her usual dignified poise. Ellyn exhaled and relaxed her shoulders as the queen left. She took deep breaths, trying to ease the tension, and release some of the anger and irritation that had been building as the queen spoke. Then she stood and left the room, quickly withdrawing to her own room. Alys had just finished making her bed and was adjusting the pillows when she entered.

"I need you to gather some information for me," Ellyn said, closing the door and talking in hushed tones.

"Of course," Alys said.

"Find out for me whether or not Prince Corbin is home. I want to go somewhere alone for a while, and this room is more like a prison cell than a bedroom. The rooms across the hall may be more suitable, but if he is there, I'm not going near the rooms. Please go and ask someone whether or not he is home."

Alys set out on her quest and returned only a few moments later with the information Ellyn had requested.

"I discovered that Prince Corbin is not in the palace currently. He is away with King Evander and will not return until early evening."

Ellyn stepped from her room and cautiously looked both directions down the wide hall. No one was in sight, so she stepped out and sought out the balcony which would take her to the other side of the floor. The balcony overlooked another passageway below, and there was a window on the floor below, and Ellyn could see bushes directly outside of it. There was a hallway running perpendicular to the balcony once she reached the end of it, and turned left and down another long hallway. At the end of the hallway, there was a series of doors. She carefully turned the knob of the first door. It eased open and she poked her head in. A table sat in the middle of the room with chairs surrounding it and a desk along the wall. She scanned the room for a moment, then closed the door again.

She looked down the hall and saw a door at the very end of the hallway, along the back wall. She treaded across the wooden flooring, the clicking of her shoes echoing in the hallway. She stopped in front of the door and looked behind her, expecting to see someone walking towards her. But the hallway was empty. When she pushed the door open, she found herself in a comfortable sitting room. It looked calm and inviting, and Ellyn stepped inside and closed the heavy door behind her. There was a fireplace at the back of the room with a tall, cushioned chair next to it. In the corner, there was a desk with a stack of papers in the middle. She walked over to the desk and looked at the writing on the paper. Bold and black, the spidery letters covered pages and pages of the cream-colored sheets.

Turning, Ellyn saw a door with a large glass window, through which she could see the blue sky and the branches of trees. She went to the door and opened, and closed her eyes as a fresh wave of chill air blew into her face. Though it was cold, it refreshed her, and she stepped out onto the elevated veranda. The view from her perspective was breathtaking. The small porch was two stories in the air and overlooked rolling hills and a pond beyond. From her vantage point, she could see past the castle wall and past a line of trees to rolling hills.

"Someday," she murmured to herself. "I will escape past those walls. I will not resort to a life of misery forever."

Ellyn was lying in bed. Nighttime darkness hovered over her, and she pulled the blankets up to her chin. The curtains were open, and occasionally the moon emerged from behind a pocket of clouds, casting shadows of tree branches waving in the wind onto her bedroom floor. Ellyn felt restless and uncomfortable. She twisted and turned, the low hum of the wind whistling through the window panes.

Just as she began to relax at last, and her eyelids began to grow heavy, there was a rustling from outside her door. She was instantly alert, and stared at the ceiling with widened eyes, lying in anxious stillness.

Then, there was a knock on the door.

She watched Alys's silhouette as she rose in the darkness from her cot in the corner and walked silently to the door. She heard the latch being unfastened and the door opening. A dark form stood in a hallway, and a few words were exchanged. Then Alys slipped out of the room and a tall figure stepped inside, closing the door. Ellyn watched the form tread lightly across the floor, not making a sound, and approach her bedside. At that moment, the moon came out from behind some clouds, illuminating Prince Corbin's dark features. He looked down at her silently for a moment, then pulled off the long robe that he had been wearing over his nightclothes and tossed it to the end of the bed. Ellyn's fists clenched and her whole body tensed.

"Why are you here?" she asked quickly.

He froze and frowned with incredulity, scoffing harshly.

"I don't know if you recall the ceremony you attended yesterday," he said dryly. "If you do, you should remember I was there also, and that the purpose of the ceremony was to perform a ritual known to most as a marriage. Should I explain the meaning and conditions of this term as well, or are you familiar with them?"

Ellyn closed her eyes and heaved a sigh.

"No, wait," Corbin said, sitting on the edge of her bed. "Perhaps I should take a moment to explain, since you do seem to be confused about your purpose here, and your place in this family."

"I do know one thing," Ellyn said, sitting up quickly and speaking rushed sentences. "Contrary to what you may think, I am not one of your subjects. I will not stoop to a level that you may think you have the authority to rule over; not you nor either the king or queen. I will make my own decisions, whether you approve or not. And if you do attempt to have lordship over me, you will regret ever having spoken to me."

"I already do regret it," Corbin replied quickly. "I regret having an affiliation with you at all, but unfortunately for me, it is a decision that I could not control. For I, like you, are not as in control of my own life as I would like to think. If I was, I would not be here right now, and neither would you. This is one of many decisions that has been made for you, so stop trying to be the ruler of your own life." to say."

"You idiot," Ellyn said, stammering to find a response to his stinging words.

"If all you're going to do is throw insults at me, keep your mouth shut and listen to what I have

"I was not aware that you had come here to say anything," she replied. "And since you have said nothing useful yet, perhaps you should not continue."

"We are now husband and wife," he said, breaking Ellyn off before she had finished her sentence. "And I am to inherit the throne one day. As my wife, you have your part to fulfill, two tasks specifically. One of them is to unite the kingdoms of Lyntirith and Eurasia through this marriage so that we may combine forces and fight the Northmen. Since this has clearly been completed, your only other task is to provide an heir for the throne so that this family line may continue. Beyond that, you have no purpose. Think of me what you will. Our marriage was not arranged for our own individual profit, but for the profit of our country. As long as you fulfill your duty, I want nothing more from you. Keep your useless opinions to yourself."

She opened her mouth to speak, but, once again, Corbin cut her off. "We have done enough talking tonight."

"I think you meant to say that you have done enough talking, while I have yet to respond."

"Exactly, that is as I intended," he replied indifferently.

"I hate you," she said in a low voice.

Corbin laughed dryly.

"That is one thing I can say is mutual between us, Ellyn."

Chapter 10 - A Stranger in the Night

Ellyn stood in her bedroom looking out through the window. The sound of clattering armory and men shouting reached her ears. Horses whinnied above the commotion and someone was yelling out orders every few minutes. King Evander was about to transport hundreds of soldiers across the country to Ellyn's home, where they would be settled at a campsite, awaiting an expected attack from the Northmen.

A tall figure strode into view and stood surveying the activity. The king looked proud and dignified, standing with his arms crossed. Someone strode up to the king's side and stood with his back to the window so that Ellyn could not see his face. But she knew it was Corbin. He stood with the same stature and dignity as his father. Ellyn withdrew from the window and closed the curtain before anyone saw her.

"How long will they be gone?" she asked Alys.

"It will take a few days just to make the journey to Eurasia. Then maybe a day or two for all the soldiers to be settled. So I presume it will be a week or so before the king and his son return," Alys replied. Her sentence was broken off by a series of coughs, and she pressed her fingers to her temples.

A loud groaning sound came from outside the window as the massive castle gate was opened, and the sound of marching feet, stomping hooves and squeaking wheels echoed in unison as the host of men departed for the northern journey. Gradually, the sounds grew more distant, and Ellyn stood again and went to the window. The castle gate was just being closed, and the gate yard that had a moment ago been ringing with the sounds of the departing soldiers was now quiet and empty. Just beyond, Ellyn saw rows and rows of soldiers, marching in straight lines, with shields, swords and spears at their sides, disappear beyond the hills and trees. It was long after the last row of soldiers had disappeared and the last voice ringing over the hills had faded that Ellyn finally turned away from the window.

She cringed as Alys began coughing again. Her maidservant had insisted she felt well, even though she had been coughing all morning, and occasionally had to sit down due to shaking and chills. "You certainly are not well, Alys," she said, when the coughing had subsided. "And your constant coughing is very unnerving. Please find a place to rest so that I may have peace and quiet."

Alys nodded and stood. "I'm sorry," she said raspily. "I will tell Hildegard I'm going to rest so that she can tend to you if you are in need of anything."

Her shoulders were shaking as she tried to control another round of coughing, and she left the room. Ellyn sighed, sinking down wearily into a chair.

She had been residing in Lyntirith for just under a week, but already, it seemed that she had been there for an eternity. Each day had dragged so tediously, and each of them had been spent in dull solitude. Every moment was spent dreading the next time Corbin would confront her and fearing her next encounter with him. His presence made her nearly speechless with fright, and even the thought of him made her shudder. Even though he was a young man, his austerity and severeness made him seem older than he was.

"He is the complete opposite of Julius," Ellyn thought to herself. "Julius is kind and warmhearted, while Corbin's heart is made of stone. Julius made me happy, and made me want to spend time with him. My life here is miserable, and it is my sole aim to avoid Corbin as much as possible. Julius was always smiling, and made me smile too. He was easy to talk to, and I was always comfortable around him. He was also brave and self-sacrificing. He didn't even think a second time about saving me when his own life was in danger. I don't think Corbin has ever smiled in his life, and he makes me want to run from the room when he enters. The only person he ever thinks about is himself. Out of all of the princes in the country, how did I manage to marry the most heartless, uncaring, unkind of all of them? What did I ever do to deserve this? Nothing so unfair has ever happened to a person before."

Now Ellyn had stood and was pacing her room, muttering to herself. She was wringing her hands tensely and glaring at the floor, her teeth clenched in anger.

"Father did not know what he was doing in sending me here. In possibly saving the lives of some of the people in the kingdom, mine is utterly ruined forever. Was there truly no other way?"

She angrily kicked the side of her bed, then winced as a sharp pain shot through her foot. She groaned and sank down onto her bed, trying to calm the feelings of discontent and anger.

"It wasn't really Father's fault," she thought, once she had calmed herself somewhat. "It was King Evander's. His firm negotiations left my father no choice. What does he expect to gain by having his son marry me? Couldn't he have formulated another method of securing the treaty with Eurasia? Why was I the one to suffer the consequences of evils that I never committed? Out of the many lives of those involved in or affected by this whole ordeal, mine is the only one that is ruined."

She sat up and stared into space, her shoulders slumped over. Images of her family and Julius crept into her head, and tears began slowly trailing down her face.

"Why can't I just accept my life as it is now and forget everything I left at home? They are gone forever. I should stop blaming everyone else for my current situation and be content with the certainty that this is now my home forever."

Then Ellyn stood up defiantly and looked at herself in the mirror over her dressing table.

"No," she said aloud to her reflection. "This is not my home forever. Someday, somehow, I will leave this place. I don't know how or when, but I will see my family again. It is not my destiny to stay here forever. But if it is my destiny to stay here, I will change my fate. I will not stay in this prison for the rest of my life. Someday, somehow, I will leave this place."

It was the dead of night, many hours after sunset. The night was still. Darkness shrouded everything. Even the servants in Lyntirith had gone to bed, and the watchman in his tower was one of only a few people who still stirred near the Lyntirith castle. There was no breeze, no clouds. The sky was clear, and the small, silver moon was a thin crescent and offered very little light to the world below.

Ellyn awoke from a deep slumber and opened her eyes to the utter darkness. Alys was not in her usual place on the cot. Ellyn had not seen her since that morning when she had gone downstairs to rest. Hildegard had prepared her for bed, then left the room. Now, Ellyn felt alone, and the sound of Alys's heavy breathing was absent, making her feel uncomfortable.

A muffled rustling sound came from behind Ellyn's bedroom door. She sat up and stared into the darkness, listening intently. It came again. This time, it was the sound of hands fumbling with the doorknob.

"Is it Alys?" Ellyn wondered to herself. But why would Alys be walking around in the dead of night? Ellyn slid out of her bed and shivered. Trying to suppress the fear in her throat, she crept toward the door. Was that faint sound she heard whispering? She couldn't tell. Her legs began to shake, and Ellyn felt around for something to support her.

A clicking sound made Ellyn start. The door was unlocked, and slowly, she saw the knob begin to twist. She covered her mouth and leaped aside, concealing herself behind a tall wardrobe along the wall.

A glimmer of light cast shadows against the back wall as the door opened, and a hand appeared, holding a candle. Ellyn peered out from behind her hiding place, her heart pounding, waves of heat rushing through her body. A form emerged from the hallway and Ellyn distinguished a person holding up the candle for more light. The person glided across the room without making a sound and stopped at the side of her empty bed. Ellyn held her breath, waiting and watching. Whoever was hiding beneath the black mask was certainly not Alys.

The person stood at the bedside for a long time, then reached a hand under the blankets that had been frantically shoved into a heap only moments before. Then, the candle was held up higher, and the black figure looked left and right, peering into the corners of the room. Ellyn cowered in the shadows and pressed her hand to her mouth. Her legs were shaking violently, and she felt drops of sweat forming on her forehead as the candlelight reflected off the beady eyes as they stared in her direction. But the light of the candle did not reach her, and the person turned away and examined the opposite side of the room where Alys's empty cot sat.

The person crept silently towards the cot, facing away from Ellyn. She saw her chance. Standing, Ellyn darted from her hiding spot on her toes and escaped through the open bedroom door. Her heart was pounding even harder, and Ellyn looked behind her, expecting to see the black figure emerging from the room, walking briskly toward her. She ran on bare feet from her room, heaving deep, labored breaths. She ran past the balcony and down the hallway toward the sitting room she had occasionally visited. She had just turned to dart down the hall when she heard a sound just behind her. She felt a hand on her shoulder and opened her mouth to scream. But all that came out was a muffled yelp as an arm reached around her neck and a large hand covered her mouth, stifling her scream.

Frantically, Ellyn fought to pull away from the person, but his strength far outweighed her own and she found herself with her back against the wall, staring with terror at a face inches from her own. The hand still covered her mouth, and she was being held tightly against the wall so that she was unable to move.

"Calm down," the voice hissed. "I'm not going to hurt you, I promise. Please calm yourself and don't scream."

Ellyn's shoulders heaved and shook as she stared at the person she had never seen before. It was too dark for her to make out his features, but she could tell he had dark hair and high cheekbones. Then she realized he looked about her own age, if not perhaps slightly older. She twisted and turned in his grasp, and finally he pulled his hand away from her mouth.

"Who are you?" she gasped breathlessly.

"Hush!" he whispered. "You're going to wake everyone else. I am Prince Corineus."

Ellyn felt faint and leaned her head against the wall. Her body was weak from the strain of the past few minutes, and she felt she was about to collapse.

"Corbin's brother?" she breathed. He nodded.

"Why did you come into my room?" she demanded angrily.

He stared at her blankly. "I was not in your room. I was walking down the hall when you dashed past me, and I followed you, wondering what was amiss."

Ellyn stared at him skeptically. "Then why were you out in the hall in the middle of the night?" she prodded.

"I was just coming upstairs from one of the sitting rooms. I always go to bed very late and was on my way to my room."

Ellyn frowned, trying to decide whether or not he was telling the truth.

"Can you please let go of me now?" she finally said. Corineus released her from his strong grip and Ellyn fell against the wall.

"Well, if what you say is true, someone is still in my room," she said. "And I am not going back in there. I know someone is there, and whether or not it was you, I don't know."

"It certainly was not me," he insisted. "But I will investigate your room before you go in. Come with me."

He pulled her down the hall and opened a door. He fumbled around the room and was soon holding a lit candle in his hands. He set it on a small table and lit another candle. Ellyn watched him with a feeling of doubt and discomfort. She was able to see him clearly for the first time. He had the same dark hair as his brother, but his features were very different. He was smaller and looked much more youthful.

"Stay here," he said, leaving the room with one of the candles.

Exhaling slowly, Ellyn tried to relax. Her back and shoulders were sore, and she could still feel Corineus' fingers wrapping around her face. She shuddered and picked up the candle, looking around the room.

A bed stood in the corner of the room and a desk was right beside it. A dark robe was hanging over the bed and a blue tunic was hanging on the wall next to the bed. A stone fireplace was situated on the other side of the room, and Ellyn wished a warm fire were in it to push away the shadows and darkness. She felt vulnerable, and frightened, alone in Corineus's room. Why had he brought her here, and what was he doing? She shivered.

At last the door opened, and Corineus entered.

"Your room is empty," he announced. "I looked in every corner and closet. No one was to be found. You must have been dreaming."

"I certainly was not," Ellyn insisted, "I have never been more awake in my life. I remember the dark, masked figure creeping across the floor." She groaned. "I'm never going in that room again."

"All the floors of our castle are always guarded. An intruder would have been caught if there was one."

"Then how do I know that the intruder was not you?" Ellyn asked fiercely. Corineus closed the door and walked across the room toward her. He stood directly in front of her and stared into her eyes.

"I was not in your room."

Ellyn stared back. Her heart was pounding, and something about Corineus made her feel uneasy. She cowered away from him.

"Then I want to go back to my room," she finally said, after a long silence.

He looked at her in silence for a long time, then shrugged and opened his bedroom door. Watching him warily, Ellyn walked past him and out into the dark hallway. Holding the candle up to light her way, she treaded down the hallway. She jumped as Corineus's bedroom door closed behind her. She turned. The hallway was empty and dark behind her. The candle flickered as she walked back to her room. Her door was closed and she timidly reached for the doorknob. She looked up and down the hallway and finally opened the door, cautiously and quietly.

Stepping into the room, she closed the door and held up the candle. She looked around, fearful of any sound or movement that might issue from the dark corners of her room. An ominous silence surrounded her. Ellyn locked the door and stepped into her room, her eyes darting left and right.

She crept around her room, looking in every corner, under each desk, inside each wardrobe and closet. Finally, she sank wearily onto her bed and set the candle on the table next to her. Her head was throbbing and she pulled her legs up, hugging them to herself. She could almost see the dark figure treading stealthily across her bedroom floor, and shuddered at the memory of those terrifying moments. The danger she had been in fully struck her as she sat alone on her bed. Who was the strange person in her room? Was it Corineus? What if she had not woken up and escaped from her room before she had been found? And then she remembered being alone with Corineus in his room. What if he had decided to harm her? He was much stronger than she, and she would have been entirely at his mercy. Was he telling her the truth? After all, it seemed very suspicious that he had been out in the hallway at just the right time.

Pulling her blankets up to her chin, Ellyn fell back onto her pillows, the candle casting flickering shadows on the walls. She tossed and turned for many hours, until she fell into a restless sleep as the sunlight began illuminating the eastern skies.

Chapter 11 - Peronell's Story

"Good morning, Ellyn."

Ellyn sat straight up in bed. She pulled her blankets up as if to hide her face as a voice at her bedside startled her out of her sleep.

"I'm sorry, I didn't mean to frighten you," Alys said.

Ellyn exhaled and fell back onto her pillow. Sun was streaming through her window and the light made her eyes hurt. The night had been nearly sleepless and she felt weak with exhaustion.

Alys pulled the blanket off her face. "You have slept later than usual."

Pulling the blanket back over her face, Ellyn tried to decide whether or not she should tell Alys about the events from the night before. What if she was worrying prematurely and nothing of the sort would happen again? On the other hand, she would feel safer if someone else was aware and could keep watch. At last, she sat up and stretched, trying to rouse her weary body.

"I would have felt more at ease had I not been alone last night. It was quite… unnerving."

Alys looked at her, trying to assess the meaning behind her words. "What do you mean?" she

asked.

Ellyn was silent for a moment. Then she slipped out of bed. The sunlight from her window

shone through the long golden waves of hair that fell down her shoulders and back. Her white nightgown rippled against her legs as she treaded to the bedroom door. She pulled the knob and felt it give way. She pushed it tightly closed and locked it. Then she turned back to Alys, who was watching her with furrowed brows.

"Someone made it past this door last night when they no doubt thought I was sleeping," she said.

Alys's eyes grew large in shock.

Ellyn gave Alys a full account of the intrusion of her room and her encounter with Corineus. "Whoever found their way into my room last night either had the key, or was an expert at opening locked doors," Ellyn said when she had finished. "Besides being accomplished in undoing locks, surely the intruder knew I was here alone. I have been here for a week, and last night, not only was Corbin away, but you were ill and not sleeping in my room. Could someone have known that and taken advantage of the opportunity to enter when I was alone? If so, only a few people would have known I was alone, and Corineus was one of them. He was acting so strange, I would not be surprised if he had been the intruder. But what was his purpose? If he had wanted to hurt me, he could have easily done so at nearly any point last night. So what else could he have wanted? Did he want to look through my belongings?

"But then, what if he is telling the truth and it was another person? If it was, I can't think of who it would be, or what they would want."

Alys, who still had not yet spoken, began looking around the room, scrutinizing it for anything that looked unusual. Ellyn also looked around her bed, feeling uneasy even in broad daylight. The experience from the night before was now fresh in her mind after she had conveyed everything to Alys. "I can't believe that you were in possible danger last night and no one was here to provide protection," Alys said. "And if the person was not Corineus, then who was it? And why did they enter?"

"I have been wondering those same things since," Ellyn said. She sank down into a chair and stared out the window.

"There are always guards just at the bottom of the stairs and no other way to come up without being seen. Whoever it was had to be upstairs already, making Corineus seem suspicious."

"But I don't understand why he would want to come into my room. Not to harm me, I don't think. If he had wanted to, he easily could have. I don't know, it's too confusing. I just hope nothing of the sort happens again and I can sleep with peace of mind after this."

"Maybe someone wanted to find out something about your past," Alys suggested. Ellyn shrugged. "No one would be interested in that."

Alys raised her eyebrows. "I don't know if that is true," she said. "Hildegard asks me questions quite regularly."

"What kind of questions?" Ellyn asked quickly.

"Oh, a variety of them, but all about what life was like before we came here. What Eurasia was like, and that sort of thing. She sometimes brought up questions about your family as well."

"My family?"

"Yes, just general questions about them."

"What have you told her?' Ellyn prodded.

"I have simply answered her questions without addressing the private issues. Her questions are general, so my answers are general as well."

"Have you told her anything about … Julius?" Ellyn hesitated before saying his name. She had barely said his name since her departure because it brought her pain to speak it, but he was nearly always in her thoughts.

"Well." Alys thought for a moment. "I think I did mention him, but did not give any details."

Ellyn sighed. "I hope she does not say anything about Julius to anyone else. I would feel uncomfortable if others knew about our… affiliation which would have probably been a marriage eventually."

"But you have done nothing to be ashamed of. You could not have foreknown what would happen in the future."

"I know," Ellyn sighed. "I would rather my past not be mentioned here. Untrue speculations might be made, so it is probably best no one knows any details."

"Very well, I will make sure that no more information about Julius or your family is passed along."

Ellyn nodded then fell into a brooding silence.

Ellyn spent the next few days in this anxious solitude, wondering who the intruder had been and whether or not it would happen again. Every night she spent sitting in bed leaning against the pillows, which she propped against her headboard, listening to the sound of the night. The darkness made her feel susceptible, and she began to realize how alone she truly was. There was no one she could turn to if she was ever in danger or needed help. Alys was the only person in Lyntirith with whom she could speak comfortably, but she was not much more than a loyal maidservant. If she were in real, desperate danger, Alys would not be able to offer the assistance she would need. She had no one to protect her if she was in danger, and no one to turn to if she needed help.

Despite Ellyn's worries, her fears were not confirmed in those slowly passing days. The nights passed with no interruption and the days faded in and out, with only Alys to speak with. The frightening events from that night began to have less of an impression on Ellyn so that she rested easier at night, especially now that she was not alone. She was careful to ensure that the door was locked every night, a precaution she had not been worried about before. Occasionally, Alys brought her news about the affairs at home. The strength of the Northmen seemed to be dwindling, from the reports, and the soldiers would be returning home soon, although no exact time was determined over the course of those days. Usually, though, Ellyn did not like to hear reports from Eurasia. They left her with a feeling of homesickness and loneliness.

Two days after the nighttime incident, Ellyn's language teacher arrived. She was middle-aged, short and dark-haired. She was certainly a foreigner, as Ellyn immediately noted. Her complexion was dark and her hair back and coarse. Her eyes were small and slanted. She was solemn and reserved and greeted Ellyn without a smile. Though she was small, she held herself tall and straight, with her broad shoulders squared.

"Good afternoon, Princess Ellyn," she said stiffly when they met in a sitting room down the hall from Ellyn's room. Both seated themselves across from each other at a round table. "I am Peronell, and am to be your language tutor for the next few months. I hope you will be a diligent and studious pupil." Her accent was heavy, one that Ellyn thought sounded familiar, but could not determine.

"I will certainly endeavor to," she replied. "May I ask where you were born?"

Peronell looked into her face, expressionless. "I grew up in Weyhill, a country west of this island and many miles from here. But that is not my heritage. I was born in the country of Northland."

"You are a Northern!" Ellyn exclaimed. "Where the Northmen come from."

He nodded.

"But I understood that though the Northerns are somewhat... barbaric, they are close-knit within their clans. Why did you leave Northland?"

The woman raised her eyes upwards and shook her head. "First of all," she said. "The Northerns are not barbaric. They are not as cultured or as civilized as Eurasia, or some surrounding countries, but they are far from barbaric. They have towns and villages just as you have, except they are called communities. Many are educated. Just because they don't have a king or strong leadership does not mean they are barbarians. This is one of the strongest misconceptions of Northerns, and it is because the Northmen have tainted the meaning of what it is to be a Northern.”

“What do you mean?” Ellyn asked. “I have seen Northmen. I heard them speak. They sounded harsh and uncouth and dressed without the signs of having been educated.”

“Yes, but the Northmen are not all from Northland. They are a large group of men, who started out when Northland was not what it is now. Northland indeed used to be a nomadic, barbaric group of tribes, and were known as warriors who took over other countries. Since then, Northland has settled into a few large communities, but many did not want to settle down. They wanted to continue in their old ways of ignorance and restlessness and warfare. This group of people, many of them men, began to grow, as people from other countries came from afar at the prospect of taking over other lands. The Northmen continued to grow, until they were the size of many armies. They lived in tents outside of the communities, and attacked small nearby towns. It was very disorganized, but the men were strong fighters and renowned warriors. Instead of killing the inhabitants, they forced the men to fight with them, thus growing their ranks. That is the reason they have grown so large, and now are laying their sights on large lands and kingdoms, such as Eurasia.”

“So, you saw the Northmen when you lived in Northland?” Ellyn asked. “No.” Peronell shook her head slowly. “I was one of them.”

Ellyn stared at her silently. “What happened?” she asked.

Peronell shook her head. “I was born to a great Northern fighter, one of the leaders. He was greatly feared by all his foes, even though he was still a young man in his youth, around twenty-six when I was born. But in his bearing and strength, he had the appearance of a warrior ten years older. My mother was very young, the daughter of a family that the Northmen had conquered, about your own age. It is a long tale which I have not the time to tell. But my father had come to love my mother. Even though she had been a prize from war, he was filled with love for her. My mother was full of sadness and grief at being separated from her family and uprooted from her homeland. I think I was her only source of happiness. She kept me always by her side and was always tender towards me.

“As I grew up, all I knew was that my father was away very often, and that my mother seemed brighter when he was away. I did not understand why, because he was always so kind to her. He did have a fierce temper. but he never showed it towards her. Then one day, when I was nine, my mother took me away and we left. I did not understand why we left, and I often asked, but she would not tell me. I still have not answered that question, even though she died years ago, when I was a young woman. I think she must have been unhappy."

Ellyn had been staring at Peronell throughout the tale. Visions of the young girl, Peronell's mother, being torn from her family's side, flooded through her head. The family that would never see her again. She had been taken away and forced to live with another man in unhappiness until she fled. Suddenly gasping quietly, Ellyn seemed to start out of a reverie. Images of the home she had left behind began filling her head, and she shook them away.

"The Northmen have torn apart many families, not only your mother's," she murmured softly.

"Yes, it is true. Many poor peasant families would never be the same again because of them."

"But not all of them peasants," Ellyn thought, but said nothing.

"I should begin your lesson," Peronell said, taking a deep breath. "I have wasted time. But the history of my people is a foundation you will need before understanding our language. Now let us begin."

Ellyn thought long and hard about what Peronell had said after her lesson. She sat in her bedroom, staring out over the wide open hills and forests beyond the castle walls. They seemed to be so open and welcoming, inviting her to come and traipse across them. She began to think about Peronell's mother, and the short life she had lived.

"She must have had so much bravery," she thought to herself. "To leave to a place that was unknown with a child. And no doubt she was not sure how she would support herself and her child. She could not return home, it was probably destroyed. How did this young woman, not many years older than myself, make such a decision? What a turmoil her mind must have been in, leaving safety and going out into danger. But at least she had a husband who wanted her to be happy and tried to be kind to her."

Ellyn leaned back in her chair and sighed, staring out the window. "I wonder what he thought when she left. Peronell said he loved her; did he try to find her? Did he grieve her disappearance? Did he miss her? Or did he just claim another beautiful young woman from another plundered town? Even though this young woman lived years ago and is separated by status and wealth, many miles and years, somehow I feel that we share a story. I wonder how she died, and where she fled to. Peronell must not have wanted to tell all of the story, since she did not say."

Ellyn sat with these ponderings for many minutes. Then, suddenly, she was struck with a strange urge. She leapt up from her chair and scrutinized the window panes until she found a small lever. She pulled it and heard a click. Then slowly and carefully, she opened the top half of the window. A bare, crisp breeze struck her face. She inhaled sharply as the wind blew through her hair and into her room. She had not felt the wind on her face for many days. She took deep breath after deep breath, closing her eyes. Then she opened them and looked down at the castle walls.

"I wonder if Peronell's mother felt imprisoned," she thought. "Imprisoned by the walls of her house that kept her from leaving, as these castle walls do for me." Her eyes once again lifted to the hills beyond the castle walls, then, slowly, she closed the window, and sank back into the chair again.

Chapter 12 - Maerynn of Wyndham

Ellyn sighed and leaned her back against the wall. She felt empty and dull after hours of looking out the window. She listlessly sank into the chair by the window and rested her chin on the sill. She felt exhausted, even though she had done nothing to exert herself. Her body felt heavy and fatigued.

"All I have done for days is sit," she said to Alys, who was seated nearby. "I need to be somehow occupied; I cannot spend the rest of my life in this way, sitting around with nothing to do and with no real purpose."

Alys looked up from her mending, but said nothing.

"I envy you, Alys," Ellyn continued. "Your days are never idle. You are always doing something with your hands, or working in the kitchens."

"If you spent your days rising before dawn and working until well past the setting of the sun, no doubt you would wish for some idleness," Alys commented.

"But surely there is some sort of balance that can be struck between the two extremes. I feel useless."

"I think you are very far from useless," Alys said. "If you had not come, the desolation brought on by the Northmen would surely be extreme. You would have had to exile Eurasia, and many lives would have been lost."

"I know, I know," Ellyn sighed. She said nothing more, feeling that any response she had to Alys's comment would sound unfeeling and callous. She heaved another sigh and stood up.

After several moments of silence, she said, "I'm going to the sitting room down the hall. I'll return shortly."

She treaded from the room and out the door. As always, she felt strange and conspicuous whenever she stepped out of her room. She expected to find Queen Guinevere lurking around the corner, or Corineus hiding behind a closed door. The upstairs halls and rooms were quiet, and Ellyn saw no one, but she could hear movement and activity on the lower floor, somewhere beyond the staircase. She did not stop to listen but continued down the hall until she reached the galley of doorways that she had been permitted entrance to. Many of her waking hours had been spent in the sitting room at the end of the hallway in solitary and woeful contemplation.

She quietly turned the doorknob, and the sound of the latch unfastening echoed in the empty hallway. The door creaked as it opened, and Ellyn stepped inside.

As she closed the door, Ellyn felt that something was amiss, and as soon as the door had closed, she heard a rustling from the corner of the room. She gasped under her breath, and pressed her lips together to keep from crying out in her surprise.

The movement had come from the corner of the room that was only visible to the person entering the room once the door had been closed. A desk sat in the corner, and at this moment, the chair at the desk was occupied by the person Ellyn had least expected and least hoped to see.

"I did not know you had returned," she said slowly.

"Clearly," said Prince Corbin wryly. He set down his pen and leaned back in his chair, looking at her intently. His features were dark and uncompromising, and Ellyn returned his glare.

"If you wish to stay, you are permitted as long as you keep the noise to a minimum" Corbin said.

"Oh, I am permitted—"

"Just sit down and keep your thoughts to yourself. I know where this conversation is going and I don't want to have it again."

Ellyn opened her mouth to speak, but no words came to her mind to say, so she closed it again. After an uncomfortable silence, she turned aside and walked to the opposite side of the room. She could feel Corbin's eyes following her as she went. She sat in her usual chair by the window and turned her face away, staring blankly at the tree just outside the window. Her heart pounded and beat rapidly, and she took quick nervous breaths. The sound of a pen scratching on paper reached her ears, and agitated the silence.

After a long time, Ellyn, without turning her head, looked toward the desk out of the corner of her eyes. She could see the form of Corbin sitting, his head bent over the desk, only his profile visible to her. She slowly turned her head and glanced at him. She felt a sort of intimidation and smallness, even without him looking at her or speaking to her. His expression was severe, and his eyebrows were furrowed pensively. She looked away quickly and stared down into her lap.

At length, the sound of the pen stopped, and the rustling of paper followed. The wooden legs on the chair scraped against the floor and echoed through the room, followed by the sound of heavy footsteps striding across the room to the door.

"I will leave you in peace now," Corbin said, his voice low and impassive.

"Wait," Ellyn said quickly, turning toward the door. Her voice sounded louder and sharper than she had intended it, and she inwardly chided herself for having spoken at all. Corbin froze in front of the closed door, his hand resting on the knob. He slowly turned and looked at her.

Ellyn took a deep breath and spoke falteringly. "I must know the outcome of the fighting that you have come from. What was the condition you left Eurasia in?"

Corbin was silent for a long time, his gaze unwavering. When he spoke at last, his cold voice matched his expression. "Why do you care about the condition of Eurasia and speak of that place as your home?" he said. "Your place no longer stands with them. The events and proceedings of Eurasia can no longer have importance to you because they no longer have any implications for you."

"Well, I have interest as it is my former home, then," Ellyn said. "Even though the occurrences that have taken place in Eurasia no longer affect me here, there was a time when they affected me very profoundly, and, if it were not for certain happenings that affected me there, I would not be here now."

"That is irrelevant, for the times that are behind you are gone forever. So there is no need to brood over them."

"So you are saying that what has happened in the past has no effect on the present," Ellyn asked.

"Not directly," he replied. "What has happened is already past. Why regret them, or wish them otherwise? They are unchangeable. It is better to focus on the present, and plan for the future."

"You have not answered my original question," Ellyn said.

"How observant you are," Corin said mockingly.

"Well if you intend to answer my question, do it," Ellyn said. "If not, leave me alone and go tend to your duties."

Corbin crossed his arms, and looked at her unwaveringly. "The outcome of the battle," he said, speaking slowly, "was fulfilling in that we completed the task that we set out to do, which was to subdue the advances of the enemies. They are stubborn and will return once they gather new strength, but this is the beginning of their decline of power. While they have not realized it yet, they will soon."

Ellyn nodded with satisfaction and turned, sitting down once again. The door behind her opened, and was slowly shut. Then footsteps were heard retreating briskly down the hallway. Ellyn leaned back in her chair and stared at the ceiling.

Several moments later, she walked slowly back into her room. Alys sat in her chair exactly as Ellyn had left her, and looked up as Ellyn closed the door.

"You look troubled," Alys said, as Ellyn sat vacantly on the edge of her bed.

She shook her head, but did not reply at first. "I just spoke with… Alys, did you know the soldiers had returned from Eurasia?"

Alys looked at her and frowned. "Of… course. I told you so this morning." Ellyn sighed. "I must have been distracted."

"Then I suppose you didn't hear about the feast either?"

"The… what are you talking about?"

Alys smiled wryly. "Yes, there is to be a feast tonight, to welcome the king home from battle. Apparently it is a custom here to hold a feast if the king returns successful from the battlefield. Also, there are several guests staying in the castle for a few days. The royal family of Wyndham is here, and will be at the feast."

Ellyn's shoulders slumped. "I wish I had known they had returned. Then I might not have encountered…" Her voice trailed off.

"You may remember the King of Wyndham and his family," Alys continued. "They live very nearby and are often here at the castle, because King Arnos is the brother of Queen Guinevere, and I believe his family was at your wedding ceremony."

"Well, I remember very little of the guests from that day." Ellyn shrugged. "So most likely, I will not recognize any of them. A feast, though? For once, I wish I could spend the rest of my day in here. The evening will no doubt be tedious and dull. And that means I'll have to see him again."

"Him? Oh, do you mean Corineus?"

"No. Well, yes, Corineus too. But I was speaking of Corbin."

Alys nodded slowly, then raised her eyebrows suddenly in realization. "That accounts for your change of temperament. You saw him, didn't you?"

"I did more than see him," Ellyn grumbled.

"I'm sorry, I don't mean to pry," Alys said quickly. "I should keep my observations to myself. It is getting later in the afternoon, though. I will lay out your gown, and then I will begin with your hair."

Ellyn sat in an elegant sitting room on a satin-covered chair near the door. The room was filled with low murmurings as those in the room talked quietly amongst themselves. Trying not to appear too obvious, Ellyn studied each member of the family who was present in the room. At the end of the room, King Evander stood with grandeur and dignity. His arms were crossed in an almost defiant manner, and his thick, black eyebrows were furrowed pensively. His shadowed face was darkened by the lighting in the room, and every now and then Ellyn felt his eyes pass over her, and she felt a tremor under his gaze.

At his side stood Queen Guinevere with austere elegance and grace. Her sharply defined mouth was turned down at the corners, and her black eyes pierced from under her arched brows. Her features were delicate, but severe. Occasionally, she turned to say a word to her husband in hushed tones.

Across the room from Ellyn, a small settee stood against the window where Corineus was sitting. Her eyes constantly met with his, and she found herself trying to translate the meaning of his expressions. Every time she looked at him, he would raise his eyebrow a certain way, or his mouth would twitch curiously. But he sat silently, not contributing to the general noise in the room. Next to him sat the member of the family Ellyn had not yet met. She was a small, pallid girl with a thin face and delicate features. Her white hands were clasped together in her lap and she kept her eyes downward and barely moved. Only her shoulders heaved slightly, but almost unnoticeably.

In the corner of the room, near his parents, Corbin stood, tall and severe. Even though he stood near the edge of the room, he seemed to be acknowledged by everyone there to be present, though he rarely spoke. When he did, his low voice seemed to cause a slight hush in the room, and Ellyn unconsciously tensed when she heard his voice, even though she could not understand the words over the conversation in the room. Amidst the royal family, small groups of people sat or stood about the room, talking quietly, or merely observing.

One of the first guests Ellyn noticed was a young woman standing in a group of people near the chair she was sitting in. Her dark hair fell in waves down her back, and she had a gold band wrapped like a wreath on top of her head. Even though there was a conversation in the midst of her group, she seemed distracted, and was constantly looking around the room with quick darting glances. While her face had the possibility of being pleasant and winsome, she glared with small, piercing eyes, which seemed to frequently meet with Ellyn's. The young woman's face seemed to hold familiarity in her mind, and Ellyn did not have to think very hard to remember that same face glaring at her near the end of her wedding ceremony and throughout the duration of the wedding feast.

At length, the young woman broke away from the group and approached Ellyn, sitting in a chair next to her.

"Good evening, Ellyn," she said coolly.

"Good evening," Ellyn replied, with equal evenness.

"My name is Maerynn," the young woman said. "I am princess of Wyndham, which you are no doubt already aware of."

"I had assumed so," Ellyn replied. She felt guarded, and studied Maerynn suspiciously as she spoke.

"You look paler than when I last saw you," Maerynn commented. "Lyntirith weather seems to have damaged your health and complexion."

"It is very different than what I was used to in Eurasia, but I am beginning to become accustomed to the changes."

Maerynn raised her chin, but remained expressionless. "Yes. But the weather must not be the only thing that has changed for you since you left your former home. No doubt at home you had your family to constantly keep you company and activities to keep you occupied. Now, you must be trying to accustom yourself to a quieter life, one of inactivity."

Ellyn winced slightly with suspicion, remembering her conversation on that topic earlier that day.

"Yes, I suppose so," she said vaguely.

"Since my father and Queen Guinevere are brother and sister," Maerynn continued, "I am very closely acquainted with both Corbin and Corineus. I know them well, since we grew up together. I know they are distant, and you must feel very friendless."

Ellyn hesitated before speaking. "It is true, my days are generally lonely, but I wonder why you are concerned about me?"

Maerynn's eyes darkened and she squinted her eyes slightly. She was about to speak in reply when a servant entered the room and announced that the food was ready.

"I will talk to you after the meal," Maerynn said with a tinge of urgency as she stood. Then she stood and turned her back to Ellyn and walked away as if they had not spoken.

Ellyn followed everyone from the room, and they entered a magnificent dining room across the hall. A long, thick wooden table was laden with dishes full of food, sitting on top of an ornate rug sat beneath the long table, and two long lines of chairs sat, spaced immaculately. The room was well lit with candles lining the center of the table and on pedestals along the walls, and a fire in the fireplace at the end of the room cast tall shadows against the opposite wall. A great chandelier with candles hung above the table.

As Ellyn took her seat, she noticed the variety of dishes on the table. In the center were preparations of mutton, veal, pork and poultry. Pots full of soups and stews with steam curling from them issued forth a pleasant, warming aroma. Other platters included loaves of bread, gravy, beans, peas and other vegetables.

The room fell silent as the plates were ceremonially filled and each person around the table given a generous portion of food. Then the sound of forks against glass plates and cups being set down on the table were soon accompanied by quiet conversation.

Eating inconspicuously, Ellyn quietly observed that which was done and said around her. The more food was consumed, the slower the eating became, and the more the conversation began to flow. Corbin was seated next to her, but did not seem to regard her, and spoke very little to anyone. When he did speak, it was to his father, or the King of Wyndham, with whom he was conversing. Maerynn was situated at the opposite end of the table, and Ellyn was glad that they would not have any interaction throughout the meal. She also noticed about halfway through the meal that Helena was not present, and wondered why she had not joined them. She did not remember seeing her leave the group, but quickly forgot about her as the evening progressed.

Focused on her food, Ellyn paid little attention to what was said, until the king of Wyndham, King Arnos, said something about

Northmen. Then, she perked her ears without lifting her head from her bowl of stew.

"Yes, I do think they will still need subduing," King Evander was saying. "They will not be so easily defeated."

"It is for the fortune of many countries that an agreement was reached between Lyntirith and Eurasia," King Arnos stated.

King Evander nodded slightly, and Ellyn felt uncomfortable, though she did not fully understand why.

The conversation then took an abrupt shift, at a comment by King Evander regarding something about the arrival of goods brought by merchants for the Eastern countries.

As soon as the meal had finished, the table was abandoned with much of the food disappeared. They adjourned to a different room, this one smaller and more intimate. This time, everyone found a chair or couch to continue the conversations they had broken off from around the dining room table.

Ellyn sat in the far corner, hoping to meld into the background and not be noticed. But Maerynn sought her out immediately and sat down next to her. She lowered her voice below the sound in the room so as not to be heard.

"You probably were confused by my comments earlier before supper about your loneliness here."

"Somewhat," Ellyn replied.

"I was only going to offer my companionship sometime this week, hopefully to help shorten the day if I may."

Ellyn looked puzzled.

"I am only offering to come and visit you, as a formality and nothing more. We will be staying here for one or two days more, so I would be happy to come visit you in your room and keep you company for an hour or so in the middle of the day."

"I only wonder why you are choosing to seek out my company," Ellyn said slowly.

"Well, there is nothing prohibiting it," Maerynn said rather sharply. "And no doubt neither of us will be better spending our time. Tomorrow afternoon?"

Ellyn straightened her back and took a breath. She was still puzzled why Maerynn seemed so eager to visit her, even though she herself was clearly not seeking the young woman's presence. But she said, "Very well, I will look for you tomorrow."

Maerynn nodded and turned her head, leaning against the back of the couch. Her face settled into its usual expression of conceited disapproval.

Chapter 13 - Maerynn's Proposition

The day after the feast, Ellyn spent almost the entire morning with her language tutor, Peronell. While she found her instructor to be patient and a knowledgeable teacher, the classes were long and tedious, and she was always relieved when they were finished.

"Maerynn will probably be coming soon," she said to Alys when Peronell had left. "I wish she wasn't, but she was very insistent upon paying a visit this afternoon. I hope she does not stay very long."

"Should I leave when she comes in?" Alys asked.

Ellyn thought for a moment, then said, "Yes. Leave the room when she comes in, but come back fifteen minutes later and start making yourself busy here. Maybe that will cause her to leave earlier than she would otherwise."

"Then she only wants your company to pass the time?"

"I don't know." Ellyn frowned. "I really dislike her very much, and I think she has the same opinion of me. I wish she would avoid me, but she seems to seek out my company, and I can't understand why."

"Perhaps it will become clear this afternoon," Alys said.

At that moment, there was a tapping on the door, and Alys rose from her place. She opened the door, and Maerynn sailed into the room. Alys slipped out and closed the door.

Ellyn remained seated in the chair by the window and watched Maerynn as she stood in the middle of the room, looking around with scrutiny.

"Why don't you sit?" Ellyn said dryly, indicating a chair next to hers.

Maerynn raised an eyebrow and pressed her thin lips together. Then she glided across the room and eased herself into the chair. She looked at Ellyn, and her eyes darkened. Ellyn said nothing, but waited for her to initiate the conversation.

"Thank you for allowing me to take up some of your time," Princess Maerynn said coldly. She leaned back and crossed her ankles, without taking her eyes off Ellyn

Ellyn nodded slightly, but said nothing.

"This room is somewhat small," she commented. Ellyn still did not speak.

"Probably much different than what you were used to in Eurasia."

"Why do you keep asking and saying things about Eurasia?" Ellyn asked sharply, cutting her off before she could continue.

Maerynn squinted her eyes. "I have an interest in the life you left behind there," she said slowly, carefully enunciating each word.

"Why?" Ellyn asked.

"Because I had a suspicion that I wanted to confirm."

"Was it correct?" Ellyn asked, anger beginning to creep into her voice.

The corners of Maerynn's mouth turned up evilly. "Of course," she said coolly. Ellyn frowned and stared at Maerynn, who intensely returned the glare.

"You had a lover in Eurasia, didn't you Ellyn?" she said haughtily.

Ellyn took a sharp breath, but did not take her eyes off Maerynn, despite her disbelief at these words.

"What are you talking about?" she pressed.

"You know what I am talking about," Maerynn laughed harshly. "Your lover's name is Julius and he is Prince of Veridell. He is currently in Brystol, but very unhappily."

"I would not call him…"

"Of course he was your lover," Maerynn interrupted callously. "You would have married him if you hadn't hadn't had to leave unexpectedly. Isn't that right?"

Ellyn's frown deepened, and she opened her mouth to speak, then shut it quickly again.

Maerynn smiled with self-satisfaction.

"Julius is a very handsome young man, and very kind. I understand why you fell in love with him," Maerynn continued coyly.

"You have seen him?" Ellyn said with a slight gasp. "Yes, I have," Maerynn replied.

"How did you find out about him?" Ellyn asked, her voice rising in anger. "And how did you find him? What business is my past of yours, and why are you telling me these things?"

"Calm yourself," Maerynn said in disgust. "There is no need to raise your voice. Now just listen and I will answer your questions."

Ellyn settled back into her chair restlessly. Her hands were clenched together in her lap, and her head felt hot.

"First of all, it is no matter to you how I found out about him. I have my own methods and ways of finding things out. It was easy enough to find him. I know where Brystol is and I know how to get there. I met Julius there, and spoke for a while with him. When he found out that I had seen you, he was so persistent, asking questions, wondering how you are, and so forth."

Ellyn lowered her eyes and bit her lower lip.

"He was especially keen when I told him that I have the power to let you see him; that I could bring him here to visit you."

Ellyn raised her head and looked at Maerynn in shock.

"I told him I would ask you if you were willing for me to bring him here. After all, I would not want to bring him against your wishes. Of course he would be devastated if he found out you don't want to see him. But the choice is yours."

Ellyn stared at Maerynn in disbelief. "Are you serious? How would you be able to bring him here secretly? It's impossible! He would be found, and then what would happen? Also, why are you doing this? Why do you want him to come?

"What does it matter?" Maerynn asked sharply. "I have given you the choice and it is for you to decide. If you agree, you have my word that no one will see him. Julius will not be discovered and he will leave safely."

"And why should I trust your word? I would be allowing you to start a false scandal."

"Why would I want others to find out?" Maerynn asked impatiently. "If word came out that it was I who brought him here, the blame would be shifted to me and I would be in disgrace, so I would want to keep it secret as much as you would."

"Then why are you doing this? There must be some benefit for you," Ellyn insisted. "If there is, that is my business. Do you want me to bring him here, or no?"

Ellyn fell silent. She stared at Maerynn's face for a minute, then shifted her gaze out the window. Her initial reaction was to decline Maerynn's offer to bring Julius. She felt sure that Maerynn had some hidden purpose in bringing Julius. And she doubted that this purpose would be to benefit Ellyn. But she was at loss to explain why Maerynn would bring up the offer.

She was about to speak, telling Maerynn she did not want to see him, when her thoughts went from Maerynn and her wiliness to Julius. She remembered their final farewells, and how rushed and incomplete they had been. She thought about the many nights she had lain awake thinking of him, and the days she had sat, staring out the window, wishing she could see him. It was not that her thoughts of him had grown less fond, or less tender. But they had grown less frequent, because of her dwindling hope. She had given up all hope that she would ever see him again, and the thought of him had begun to cause her pain. So she had purposefully tried to think less of him. But, by thinking less of him, she had grown even more dismal. And, lately, she had been waking up in the middle of the night with tear stains on her face, and thoughts of him penetrating her memories.

What if she were to agree to Maerynn's proposition? The thought of seeing Julius, something she had given up all hope for, suddenly seemed overwhelming, and the yearning to see him was so great, that she almost spoke at that moment in concurrence, and looked at Maerynn, opening her mouth to speak. But then she stopped. Maerynn was watching her intently. The sight of her face, set in an expression of cunning anticipation made Ellyn rethink again. She took a deep breath, then exhaled loudly, leaning her head back against the chair and staring at the ceiling.

"I don't know," she murmured.

"I promise, no one will ever find out," Maerynn said slowly, in a low voice.

Ellyn squeezed her eyes shut, and it seemed that each second, she made up her mind, only to change it again a second later. The idea of seeing Julius again was so overwhelming, something she never thought would be possible again. But to possibly be at the mercy of Maerynn made her uncomfortable. Back and forth, Ellyn's thoughts tossed, one moment leaning towards one alternative, and the next the other way. She pressed her palms against her temples and took a deep breath, holding it between tight lips.

With a suddenness that startled even her, she sat up and let out her breath, sitting erect on the edge of the chair.

"Alright," she said sharply. She took a deep breath and closed her eyes. "Alright," she said again, lowering her voice. "Bring him."

Maerynn's shoulders relaxed, and she nodded. "I will," she said. "I cannot say how long it will take, or when I will be able to bring him here. But soon, Julius will be in Lyntirith."

Then she glided out of the room and was gone. Ellyn sat in the chair, frozen in place, staring at the door Maerynn had just closed. Then she stood and began pacing the room. Would she regret her decision? She thought of Corbin, and what he would do if he found out. She shuddered at the thought. She began chiding herself for her decision, wishing she had asked for time to think about it. Was it too late to change her mind? But somehow, she couldn't change her mind. She didn't want to go back to Maerynn and tell her not to bring Julius. She didn't want Maerynn to go back to Brystol and tell Julius that she didn't want to see him, because that was not true.

Ellyn stepped out into the hall a few minutes later. She felt restless and couldn't stay within the confines of her room. Alys walked quickly around the corner as she was closing the door and stopped short when she saw Ellyn.

"Maerynn's already gone?" she asked in surprise.

Ellyn nodded and started down the hall, staring at the ground.

"Ellyn?" Alys turned as Ellyn brushed past her. She stopped and turned, looking at Alys. "What happened?"

"I—I'll tell you later," Ellyn said. "I'll be back." She turned the corner and walked quickly down the hall. As she reached the second corner, she met Corineus coming around the corner and stopped quickly to keep from running into him. She tried to walk past him but he grabbed her shoulders and pulled her to face him.

"Where are you off to in such a hurry?" he asked, looking down at her slyly.

Ellyn frowned and shrugged her arms, trying to rid them of his hands, but he only tightened his grip.

"Let go of me," she said in frustration, and pulled his arms away with her hands. "What does it matter to you where I am going?"

She stepped aside but he blocked her again. Ellyn looked up and scowled at him. He only returned her gaze with a grin.

"Corineus, please step aside and let me go," Ellyn said.

Corineus opened his mouth to speak, but just then, there was the sound of feet coming up the stairs. He looked over Ellyn's head toward the stairs, and then walked past her, continuing on his way down the hall. Ellyn darted around the corner, then heard a low voice echoing from the hall. A voice answered a reply, and though Ellyn could not see around the corner, she knew Corineus had encountered Corbin at the top of the stairs.

"Oh, please don't come this way," Ellyn muttered under her breath. She hurried down the hall and into the sitting room at the end of the hall. Then she stood at the door and leaned her ear against it. She could hear vague voices from the hall, but could not distinguish the words. After about a minute, they fell away, and Ellyn waited at the door.

But there was only silence. When she was sure she would be alone, Ellyn heaved a sigh of relief, then leaned her back against the door. She stared straight ahead at nothingness, thinking again about her conversation with Maerynn. She went to her usual chair to sit, but stood up almost immediately. She went to the window and stared out, then turned away and began pacing the room.

Her stomach was churning and her hands felt sweaty. She rubbed her hands down the sides of her dress as she began walking restlessly back and forth, letting her feet fall gently on the hard floor to keep them from echoing through the room.

Was Julius really coming to Lyntirith? It seemed impossible. The thought of seeing him again, for the first time in months, of speaking with him for the first time since the day she left Brystol; how could that happen? She began to think of him, his laughing eyes, his kind, warm voice, his gentle smile. She stopped in the middle of the room and closed her eyes, smiling gently. Then she opened her eyes and her face grew solemn again.

She had never trusted Maerynn before, and still did not, and here she was taking a great risk in allowing her to bring Julius. Yes, she could be blamed if he was discovered and it was found that she had brought him. But in the end, she would be able to defend herself by saying it was by Ellyn's leave that he came, and then what could she say in response? And the thought of Corbin finding out still haunted her. What would he say? She squeezed her eyes shut and shook her head. Then she continued pacing.

Even if Maerynn did want to do mischief, what would be her motivation? Ellyn had never done anything to offend her; in fact they barely even knew each other. And why would she do something that would risk her own reputation just to spite someone she barely knew, and for no other reason? But she had to have some reason, there was no other explanation. And the more Ellyn considered this, the more fearful and suspicious she became.

"I will have to be on my guard," she thought to herself, stopping at the window to peer out towards the horizon. "Maerynn could do something that would ruin my life here, or at least make it worse than it already is. Why did I agree to her plan? I should just recant. I need to tell her I changed my mind. I am already married, and to see another man in secret, wouldn't that be wrong? But we are only going to talk, and very briefly. There is certainly nothing wrong with having a conversation. Is there? Oh, I don't know. It feels so wrong. Maybe I should change my mind."

But the thought of seeing Julius again had become so imprinted in her mind that she could not bring herself to go to Maerynn, requesting her to leave Julius in Brystol.

After a long time of pacing about the room with these thoughts tossing in her mind, she at last went to the door and stepped out into the hall. She decided to go back to her room and tell Alys everything. Her maidservant could be trusted to keep a secret, and she nearly always had sound advice. As she turned the corner, she heard movement from within Corbin's room and stopped short in the hall. Then she continued, treading silently on her toes. But just as she was reaching for her own door, his door opened behind her, and she whirled around.

She felt overcome with guilt and remorse as she looked up at Corbin, who stopped in his doorway and was looking at her.

"Sorry," Ellyn said hurriedly, and turned, turning the door handle.

"Wait," he stopped her. She tensed and turned around slowly, her heart pounding.

"I wanted a word with you about something. I was going to wait until later tonight, but you are already here. Can you step in please?"

Ellyn felt a sinking feeling in her stomach. Had Maerynn laid a trap for her? Did she tell Corbin everything that had been said? He looked and sounded calm, but she never knew what was hiding behind his mask of expressionless severity. Finally she nodded and let go of the handle. She could tell she was quaking as she stepped past him into his room, and took deep breaths, trying to calm herself. She took several steps in and stopped, turning around. He closed the door quietly and turned to face her.

He started to talk, and then stopped and frowned. "You look white," he said. "Are you ill?"

"No," Ellyn said quickly, looking down. She clasped her hands behind her back and wrung them together.

"Well, there is no need to be afraid," he said, somewhat harshly. "Sit down if you wish." Ellyn shook her head and said, "I'm fine."

"I just wanted to say a few words about Princess Maerynn," he said.

Those were the words Ellyn least wanted to hear. Her heart seemed to stop and she looked up at him quickly, expecting him to be furious, and tell her he knew all about Julius and her conversation with Maerynn. But his expression remained unchanged. She pressed her lips together firmly.

"I noticed she spoke with you at the feast yesterday, somewhat extensively."

Ellyn nodded her assent.

"I merely want to warn you against her. Maerynn is a cunning woman. She has clear ideas and motives and knows how to carry them out. I have known her for many years, and, ever since we were children, she knew how to get her way and have her wishes carried out. She wouldn't bring harm to anyone but... " He paused and looked straight into Ellyn's eyes. "Be careful. You don't know how determined she can be. I'm not saying she is plotting any harm, but if you have further conversations with her, be careful that you don't let her take advantage of you, and don't submit to her devices without having a clear view of them. Is that clear?"

Ellyn's heart was now racing. He obviously had no idea of their conversation, or else he would have said so, and he would be much more direct. But now she really did feel ill, and took a deep breath to calm herself.

"Yes, it is," she said evenly.

"You see..." Corbin began thoughtfully, then hesitated. "I probably shouldn't say this. But you might as well know. In fact, maybe you already do. But Maerynn and I were engaged to be married. It was a marriage our parents arranged at our birth. So, all her life, Maerynn has been expecting to be the future queen of Lyntirith. Since that was taken away from her, she may want to get revenge. Revenge from Maeryn can be deep and hurtful, or it can simply mean she treats her victim thoughtlessly. Whatever the case, try to avoid her."

Ellyn nodded slowly, but inwardly, she was shaking with disbelief. Maerynn had been engaged to Corbin! That explained why she had treated her with such sourness. But what did that have to do with Julius, if anything?

"I'll be careful," Ellyn said in a small voice.

Corbin nodded, then opened the door and stepped aside. She walked past and across the hall to her own room. Once inside, she leaned against the door and exhaled slowly. Then she went across the room and collapsed on her bed.

Chapter 14 - Corineus Makes Trouble

"So, she actually offered to bring Julius here? Here to Lyntirith?" Alys asked incredulously. Ellyn had just finished telling her about all that she had been told in the past few hours by both Maerynn and Corbin.

"That is what she said," Ellyn said wearily. She sat up in her bed and looked into the face of her shocked maidservant.

"And you… agreed?" she asked, the disbelief in her voice rising. Ellyn sighed.

"Yes, I did. And since, I have been debating with myself as to whether or not I made the right decision. She could easily take advantage of me. Even if she is telling the truth and she allows him to escape undiscovered, she could use it as a threat and hold it over me so that I submit to her, for fear of her telling others. But then that wouldn't make complete sense, because she is the one bringing him here, so wouldn't she want to remain undiscovered as well?"

"I can think of many negative outcomes for her to bring him here, and few positive ones. She does not seem like someone who would do something just for the sake of doing it."

"I know." Ellyn frowned. "But imagine if I could see him again! I think I am willing to risk what consequences may come just to be with him for a few moments. Our last time together, we were not even able to say goodbye. The mere thought of him is painful to me, but if I could just see him once more, I might be able to think of him with fond memories, rather than with regret."

Alys was silent, thinking.

"This will probably be my only chance to ever see him again, Alys. Ever!" Ellyn said in a hushed voice. "I would feel guilty refusing the last chance I will get."

Alys nodded slowly. "I suppose so," she said slowly. Ellyn could hear the doubt in her voice. "Maybe," she continued, "You should do something to make yourself more… protected. I don't know what it would be, but you seem so susceptible to anything Maerynn is planning."

"I know," Ellyn moaned. "I thought I had made up my mind, and then I started doubting my choice, and now I just don't know. Maybe I should go to Maerynn and tell her I've changed my mind."

There was silence. Ellyn rolled her eyes upwards in exasperation. "I really don't know," she groaned, and she flopped back down on the bed and stared at the ceiling.

"I think, since you have doubt, maybe you should reconsider," Alys said slowly.

"I have been reconsidering," Ellyn said. "But there doesn't seem to be a clear answer. I've already given Maerynn my answer; maybe I should keep it, and if something happens… I don't know. I would feel guilty either way."

"Well, which decision would you feel the least guilty with?" Alys asked.

Ellyn was silent. Throughout the conversation, she had been imagining in her mind the moment she would be able to see him, and the happiness she felt just thinking about it seemed to cover up all of her doubts and uncertainties. Finally she sat up.

"Maybe I will speak to Maerynn again," she said slowly. "I don't think I asked as many questions as I should have. I need to clarify some things; maybe her motives will become more clear. But I think I'll consider it tonight and think about it more. I've only had a few hours to contemplate, and everything still seems so muddled. Maybe once some time has passed, I'll feel more settled with one of my options."

The day passed slowly, with no decisive decision on Ellyn's part. She carefully considered each possible risk, outcome, effect and consequence, but, as soon as she had made up her mind, she felt that it was the wrong one and found herself reconsidering again. She began to grow frustrated and unsettled, angry with herself for not being able to feel at ease with either resolution. At last, late that night, she fell into an uneasy sleep after deciding she would talk to Maerynn again in the morning, hoping that would make her decision more clear.

The next morning, Ellyn still did not feel ready to approach Maerynn. She spent most of the morning much as she had the day before in the back room down the hall. She paced the room, stared out the window, sat gazing at the ceiling, paced again and struggled with her decision and whether or not she had made a mistake. At last, when it was almost noon, she left the room and walked slowly back to her room. Still deep in thought, she walked with her head down, a pensive frown on her face.

When she reached her room, she opened the door and stepped inside. But when she tried to close the door, it stopped just short of closing. She pushed harder, but it did not budge. Confused, she looked down to the floor and saw a shoe stuck between the door and its frame. Opening the door and peering out, her heart sank when Corineus's grinning face appeared behind the door.

"You were able to escape me yesterday," he said with a wry laugh. "But not today, Ellyn."

"Please leave," Ellyn said angrily, and tried to dislodge his foot with her own. But he only pushed against the door and forced his way in, looking victoriously at Ellyn as he did so. She crossed her arms and glared at him, but he was unrattled by her menacing expression.

"Many times have I wanted to speak with you since that night that was interrupted by the mysterious intruder. But every time I have made an attempt I have been somehow thwarted."

Ellyn squinted at him suspiciously.

"I don't know why you seem so mistrustful," he said.

"You haven't given me any reasons to trust you," Ellyn returned.

"I don't mean any harm," he said. "But you can have your suspicions if you'd like."

"Well, why don't you just say what you came here to say and then leave," Ellyn suggested harshly, leaning her back against the wall.

Corineus held up a hand. "No reason to be agitated," he said coolly, causing Ellyn to scowl angrily. "All I want to say is, if you ever have any concerns about your safety, you can feel confident bringing them to me."

"I don't think I can," Ellyn said haughtily.

"Why not?" he leered, taking a step closer. "I know a great deal about this place and the people who live in it, and the people who come and go. I am an observant person, and people trust me. They trust me to help them, if they need it."

"What people?"

"Oh, anyone," he said. "And if you are worried about keeping your secrets hidden, you can rely on me." Now he took a step even closer and leaned close to Ellyn. She tensed and turned her face away from him. "Because I know your secrets already, Ellyn. But you can trust me not to tell anyone."

Ellyn's eyes widened but she did not even flinch. "What secrets?" she asked through clenched teeth.

"I know about the prince who will be paying you a visit soon, and all about your acquaintance with him."

Ellyn jerked her head up and looked straight into his face. "You speak of my acquaintance with him as if it were dishonorable," she said bitterly. "I am unable to see how that is true."

"It may be since you requested he come here."

"Yes, I do want to see him, but there is nothing dishonorable about that. Besides, you realize I could change my mind, don't you? I could go find Maerynn right now and tell her I've changed my mind."

He smiled slyly. "Not now, Ellyn. It's too late. Maerynn and her family already left."

"Well… I could send her a message then."

"But you won't, will you?" he said.

Ellyn fell silent and looked down at the floor. Corineus finally stepped back, but Ellyn remained tense and rigid. Her brows were furrowed.

"So why did you come to tell me these things?" she asked angrily. "All you have said is that you know about Julius, but you will keep it a secret. That's all?"

"Yes." He shrugged. "I just wanted you to know that I know. That way, if you find yourself in trouble regarding this issue, you are aware that you can turn to me."

Ellyn frowned. "If I was in trouble, you would be the last person I would go to," she said in a low voice.

"Maybe so," he said. He turned to leave. But before he turned the handle, Ellyn said, "How did you find out about Julius, and when?"

He turned slowly back towards her, his mouth curved into a malicious smile. "Why do you want to know?"

"Just tell me," Ellyn ordered impatiently. "And I want to know who else knows."

"No one else knows, of course. Your secret is safe." With that, he turned to the door, and Ellyn sighed with exasperation.

He opened the door wide, but lurched to a stop in the doorway. Ellyn looked past him and saw that Corbin had just been walking past the door, and was now standing in the middle of the hall, glaring at his brother.

"Corineus, what do you think you are doing?" he asked angrily.

Corineus let his hand fall from the door and took a step into the hall, returning Corbin's glare with a grin.

"Only talking," he said mockingly.

"Listen, you fool, do you think this is a light matter? How dare you intrude into her room?"

"She let me in," Corineus insisted.

"That's not true," Ellyn said angrily before Corbin could speak.

"Of course it's not, now clear out of here," Corbin said. His brows were knit together so low, they looked as if they were touching his eyes, and his jaw was pulsing with rage.

"Alright, alright, I wasn't doing any harm," Corineus said.

"Of course, you never mean to do harm," Corbin said, rolling his eyes. "Now if I find you around here again, you'll regret it. Now go!"

Corineus slinked away without looking back.

Corbin watched him until he turned around the corner. Then, he turned to Ellyn, who was partially hiding behind the door. The fury left his face, and he said with agitation, "What was he talking about?"

Ellyn opened her mouth to speak, then pressed her lips together. "He just… I don't know," she stammered. "He wasn't here for very long."

Corbin heaved a sigh. "He won't do anything to hurt you, he's too cowardly," he said with a scoff. "But he's always causing some kind of trouble."

He turned to walk away, but after a few steps, turned around quickly. "If he does that again, don't keep it to yourself." Then, without another word, he strode quickly down the hall.

Ellyn waited until he had turned the corner, then began taking deep, gasping breaths. She grabbed her throat, as if she were being strangled, then shut the door quickly behind her. She leaned against it and closed her eyes. Her head was throbbing, and she pressed her hand against her mouth, staring with disbelief into nothingness. Weakly stepping across the room, she crumpled onto a couch near her bed and tried to calm herself.

Corineus's words and his conduct had terrified her, and now she realized it truly was too late to rethink her decision. Julius was coming to Lyntirith. Part of her felt relief and anticipation, but it was smothered with an overwhelming feeling of dread and guilt.

Chapter 15 - Michaelmas

Autumn came early in Lyntirith, and leaves began to fall from the trees, and the days began growing shorter. The air felt crisp, and a chill breeze blew through the bare branches of the trees. Flocks of geese flew southwards overhead, filling the bleak air with their echoing calls. The daytime sky was clear and blue, with hardly a cloud to be seen, and the nights brought a thin layer of frost that glistened in the morning sun on the hard ground.

From her window in the castle, Ellyn was only able to observe some of these changes in the air. She saw the bare branches of the trees, trembling in the wind. She saw the frost, creeping up the window panes in the morning. One morning, she awoke to a fire crackling in the fireplace and to Alys replacing the white, lacy curtains with thick, dark ones to keep out the cold.

It had been over a week since Maerynn and her family had left the Lyntirith castle, and Ellyn expected every moment there would be a knock on the door, and Julius would be standing there. She felt that she was living in a state of dreadful expectation. Even though the days were long and dull, it seemed that something was about to happen. She often sat next to the window, staring outside, listening, watching and waiting in a dull state of apprehension. But she heard not a word from Maerynn, and wondered if it had all been a hoax. But this presumption seemed to her misleading, but whether hopeful or disappointing, she could not decide.

The end of September approached, which meant the annual celebration of Michaelmas was nearing. Homes and kingdoms all throughout the country would be holding a feast honoring the saint of old. In the village, breads and pastries were sold to families preparing for the feast, and cages of fattened geese were kennelled in the village markets.

Being one of the largest kingdoms in the country, Lyntirith had several royal families under the king and queen. Dukes oversaw the ruling of given territories or provinces, and standing below them in status were the earls and countesses, who would also be invited by the king and queen as guests for the celebration in the castle. The servants began preparing for the feast, planning the food and dishes and preparing the room where the feast would be held.

The morning of Michaelmas dawned clear and cold.

Ellyn awoke to a fire burning in the fireplace in the corner and Alys folding a small pile of linens. She sat up and pushed off her blankets. Sliding off the edge of her bed, she pulled on her slippers and put on her robe, which had been laid at the end of her bed. She went across the room and stood in front of the fireplace, where the warm flames pushed away the chill air. She stared into the fire for a while, watching the flames dance and flicker.

"I wonder what Mother and the girls are doing," she murmured aloud. "It must be very strange for them, not being at home on this day. It may be almost as strange for them as it is for me. I wonder if they are home in Eurasia yet? Or are they still in Brystol?"

She suddenly realized her face was growing warm from the heat of the fire and turned her back to it.

"Your breakfast tray is ready when you want it," Alys said, hanging up Ellyn's gown that she

would be wearing that evening during the feast.

Ellyn wrapped her robe tightly around her and sat on the chair next to her bed. Alys brought her the tray of food and she began eating slowly.

The dining hall was lit brightly, illuminating a long table full of delicacies. Platters and bowls lined the long table, filled with carefully prepared dishes. At the center of the table sat a large platter covered with a silver lid, under which the goose was hiding, the center of the feast.

The room was spacious, built to hold many people as well as the long dining table, and groups of people stood around the edges of the room, surrounding the table. In the corner of the room, several young boys stood, their hands clasped behind their backs and their tunics immaculate. Little girls dressed in long dresses with intricate floral patterns covering the fabric stood at the fringe of the crowd. Their hair was braided in long tresses over their shoulders, or pinned up on their heads. They looked around the room with bright, excited eyes. The youngest children had been left at home, but the older children were allowed to attend the feasts on Michaelmas, as it was a celebration for all ages to participate in.

Ellyn stood quietly at the end of the room nearest to the door. She felt uncomfortable, and it seemed that pairs of eyes were always staring in her direction. Everyone in the kingdom had heard that the future king of Lyntirith had married, but none had yet seen his wife. On either side, groups of people talked in hushed voices, often glancing her way, but none attempted to initiate conversation with her outside of wishing her a merry Michaelmas, or greeting her courteously. She felt small and alone, the focus of so many pairs of eyes.

Not long after everyone had gathered in the dining room, Corbin left his place at his father's side and walked slowly through the room, nodding at those who greeted him as he walked past. Ellyn felt her face flush with heat and she looked down at her shoes as he approached her.

He stood next to her and scanned the room scrutinizingly.

"Why have you left the group of conversationalists to come to this corner of the room where the dull, silent people are?" Ellyn asked, lifting her head and looking straight ahead.

"There is only one of them that I see who has not attempted to join in the conversation," he replied.

"I know none of them," she whispered sharply, looking downwards darkly. "They would think it strange if I approached them without any introduction."

"Perhaps less strange than standing monotonously in the corner."

Ellyn pressed her lips together and looked up at him. He was standing with his head slightly lowered looking across the room, but she saw his eyes dart towards her for a brief moment when she turned to him.

"Then are you implying that you yourself do not do this which you are accusing me of?" she asked pointedly.

Now, he did turn to her. His eyebrows were knit together in an expression of annoyance, amusement, and something else that Ellyn could not interpret. She expected him to return her pointed comment with one of his own, but instead, he looked away again and stared out into the room again.

Ellyn followed his gaze and saw that King Evander was standing behind his chair at the end of the table, and his wife had come to his side and was being seated by one of the servants. The guests had begun to circulate towards the table, finding their assigned spot.

Corbin began striding across the room to the other end, where his place was designated next to his father. Ellyn followed just behind. She noticed that, although the room was very full, there was no need for him to wind his way through the crowd. They immediately made space for him, stepping quickly aside if they stood in his path. His feet landed heavy on the floor and he strode with steady resolution. The children quickly glanced up if he walked past, and in their faces, Ellyn saw the same intimidation she had felt when she first saw him the day she arrived in Lyntirith. It was then that it struck Ellyn that things had changed since that day. It now seemed so long ago, and she felt a different person from the one who had stepped off the ship in Lyntirith. How had things changed, though? She was pondering this question as she sat down.

"You look troubled," Corbin said as he took his place next to her, almost causing her to start. "I'm sorry." Ellyn shook her head, the cloud clearing from her eyes. She darted a quick glance at Corbin then looked quickly at her plate. "I was only thinking."

Just after she spoke, the murmur of voices in the room dwindled, and then silenced completely.

A bishop had stood from the opposite end of the table and folded his hands together reverently. All heads turned to him.

"Your Majesty King Evander of Lyntirith and her Majesty Queen Guinevere of Lyntirith," he said in a low, even voice, bowing as he spoke. "Greetings and good evening to the King and Queen of Lyntirith on this fair Michaelmas Day feast. I have with me a manuscript, detailing the deeds and events surrounding the venerable Saint Michael, so that you will be reminded why it is we celebrate this honored saint of old."

He lifted several pieces of parchment from the table and began reading. His smooth voice rose and fell as he read, and the words seemed to grow quieter and quieter to Ellyn and soon it was only his voice that reached her ears. The words themselves were merely phrases and syllables that did not make sense to her. While her gaze was directed towards the bishop, her focus was not on his face, but settled on the empty space past him. The words he spoke were from the exact account that was read at Eurasia's feasts on Michaelmas. They took her to another time and another place. She saw herself as a child, sitting primly at her mother's side, listening to the words about the saint, but wishing it would end quickly so that she could eat. She saw her father sitting in his chair, tall and kind. She saw her mother, her gentle eyes, and glowing countenance. And now, looking around the table, she no longer saw the young children of the surrounding royal families, but her own young sisters, their round eyes glowing, sitting with contained anticipation. The faces of the men and women morphed into the faces of those imprinted in her mind who had sat around the feast in Eurasia. Even the room itself seemed to take on the shape, colors, and smells as the grand dining hall in Eurasia. For the first time since she had left home, it was not only the memories of those she had left behind that stretched across her memory. It was now as if they were sitting in the very room with her, as if time had erased and she was in her own home with her own family, and her heart was light and happy. Her memories had become almost tangible as she sat in that room, many miles from that place she had called home.

She was stirred from her reverie when she suddenly became aware that the bishop had just finished and had lowered his head to pray. She looked quickly into her lap, wondering how much time had elapsed since the bishop had begun speaking, as it had seemed to pass in only a few fleeting moments.

All at once, the sound of the silverware clanking and the dull sound of plates against the wooden table echoed the room, but was soon drowned out by the merry conversation of the guests. Ellyn's plate was filled and she began to eat slowly.

As she took her first bite of the tender goose meat, she looked across the table. Corineus was seated across from her. Next to him, Helena was seated, her head lowered so that her face was mostly hidden. But as Ellyn gazed at her, she thought she saw a tear roll down the girl's face. But her face was mostly obscured, so that Ellyn could not be certain. The girl's hand moved the fork slowly and methodically from the plate to her mouth, but not another of her muscles moved. Ellyn found herself often casting quick glances towards Helena with a feeling of sympathy, although she did not know with what she sympathized.

It was a long time before everyone's appetites were satisfied, everyone's plates empty and the conversations subsided enough that the signal was finally given to adjourn to the parlor nearby, where the guests would mingle until the hour for departure came. The king and queen led the way, with both Corbin and Corineus not far behind. As

Ellyn fell into stride behind them, she found that Helena was walking just beside her. Looking aside, she saw that the girl's fragile features were bent with distress and pain, and she seemed to notice nothing around her. As they walked through the short hall, Helena suddenly turned and opened a door and slipped inside, closing it quickly behind her. Surprised, Ellyn stopped short and stared at the closed door. A few guests behind her halted abruptly, and Ellyn apologized, stepping aside for them to pass. She stood in the hallway across from the door, looking at it with a puzzled expression. She looked down the hall. The line of people was steadily moving, and the parlor was filling quickly.

Then, partly out of curiosity and partly out of concern, Ellyn went to the door and slowly turned the handle. A dim light glimmered within. She stepped inside and closed it quickly.

The room was small, and only a few candles sat on a small table in the corner. But Ellyn's eyes were immediately directed to the end of the room where Helena was, lying nearly prostrate on the floor. Her body was shaking, and Ellyn approached her, eyes wide.

She slowly lowered herself to her knees next to Helena and rested a hand on her shoulder. It felt cold. Ellyn reached toward her hands. They were also cold, and trembling uncontrollably, it seemed. But the girl did not even turn her face, or seem to notice that Ellyn was there.

"Helena, are you well?" Ellyn asked quietly. There was no reply.

Ellyn gently rolled her over and saw that her face was deathly pale. Her face was wet with tears, yet none were coming from her eyes. She stared up with a locked expression, and rough, intermittent breaths escaped her lips.

Instantly alarmed, Ellyn jumped to her feet, but then stood frozen, unsure what to do. Then Helena made a strange gasping noise and reached her hand up. Ellyn immediately lowered herself again and took the girl's icy grasp. Helena's cold fingers wrapped around Ellyn's wrist and she was now staring straight into Ellyn's eyes. Small sobs began issuing from her, but her face remained frozen in its expression of distress.

"Helena, what is wrong? Should I get help?" Ellyn asked. Her heart was pounding, and she looked towards the door, hoping someone would come in and aid the suffering girl. But the only sounds she heard beyond the door was mumbled conversation, coming from the parlor at the end of the hall. She waited a moment at Helena's side, but there was no change in her condition. Her breathing seemed to lessen and become more labored, so she pried her fingers from her wrist and stood, turning to leave the room. But at that moment the door opened, and light flooded into the room. Corbin stood in the doorway.

"Something is wrong with her," Ellyn said in a rushed voice, indicating Helena behind her.

Without a word, Corbin closed the door and walked quickly to his sister's side and knelt beside her. He took her hand, which was groping on the floor for something to cling to and looked into her face. Ellyn dropped to her knees near Helena's head and looked at Corbin's face. Instead of surprise and dismay, which she expected to see, his expression was worried, but calm. Helena began writhing and twisting on the floor, making gagging noises, but still he did not stir. Ellyn held her breath, not daring to move or speak, but looked at the suffering girl with dismay.

After a long moment, the shaking and coughing finally began to subside, and the color slowly began to return to her face. She looked up at Corbin, then let out a long sigh.

"Has it passed?" he asked.

She nodded, closing her eyes with exhaustion.

Carefully, Corbin lifted her and set her on a small couch nearby, and she laid her head back, letting her arms droop at her sides.

Corbin looked at her for a moment, then turned to Ellyn, who had stood and was now standing, frozen in place, watching Helena's face keenly.

"So this is not the first time this has happened?" she asked in a hushed voice as Corbin turned to her.

He shook his head, frowning. "No," he said in a low voice. "Certainly not. She is…" Then he stopped and turned to look at Helena again. "Well, never mind," he said slowly. After a long silence, filled only by the sound of Helena's soft breathing, he turned back to Ellyn. "You should go now," he said. "She won't want any disturbance."

Ellyn nodded and walked quietly to the door. She blinked in the light as she stepped out in the hall. But instead of joining the guests in the parlor, she turned the opposite direction. A sudden feeling of weariness had swept over her and she went up to her room.

It was with a heavy heart that Ellyn retired to her room that night, filled with so many thoughts and memories that they seemed to be a weight on her head and shoulders. She stood in silence while Alys helped her into her nightgown and undid the long, elaborate braids that twisted over her head. All the while, she sat at a chair in front of a mirror staring at her reflexion, deep in thought. Alys noticed that she was unsettled and did not try to initiate conversation.

It was over an hour later that Ellyn finally went to her bed. She sat on the edge and stared fixedly at the floor for a long time, thinking. And that was how Corbin found her when he entered the room a few moments later.

She lifted her head as he approached her, still dressed in his elaborate attire. He sat down next to her, and neither spoke for a moment.

"Why are you so troubled?" he finally asked, breaking the silence.

"I—I don't really know," Ellyn said, pressing her hand to her forehead and looking away. "I must just be tired. I have been thinking so much about days similar to this that I remember from past years."

"It has been many months since you have been here. And yet are you still grieved by all that you left behind?"

"Of course," she declared. "How could I not be? It was not only my home I left behind, but my family, everything I knew; my whole life was left behind. Even if I try to forget, it is a part of me.

Every moment I spent in Eurasia: practicing archery with my father and brother, talking with my mother, playing with my sisters, riding horseback through the woods, walking through the gardens, looking at the stars out my window, everything I left behind is so imprinted upon me that it is impossible to leave the memories behind forever." Ellyn had spoken with such fervor that she now felt herself taking deep, gasping breaths, and tears were gathering in her eyes. She felt ashamed of herself, and dared not look at Corbin's face, dreading to see his expression. He did not speak.

"I'm sorry," she said, inhaling deeply. "I must sleep. But first, how is your sister?" She finally looked up. Her eyes were brimming with unfallen tears, but her face was now calm and serene.

Corbin's eyes met hers and he opened his mouth to speak, but seemed to be searching for words. His face was tense and solemn, but he spoke in his usual even tone. "Helena is fine, she is sleeping now."

Ellyn nodded and looked down.

"She wanted me to express her apologies to you, and thank you for staying with her during her attack."

"Of course," Ellyn murmured.

"Helena has… Well, she has always been susceptible to illness, but especially these past years, after a certain episode that drained her of much of her strength. Since then, she has always been weak."

"So she had a severe illness?" Ellyn questioned.

Corbin hesitated, then nodded. "Yes, a severe illness." Then both fell silent.

"You said a few moments ago that you often rode horseback in your home," Corbin said after a few moments.

"Nearly everyday."

"And it has been many months since you have, of course," he continued. Ellyn nodded.

"I ride very often through the woods near the castle," he said. "I always ride alone, although I would not mind company tomorrow, if you are willing."

Ellyn looked up. She felt confused, and somewhat leery. But she answered quickly, saying, "I am."

He nodded, then stood up and left without another word. As she watched him leave the room,

Ellyn felt a twinge of guilt. It was a feeling that had been lying in the back of her mind for many days and now suddenly rose to the surface. This feeling of raw guilt made her hands suddenly begin to tingle and she laid back on her bed, feeling lightheaded. But what was the source of her feelings of culpability and anxiety? It was Julius.

Chapter 16 - Riding in the Woods

Ellyn placed her foot in the stirrup and pulled herself into the saddle of a snow-white palfrey. She stroked her fingertips along his strong neck and adjusted the reins in her hands. The horse shook his mane and bobbed his head up and down in anticipation. Corbin stood a few feet away, adjusting the saddle on his own mount. A stable boy was standing at the horse's side, holding the reins and waiting to hand them over to the rider. Heavy breathing and occasionally whinnies echoed from the stalls nearby, and Ellyn's horse gave a gentle nicker in response.

With a quick, effortless movement, Corbin mounted his horse and took the reins from the boy at his side. Then, the boy handed him his bow and a quiver of arrows, which he slung over his back. He looked at Ellyn, who was fiddling with the reins in her fingers. Seeing that she was ready, he urged his horse into a slow walk, and Ellyn did likewise. As they emerged from the stables and into the open field, the late afternoon sun glared from the west, where it was on its downward descent. A chill autumn breeze blew through Ellyn's blonde hair, which was cascading down her back. She inhaled the fresh air and her face relaxed into an expression of tranquility.

She followed Corbin's lead as he rode at a walk, and then at a slow trot down a dirt path leading from the stables. The path was lined with a wooden fence, which ended when it reached an open meadow. Here, Corbin's horse slowed to a walk again, and Ellyn fell in stride beside him. The meadow was dotted with trees, beyond which stood the edge of the forest. Tall, bare trees were standing at its edge.

"I hope the air is not too cold for you," he said.

"No." She shook her head, squinting up into the sky. "I don't mind it. I forgot how clear the sky is during the autumn. Everything is so fresh."

He nodded, but did not reply.

"Do you usually ride in the forest?" Ellyn asked.

"Sometimes," he said. "It depends on the weather, and my preference any given day. Some days I ride through the forest, other days over the meadows."

"I often rode through the forest in Eurasia. I rode nearly every day, until it became too dangerous during the final weeks."

Corbin gave a low grunting noise in response. Ellyn fell into silence. She hoped she wasn't talking too much, but the silence made her feel uncomfortable.

"Why did he request for my company, yet say nothing?" she wondered to herself. "Perhaps he prefers silence, or wanted only a companion, not someone to talk to."

She glanced over at him for a moment. His eyes were trained forward, his face settled in its usual expression of dark resolve. Even when he was calm, his face always held a look of coldness and unwavering solemnity. His speech was always short and pointed, and he never spoke when the occasion did not call for it.

Ellyn always found herself at loss of words in his presence. She never knew what his response or reaction to her words would be. His mask of seriousness kept her from ever feeling comfortable near him. Over the past few months, she had become less frightened in his presence, but, even now, Ellyn felt pangs of nervousness and uneasiness, especially riding alongside him in silence.

The horses bore them into the confines of the forest, and the air now felt more cool, sheltered from the sun. But the trees also blocked the steady breeze that had been blowing across the meadow, and the branches hung still above them. Ellyn gazed above her at the ceiling of the forest. Even though the branches were leafless, the trees were so close together that only in a few places did the sunlight leak through.

They rode down the woodland path, over the dried leaves that lined the trail. Birds twittered in the branches and squirrels chattered high in the trees. Ellyn contented herself by looking at the scenery in the forest. The path twisted and turned, rose and fell, widened and narrowed.

The forest reminded Ellyn of Eurasia's woodlands, and the many hours she spent riding through them. As she looked at the wall of trees on either side, she began thinking about the last time she had ridden horseback in those woods. It had been a fateful day that she would never forget when the Northmen attacked, and she had been saved by Julius. Even though only a few months had passed since that day, it seemed much longer ago since it had taken place, and felt more like a dream than a past event. Even still, those harrowing moments in the forest—the shouts of pursuing Northmen, the sound of arrows whizzing through the air, the dead bodies lying alongside the path—were vividly imprinted in her memory.

As they rode deeper into the woods, the landscape on the forest floor began to change. Tall clefts, shaped with deep fissures and abysses, delved upwards into tall summits, and the trickling of a stream could be heard somewhere beyond the trail. They took a sharp turn to the right, following the curve of the path. The ground beside the trail began sloping downwards, growing more and more steep, until Ellyn found herself looking down into a deep gorge with a pool at the center of the flat plain, from which a creek went gurgling down a slope and around a bend. The trees were sparse at the bottom of the gorge and bright sunlight streamed through the trees, casting long shadows on the forest floor. Afternoon was waning and evening approaching; still they pressed on, Corbin leading his horse just ahead of Ellyn's. The sounds of horse's hooves thumping on the dirt trail, the distant sound of rippling water and the twittering of woodland creatures were the only sounds that reverberated through the trees.

As the afternoon progressed and the shadows lengthened in the forest, the horses bore their riders at a brisk walk along the trails. Ellyn admired the beauty of the woods in silence. Sitting tall and proud in the saddle, Corbin did not turn to her, or attempt to initiate conversation. Ellyn found this perplexing, but after nearly three quarters of an hour, had grown accustomed to the silence, and listened instead to the calming sounds of the forest.

At length, the path widened into a small clearing, from which several trails leading different directions went. Here, Corbin maneuvered his horse around and pulled it to a halt, facing Ellyn. She slowed her horse to a stand.

"The shadows are growing long," he said. "We should turn back. The sun sets quickly and the forest will soon be cold and dark."

Ellyn nodded her acquiescence.

"The trees in the Lyntirith forest are thick and will block out the light quickly," he added, looking into the trees, through which the evening glow radiated.

"It is beautiful, though," Ellyn said quietly. "Have you ridden through all of the paths?"

"Yes, few others have access to or ride through these woods. Many of the paths were trodden by my repeated excursions over them."

The forest was filled with a unanimous hush, and the sounds of the woodland creatures began dwindling, and fell away altogether. Somewhere deep in the recesses of the forest, a lonely bird sang over the silence, but all else was silent.

Ellyn looked at Corbin, and saw he was looking at her thoughtfully with furrowed brows. As their eyes met, his mouth opened as if he were about to speak, but then he closed it again and urged his horse into a walk.

"We should go now. It will be nearly dark by the time we arrive at the castle," he said briskly as he led his horse past Ellyn's, and started down the path again. She turned her horse and followed.

During the ride back toward the castle, the light in the woods grew more dim and the colors changed from warm sunlight to the golden hues of evening. The sound of the woodland creatures settling down for the night echoed through the unmoving trees, and everything seemed to be calm and quiet. Even the horses treaded carefully over the path, as if they were trying not to disturb the peace of the forest.

By the time they emerged from the woods, twilight had fallen over the castle, and a few stars were already twinkling in the blue, cloudless sky. The sun had only just set, and its rays could still be seen shining from the horizon. It was suddenly very cold and Ellyn found herself shivering, even under her hooded riding cloak.

"You do not need to wait for me," Corbin said as she dismounted her horse. "It has grown cold; go inside where it's warm."

Ellyn ran her hand down the horse's back, and then turned and walked back to the castle. It was now nearly completely dark and an owl called from the trees along the edge of the forest. Trembling in the cold, she quickened her steps and slipped through the castle door, relieved to be sheltered from the frigid air.

She began walking slowly up the stairs, thinking, wondering and pondering. Why had Corbin offered to take her on a ride? She thought he might seem more at ease, or at least try to converse, but he had been distant and silent nearly the entire ride.

She sighed audibly as she reached the top of the stairs. A servant passed, holding a pile of linens, and somewhere down the hall, a door closed, the sound echoing through the dark hall. The glow of candles along the walls lit the way to her room, and Ellyn opened the door slowly, her head lowered in thought. She closed the door behind her and began to unfasten her riding cloak.

Alys had already lit the candles in her room and warm embers were glowing in the fireplace. She lifted her head as she stepped into the room and suddenly froze and gasped in astonishment. She clasped her hands over her mouth and her eyes grew wide with disbelief.

Julius was standing at the end of her room.

Ellyn was shocked and at loss for words, but Julius smiled and strode to her side. He held her arms and looked into her eyes with his kind, gentle expression that Ellyn had almost forgotten.

"Julius," she finally was able to murmur, and she felt tears gathering in her eyes.

Julius pulled her into a tight embrace and held her. She was stiff with amazement, and wrapped her arms around him, her movements slow from her shock. She felt her hands trembling, and pressed her lips together.

A strange feeling of wariness and apprehension coming over her, she pulled herself from Julius's arms and looked into his face. He smiled sympathetically and said, "Are you alright? You look tired, and pale."

"Yes, yes," she said hurriedly, trying to keep her voice from quavering. "I didn't expect you though."

"What do you mean? I thought you were aware I was coming."

"Oh yes, I was, but I didn't think you would really come. Or I never really thought of you actually coming." She laughed, a short, confused sort of laugh that seemed to escape without her bidding.

"How did you get here?" she asked, lowering her voice.

"Maerynn helped me. I didn't think it was possible, but she is shrewd, and was able to bring me here without so much as a suspicion from anyone else. See, I am dressed as a servant."

For the first time, Ellyn noticed his attire that exactly matched that of the servants in Lyntirith. "We should come away from the door now," Ellyn said, feeling worried. "I wouldn't want anyone to find you."

She grasped his wrist and they went to a couch at the end of the room, out of sight from the doorway.

"How have you been?" Julius asked as they sat down. "I have been so anxious."

"I—I don't know. That is a hard question. Sometimes, I feel disheartened, but usually feel restless and empty. The family here is not like mine. They are cold, and distant. They don't mistreat me, but the days are lonely and cheerless."

After a pause, she asked, "Are my mother and sisters still in Brystol? Are my father and brother well?"

"The attack by the Northmen caused much damage to the castle, and there is still the danger of an attack, so yes, they are in Brystol. But great destruction has been made among their ranks by your father and his army, so they will not last much longer. I expect your family will be home soon."

Ellyn lowered her eyes. The thought of her family safely united home once again after such a long period of unrest and upheaval made her dejected, since she would not be there with them.

"And where have you been?" she asked, looking up again.

"I could not stand the tediousness of doing nothing in Brystol, overwrought with the dispiritedness of my thoughts. A few days after you left, I went to Eurasia and have stayed with your father and brother, aiding in the fight."

"But don't you want to return to your home and reclaim your kingdom?

Julius shrugged and looked away. "Maybe someday," he said. "But the time is not right, and I don't have the incentive yet. Besides, I will need an army, and other resources not in my possession."

Ellyn studied Julius as he spoke. He was changed since she had last seen him. He seemed more careworn and solemn. Then she realized he must have been thinking the same about her. She dropped her eyes into her lap, and both were silent for several moments.

After a while, Julius took a deep breath and spoke in a low, serious voice. "I know it is very wrong of me Ellyn, but I often try to think of a way to reverse this situation."

Ellyn looked up at him and frowned.

"There is no way, Julius. Even though the problem with the Northmen may be temporary and Eurasia will be peaceful once again, marriage is not temporary. It is a bond that cannot be broken."

"Unless unusual circumstances arise," Julius said, in a low, almost inaudible voice.

"Julius, what are you talking of? What do you mean by 'unusual circumstances'?" Ellyn asked, her voice rising with concern.

"Well, if one spouse abandons the other, or if one commits some grievous sin. Then, the bond can be broken."

"Julius, don't say such things. It is no use; the decision of my future has already been made, and it cannot change."

"I'm sorry," he said, looking away. He sighed and buried his face in his hand. "Sometimes I feel I have gone mad with grief that I do not know myself or what I say."

Ellyn laid a hand gently on his shoulder. "I'm sorry, Julius. I wish as much as you that things had turned out differently. But they didn't, and there is no way we can undo this."

His shoulder heaved heavily, and he turned his head, looking at Ellyn.

"But why should this be our last time seeing each other again?" he asked, clasping her small hand in his.

Ellyn shook her head and looked down.

Julius raised his head and looked out the window. It was dark, and the moon had risen, and its light flooded onto the floor through the uncovered window.

"My home is so far from yours, and once I leave it will be dangerous, perhaps even impossible to return. This may be our last meeting." His words were sad and grave.

Ellyn sighed. "I know," she said slowly. "But that is how it must be."

Julius stood from the couch and went to the window, staring out into the darkness. He was silent for a long time, looking out the window, deep in thought. Ellyn watched him. His face was expressionless, but his jaw and temples pulsed rhythmically.

Finally, he turned from the window and faced her again. Ellyn rose from the couch and he slowly walked towards her, studying her face. As he approached her, he rested a hand on her shoulder.

"Somehow, I will find a way for us to meet again."

"But it may be unsafe."

"I don't care," he said sharply. "Every day since you left, I've waited to see you again, holding some hope I could change the circumstances which have come upon us, and I don't want our meeting, after all of that time, to be only a few moments in secret. I know it is, as you have said, impossible to undo this fate by which we are bound. But does it mean we must be separated forever? What is the shame or danger with me coming here? Couldn't you speak with Corbin, and explain I am a friend who wants to stay acquainted?"

Ellyn shuddered and shook her head. "You don't understand him," she said. "I wouldn't dare to tell him that you exist. I don't know what he would say or do, especially after you have come here in secret. But he would not be pleased."

After she finished speaking, she thought she heard a rustling in the hallway. Whipping her head towards the door, she held her breath and listened.

"I didn't lock the door," she said under her breath after a long period of silence. "You should go. Do you know how to find your way safely from here?"

"Yes, Maerynn is waiting for me in a room down the hall."

She looked warily at the door handle, still listening intently. Then she looked at Julius and took his hand, squeezing it gently. "Goodbye, Julius," she said softly.

He held her hand with both of his, looking into her eyes. Then he wrapped his arms around her, and rested his chin on the top of her head.

The latch on the door clicked. The door creaked open and the sound of footsteps entering echoed through the silent room. Ellyn's heart fell and she gasped, pulling herself from Julius's arms.

Corbin was standing in the doorway. He was staring at Julius with an expression of bewilderment.

Chapter 17 - Corbin and Julius

Corbin's expression quickly changed from a look of bewilderment to a look of fury and anger. He glared with enraged intensity at Julius, his face contorted into an expression of fierce anger. Ellyn quaked and backed away from Julius and stood frozen and shuddering. However, Julius stood his ground and faced Corbin defiantly, crossing his arms and glaring directly back at him. The two young men stared at each other for what seemed like an eternity, and all the while, Ellyn's heart was pounding, and her hands were damp with perspiration.

After several long minutes, Corbin shut the door loudly with a sudden movement that made Ellyn jump. She took a deep breath and held it, trembling from head to toe.

"Who are you." Corbin pronounced each word through clenched teeth, taking slow, heavy steps into the room. His icy glare never once wavered from Julius, and his hands tightened into fists at his side.

At last, Julius moved, holding up one hand. "Perhaps it would be better to speak." Corbin continued to advance, his face darkening. Ellyn cringed.

With one swift movement, Corbin strode across the room and grabbed Julius's shoulders, thrusting him against the wall. Ellyn gasped and started, backing further away pressing her hands to her mouth.

"You are asking to talk, and discuss this situation?" Corbin said in a low voice that Ellyn could barely detect. "You fool, you cowardly fool."

His grip on Julius tightened, and his face was red with rage.

"It's not what you think," Julius began. But Corbin cut him off. "What does it matter what I think? I don't want an explanation, and don't care what yours is. The fact is, I have found you in a place you should not be with someone you should not be with. You will pay for this."

Suddenly, he reached his hand towards Julius's throat and wrapped his hands around his neck. Julius choked, his eyes growing wide. He wrapped his hands around Corbin's wrists and tried to pry his hands away. Corbin's grasp only tightened.

Ellyn cried out and looked away, trembling violently. There was a thump, then a groan. She looked up. Julius was leaning breathlessly against the wall, and Corbin had taken a step back and was bent slightly. Julius took a few steps to the side, away from the bent figure, but Corbin leaped at him again, blood dripping from his mouth. His face was wrenched into an expression of terrible anger that Ellyn had never seen before, and she quaked in her corner.

"You will regret this, I will make you pay for this," Corbin raged, pinning Julius to the floor. Julius did not reply, but fought his way to get free once again, using his fists to try to break from Corbin's ironlike hold. As minutes passed, Julius began to lose strength, and his face was plastered with fear and defeat. He fell back onto the floor, letting his hands drop to his sides. He groaned in pain, his face bruised and bleeding.

At last, Corbin released him from his grip, but not from his icy glare.

"Who are you?" he asked, heaving deep breaths, but from anger or weariness, it was hard to tell. Julius pressed his lips together and did not speak.

"Who are you?" Corbin asked again, his voice rising as he lunged toward Julius. But with deft agility, Julius leapt from the floor and dealt a fierce blow on Corbin's head, then jumped to his feet and began to run from the room.

Corbin gave a shout of anger and jumped to his feet. He looked in astonishment as Julius ran from the room, and immediately began the pursuit, disappearing from the room only a few seconds behind. Ellyn heard their heavy steps retreating down the hall.

At last alone, Ellyn began to tremble. She felt faint and clutched at her stomach, falling to her knees. Then she began to weep, tears streaming down her face.

"Ellyn?" A voice came from the doorway. Looking up, she saw Alys through a layer of tears.

She looked away and covered her mouth with her hand, continuing to sob. "Ellyn, what is it?" Alys asked, running to her side.

Ellyn shook her head and tried to speak, but was unable to through her tears. Several minutes passed, and the only sounds that came from her mouth were heartbroken sobs, and the words "It's all my fault" were repeated over and over in a hoarse and devastated whisper.

Hours passed. The sun had set long ago, but Ellyn did not even attempt to sleep. She paced her room, muttering to herself. Occasionally, she stopped at the window and stared out in the darkness. Sometimes, she would sit dejectedly on the side of her bed and stare down at the floor. Other times, she leaned against the wall and covered her face in her hands.

At Ellyn's request, Alys had left the room long ago, and she had been in solitude for many hours. The more the night wore on, the more distraught and depressed she became. Her head throbbed with weariness and her eyes were sore from weeping.

After a long time spent in this way, Ellyn heard footsteps nearing her room. She stopped short in the middle of her pacing and stared at the door, listening. A few moments later, someone knocked from their other side, and a feeling of sickening dread grew inside her. She went to the door and opened it. Maerynn stood in the doorway, her features darkened in the shadows. Without a word, she swept into the room and Ellyn closed and locked it behind her.

"You must have told him, didn't you," Ellyn asked in a rough, low voice when the door was closed. "Why did I agree to your plans? I erred in choosing to trust you, and now my life is ruined."

Maerynn scoffed. "Your life is barely worse than it was before," she said with disdain.

"That is far from true," Ellyn insisted with exasperation. "It is much worse. I may have been shunned and ignored before, but that is far better than what I shall have to endure now. The shame, the dishonor and the judgments I will receive now are much worse, and there is no way to undo this. Why did I ever let you convince me to do this? And for what purpose did you bring him, only to give him away by telling Corbin he was here?"

"You are wrongly accusing me," Maerynn said sharply. "I did not tell a living soul that Julius was here. I can assure you he was not seen in his entrance to the castle, and no word passed from my lips about his coming to anyone, save you."

Ellyn stared at Maerynn with distraught confusion. "That cannot be. It is too coincidental that he would happen to come into this room during the few minutes that Julius was here!"

"Coincidences are not impossible. Believe, or don't, but I swear Corbin did not know that Julius was in this room. There is absolutely no possible way. And I am the last person in the world who would want him to know Julius was here, mark my words."

Ellyn scowled, regarding Maerynn with doubt and uncertainty. Then she fell once again into grief and despair.

"Julius will be imprisoned; no doubt he already is. And it will all be my fault," she said falteringly.

"He most certainly is not. Do you really think I would let that happen?" Maerynn said, as if offended. Then her voice dropped to a whisper and she said, " As we speak, he is fleeing from this country. He is far from the castle now."

"What do you mean?" Ellyn asked. "He was surely outrun by Corbin. There was no way he escaped."

"You underestimate me, Ellyn," Maerynn said with a dry laugh. "I did not expect Corbin to be a consideration in my plan, but I did not entirely ignore the fact that he could be as well. I had everything planned, and extra plans for in case something went wrong, which it obviously did."

"What happened?"

"I was waiting in the room where Julius had been hiding. I was standing in the doorway, just in case the need arose for quick concealment. As soon as he came racing around the corner, blood dripping down his face, I guessed what had happened. In only a few seconds, he was hidden within the room, and Corbin thrown entirely off his trail. No doubt he thinks Julius disappeared into thin air."

"But weren't their guards searching? Didn't they search every room on the upper floor?"

"Yes, every room was thoroughly searched. But he was not found, because he was not there. I know how to prepare a good disguise."

Ellyn frowned.

Maerynn rolled her eyes. "Honestly, Ellyn, you really do underestimate me. It's simple! Dress him as a guard and make him look like he's searching madly for... well, himself."

Ellyn stared at Maerynn for a few moments, then hung her head. "That is certainly fortuitous for him, but what benefit does it have for me? I am still left with the realization of my unfortunate future, with no way to undo it. It is too late. And at my own doing that my life is ruined."

Maerynn laughed dryly. and looked at Ellyn slyly. "You despair too easily, Ellyn. You haven't even heard all that I have to say yet.

Your final moments together must not have been what you had hoped for, am I correct?"

Ellyn shrugged, but did not speak.

"I have concealed him in a place far from the castle, but where he will never be found," Maerynn continued. "I told him I would notify him when it is safe to leave this place, and he is at this moment waiting there for my signal. It would be simple, and not at all risky if you were to go to this place and just see him for a few seconds, just to say a proper farewell. He has no idea it would be possible; you could surprise him, perhaps cheer him up."

Ellyn stared at Maerynn in disbelief. "Who do you think I am?" she said indignantly. "After all of this, do you really think I would agree to your proposals again, or even want to see him again after what happened? It's ridiculous, preposterous, madness! I made a mistake in trusting you, Maerynn, and I promise you I will never make that mistake again."

"But Julius is far from the castle, Ellyn, he is perfectly safe. No one would ever know, and there would be no danger whatsoever. How can you doubt me, after all I have done to ensure that Julius escaped without harm?"

Ellyn stared at Maerynn in disbelief. "You really are mad, aren't you? There is no way I will agree to this, and you are mad to think that I would. Even if I was absolutely certain that no one would see me, I still would not agree. I have already made a mistake, I will not make it worse, even if I am the only one who will ever know it."

Maerynn looked at Ellyn with disdain. "Now I see who you are, Ellyn. What do you care about Julius? You don't seem to care if he lives or dies! If you did, you would not refuse this offer to see him once more. Do you want me to tell Julius your love for him was false, and you don't and never did care for him?"

Ellyn was speechless. She stared at the Maerynn with utter repulse and disbelief. She could not believe the words she was hearing.

"If you told him those things, it would be a lie," she said bitterly, looking at Maerynn in the eyes. "My love for him was once whole and unwavering, but things have changed since then. Even when I agreed to your bringing him here, things had already changed, and it was wrong for me to want to see him again. It is a choice I already regret deeply. Things cannot be how we once thought they could be, and in bringing him here, I was deceiving myself that there was a way to defy my fate. But it is pointless. Nothing you say, even all your threats, will not convince me to agree to see him once more. Tell him all the lies you want, but I am not leaving these castle walls, and your persuasions are all in vain."

At Ellyn's words, Maerynn raised herself and lifted her chin, looking down at Ellyn with disgust.

"Very well," she said. "Have it your way. I'm sure you realize you are turning down the last chance you will ever have to see Julius again. This time tomorrow he will be far away from the borders of Lyntirith, never to return again, while you remain stuck like a prisoner in these walls. But it is your decision."

Then she swept past Ellyn and out the door.

After Maerynn left, Ellyn collapsed in her bed and tried to sleep. But her thoughts were so agitated and upsetted that she soon got up again and walked across her room, thinking and despairing. She was exhausted, but unable to sleep, depressed but unable to cry. She felt empty and filled with shame. When the first hint of daylight appeared in the sky, she fell into the chair by her window and, resting her head against the wall, fell into an exhausted coma.

It was only an hour later that Ellyn opened her eyes and winced at the pain and stiffness throughout her body. Then she remembered what had caused her to wake up. There had been a sound that caused her to open her eyes. She lifted her head and looked towards the door. Corbin had just entered the room and was standing, watching her from across the room.

Ellyn lowered her head and looked into her lap, filled with dread and shame. Slowly, he walked across the room towards her, his footsteps echoing hollowly in the silent room. He was soon standing just in front of her. Ellyn bit her lower lip, but did not lift her head.

For a long time, neither spoke. A tense silence filled the room. After a long time, Corbin spoke. "Who was he?"

Ellyn shook her head, unable to speak.

"Tell me who he was!" Corbin said forcefully.

His words struck Ellyn like physical blows, and she shuddered.

"I—I don't know," Ellyn said, her voice trailing off. Her words were not meant to deceive him, or make him think she truly did not know who he was. She was at a loss for words, and unable to articulate anything sensible, so that she seemed to speak without thought.

"Of course you know," Corbin said sharply. He took a step closer and knelt just in front of her so that she thought she could hear his heart pounding, until she realized it was her own.

"Who was he," Corbin said in a slow, calculated voice.

There was a long silence. At last, Ellyn looked up. Corbin's head was lowered, but his eyes lifted and locked with hers. His face was ashen and drained. Ellyn sighed and looked down again.

"His name is Julius," she said in small, quivering tones. "I knew him before I came here."

"Continue," Corbin said severely.

"We had known each other for only a short time, but our engagement was imminent, until we were separated by choices that were not our own."

There was a long silence. Then Corbin said again, "Continue."

"Then he was given an opportunity to come and see me, and he took it. I only saw him for a few brief moments, during which we exchanged a few words, and the rest you already know."

Another prolonged silence followed. Then Corbin said, "How did he come here? This castle is well guarded and fortified."

Ellyn shrugged.

"You know the answer to this question. Tell me!"

Ellyn still did not speak. Corbin sighed. "Then tell me where he is now." Ellyn looked up at him for a moment, then looked away.

Corbin grabbed her shoulders and forced her to look at him. "Answer me, Ellyn," he said, his features dark and menacing.

Ellyn tensed and stared back at him, searching for words. At last she said, "I don't know where he is. All that I know is that he is no longer within these castle walls."

Corbin looked at her with disbelief. "Impossible," he muttered. "How do you know this, and how did he escape?"

"I don't know," Ellyn said bitterly. She shook his hands from her shoulders and stood, turning her back to him. "I can't speak of it anymore. I don't know where he is, or how he escaped, I only know he is no longer here."

Tears began flowing from her eyes and she pressed her hand to her mouth to keep from sobbing.

There was a shuffling behind her. Then Corbin said, “I will leave you for now. But this is not the end of this conversation. Julius will be found, and will be properly punished.”

After these emphatic words, he strode from the room, closing the door forcefully behind him.

Chapter 18 - Corbin's Hunt

After he left Ellyn's room, Corbin strode down the hallway, troubled and weary. He had spent the entire night searching for Julius and pacing his room, wondering how he could have disappeared without so much as a trace. To learn that he was no longer in the castle made him more bewildered and now he felt his anger, which had been subdued under a wave of exhaustion, rising again. He went to his sitting room at the end of the hall. Scowling, he strode to the window and looked about. Dawn had arrived. Frost covered the ground and the sun had crept over the horizon. The morning was clouded and hazy.

"Who could have brought him?" he mumbled under his breath. Then he turned from the window and began pacing the floor.

Someone had brought Julius to Lyntirith who had the means to give him entrance to the castle without being seen. It could not have been Ellyn. She had no way to communicate with him and arrange a meeting, or have a way to get past the guards and watchmen with a strange man without being noticed or questioned. But who could have? It would have to be a member of the family. No one else could have been able to bring Julius in without notice.

He stopped at the end of the room and rested his arm on the mantle that hung over the fireplace and stared into the cold, unlit fire pit. He immediately dismissed his parents and Helena from his suspicions. But could it have been Corineus? He frowned. It seemed unlikely, but not impossible. How could Corineus have found out about Julius, and for what reason would have done this? He remembered finding Corineus conversing secretly with Ellyn, and his guilty behavior when he was found. What words had been spoken between them?

Corineus was notorious as a troublemaker, but why would he do something that would be so destructive to the family, and their honor? A story such as this could quickly spread. Scandals, rumors and gossip would spark, and then what would happen to the reputation of the family? It could be ruined.

"Corineus may be foolish, but he is not blind," Corbin thought with frustration. "He would have to realize that doing this would bring severe consequences for our family. Besides, he probably wouldn't have the courage to do something like this in the first place, especially if it were possible he could be found out."

Corbin shook his head and ran his fingers through his hair. He crossed his arms and walked across the room slowly, staring at the floor. "Is there anyone else?" he thought. "Someone who has easy access to the castle, who comes often and would be allowed entrance without suspicion, who is smart enough to keep him hidden and help him escape, who would have a reason for bringing him here, and who must be in the castle at this very moment, or has only just left."

Suddenly he stopped short in his pacing and looked up. "Of course. Why did I not think before? My mind must be muddled from this long night. Who else can it be but Maerynn?"

He pressed his lips together wryly. "She claimed to have come to keep Helena company during her illness. But was that entirely true? She arrived yesterday afternoon, which is the perfect timing for all of this to fall in place. And she is wily. She could make something like this happen if she wanted. And her motive?" Corbin rolled his eyes. "She has a motive, there is no doubt. She must have had him hiding in her carriage when they arrived."

He stopped short again. Her carriage! Only an hour before, Maerynn had left for home again, and could not be far. Corbin walked hastily from the room and down the hall, striding with a quick and determined step. He went to his room and hurriedly pulled on a warm riding coat, then ran downstairs and outside towards the stable.

One of the stable boys was cleaning out a stall when he entered and looked up surprised when Corbin entered.

"Quick," Corbin said hastily. "Prepare my steed. I need to leave immediately. Saddle her quickly, don't waste a second."

The boy dropped his pitchfork and ran to fulfill his errand. Corbin waited restlessly until the boy appeared a few minutes later, leading the horse. Leaping into the saddle, Corbin took the reins and urged his horse forward, and she bolted from the barn, running down the path toward the road that led toward Wyndham. Her mane and tail flowed out behind her as she ran, her rider leaning forward in the saddle, with dark determination.

The sun had now fully risen, and the ground was damp with thawed frost. In the shadows of the trees beside the road, a thin layer of frost still coated the grass where the light of the sun had not touched it yet. The air was still and cold, and Corbin's breath was a cloud of vapor in the air every time he exhaled.

For almost half an hour, he rode at a run, only slowing once to a fast trot so his horse wouldn't lose strength before he urged her into a run again. At last, he could see a small form of a carriage down the path, rolling slowly down the trail. The wheels slowed as he approached, and the driver turned, grasping the hilt of his sword.

"Halt this carriage," he said in a loud voice of command.

As he spoke, the curtain of the carriage was pulled aside and Maerynn peered out with a look of consternation. Corbin dismounted and walked to the carriage, resting his arm on the frame, and looked at Maerynn in the eyes.

"So you thought you could get away," he said wryly. "Don't think it is this easy, Maerynn."

She raised an eyebrow. "What do you think you are talking about?" she asked with exasperation. "Get a hold of yourself, Corbin. Have you fully woken yet?"

"I never slept," Corbin said dryly.

"Well, that makes even more sense," she said with a dry laugh. "Go back home and rest." Corbin looked at her in silence for a moment, and Maerynn returned his dark look. Finally, Corbin said, "May I search your carriage?"

Maerynn began to laugh. "Corbin, you have really gone mad. But if it would humor you, I have no objection."

Corbin flung the carriage door open and looked inside. Besides Maerynn, the carriage looked empty. But his eyes scrutinized any place that a man could hide. Under the seats, behind them, he looked for a compartment that could be under the floor, or on the outside of the carriage. Maerynn watched him searching with quiet triumph, occasionally chuckling as she watched his frustration grow. At last, he leaned against the frame of the carriage and crossed his arms, looking directly at Maerynn, who was watching him coyly.

"Do you have time for a few words?" he asked in a low voice. She shrugged indifferently.

"It doesn't matter what you say," he said with disdain. "I know it was you who brought that prince into Lyntirith. There is no other possibility. Keeping Helena company was not the only thing you did during your visit. You entered our castle with someone whom you left without. Where is he?"

Maerynn looked at him incredulously. "I really have no idea what you are speaking of!" she said with disbelief. "Explain yourself."

"I don't need to," Corbin said slowly, looking at her angrily. "There is no doubt in my mind.

Not only do you have the means and cunning, you have a motive." She frowned with bewilderment.

"Stop pretending you don't know what I am talking about," he said sharply. "I know what you hoped for nearly all your life. It was your aim to be the queen of Lyntirith someday. And that hope was dispelled without warning, and I know it enraged you. I know, because I have seen it. Do not think your bitter words, your harsh words to Ellyn, and your looks of jealousy have gone undetected by me."

"Jealousy?" Maerynn said angrily. "Why should I be jealous?"

"Maerynn," Corbin said with exasperation. "It is hopeless. I can read your thoughts as if you are telling them to me. You have not given up hope that you may become queen of Lyntirith. Isn't that true? You had a vicious scheme to embroil the current future queen in a scandal that would banish her forever. Either that, or you gave her the opportunity to escape the castle forever. I don't know how you found out about this former lover of hers, but I know you are cunning enough to have done it and crafty enough to complete your plan. Let me tell you this, Maerynn. Enough! Give up. It is not only hopeless, but madness. I don't know why you have done this, but it is pointless." He stopped talking and stared into Maerynn's eyes. She looked at him defiantly, and neither spoke for a moment. Then Corbin dropped his voice in a low whisper and said with bitterness, "Even if your plan had been successful, I would never have you."

Maerynn's scowl deepened. She glared at him, and then spoke in a terrible voice, full of hatred. "You are clever, Corbin. But you have no way to prove what you have just said."

"Wrong," Corbin said forcefully. "All I need to do is find him and the truth will come out. And be assured, I will find him. But I did not need his confessions to come to the truth. It was only too clear for me; it did not take much contemplation. You had better give it up now, Maerynn. You have already caused enough trouble. Don't try again. It would be madness. Find another man and forget about everything."

For several moments, they stared at one another with unbroken tension. Then Corbin broke the silence. "Where is he, Julius?"

Maerynn did not speak.

"Very well, you will not tell me, though I know that you know. But I will find him. The whole castle has been searched. Today, we spread out and search the forests. He will be found."

With these words, he stepped from the carriage, and forcefully closed the door.

In the carriage, Maerynn was seething with anger at his words. She was trembling with violent fury. "So you think you can read my thoughts, do you, Corbin?" she hissed between clenched teeth. "You think you understand my motives and ways? You are far from right."

Her face was contorted into rage as she listened to the sound of horse hooves beating down the path. As they faded away, she leaned out the window and said to her driver. "Make haste for Wyndham. I must reach home immediately. There is no time to lose!" With a spray of dirt and pebbles, the carriage sped away.

Corbin arrived back at the castle, weak from lack of sleep. He trudged up from the stables and inside the castle where he went to rest for a few hours before setting out with guards to search the forest for Julius. He didn't want to lose any time, but he felt that they could still overtake him, even if he had several hours of a start. He was numb and heavy from exhaustion and knew he would be unable to lead a search party. He went upstairs, his shoulders bent and his step slow and heavy. When he reached the top of the stairs, he met his father coming around the corner.

"What troubles you?" he asked, falling in step alongside him. "I was told you left in a hurry on horseback over an hour ago. For what purpose? And you look exhausted."

"I am," Corbin said, turning to his father. "I can't explain now. I need rest. I will speak with you tonight and tell you what I can."

King Evander's brows furrowed. "Are you sure it is not urgent?"

"Everything is taken care of," Corbin said. "It is not of immediate importance."

Then he walked ahead and went into his room. He collapsed onto his bed, still dressed in his riding clothes, and looked at the ceiling with glazed eyes, and soon fell into a restless sleep.

"Are you sure we should not turn back now and give up the search, Your Highness?" A man on horseback approached Corbin, who was sitting tall in the saddle, looking out through the forest from his horse with gleaming eyes.

He shook his head. "No, we must press on. Keep searching."

"But we have been for over four hours now, and the sun is setting, Your Highness."

"The darkness sometimes brings out the secrets of the forest," Corbin said. "We search for one more hour. Then, if he is not found, I will give up. For today, that is."

The man grunted, then led his horse away. Corbin urged his horse into a slow walk, looking with piercing eyes into the concealing darkness of the forest. The sun had almost disappeared, but the forest was already very dark, shrouded by shadows and mist.

Five men rode just behind him, part of the band of searchers. Six groups of men had been dispersed through the forest and every hour, one brought Corbin word of their findings. So far, absolutely nothing had been discovered.

"We will cover the western edge of the woods," Corbin said to his men. "Keep a sharp lookout and tell if you see so much as a movement."

He pulled a torch from his pack and lit it, alighting the torches of the five other men as well. With Corbin leading the way, they pressed on through the darkness, holding up their torches to light their way.

Corbin's eyes darted back and forth, scrutinizing every part of the forest he could see. Many times, he thought he detected movement behind some rock or tree, but closer scrutiny showed it was either an animal, or his mind playing tricks on him in the dark. His frustration grew, and he began to regret his decision to rest before setting out to search.

"He could be miles from here by now," he thought angrily. "With no hope of ever being found."

He did not voice these thoughts, but pressed on as the darkness closed around them, and night settled in.

It was a dark night. The moon was bright and almost full, but clouds rolled continuously over it, blocking the light, and illuminating the sky with a dim light. It was very cold, especially in the woods, full of shadows and strange sounds.

The final hour of the search had almost ended when one of his men gave a sharp whisper.

Corbin pulled his horse to a halt and the others did likewise.

"I saw something," the man said in a hoarse whisper. "Just up ahead, to the right up the path."

Holding up his torch, Corbin squinted his eyes and strained his vision. As he looked, he saw something glint in the torchlight. Something was moving, almost indetectably, behind a tree alongside the path.

Corbin urged his men forward and pressed forward at a slow walk, staring at the place of the movement.

"Remember, don't kill unless it is necessary," he whispered harshly. "We don't want him dead. Yet."

Suddenly, there was a loud rustling, and a flurry of movement. Corbin let out a shout and urged his horse to a run. In a second, he had reached the spot where the movement had come from and dismounted, holding up his torch and peering behind the tree. No one was there. His men surrounded him and looked out into the night.

"The grass behind this tree has been pressed down, and it wasn't by an animal," Corbin said grimly. "I think we have found his trail."

Again, there was the sound of rustling further down the path and one of the men let out a shout. A black figure was running along the path about thirty feet beyond.

"Quick!" Corbin shouted, mounting his horse and urging it to a run.

The six men streaked down the path towards the figure, but, somehow, the man had vanished from the path and into the darkness. Corbin was enraged. "How can a man be so elusive?" he muttered. "He was just here only seconds ago. Did anyone see what direction he took?"

Not a man spoke. Corbin sighed with exasperation. "Press on," he said.

Barely a minute had passed when one of the men let out a sharp word, and the horses were halted again. "Look, off the path in the thickets. I saw movement," he said in a low voice. All men looked out into darkness, and stared into the blackness for several moments.

"He has the advantage, because we are many, and herald our presence with our lights and horses," Corbin said in a hushed voice. "We should extinguish them and leave our horses on the path for a moment while we scout the area on foot. Two men will stay here and keep a lookout. If you need help, or see him, shout. Now three of you, come with me."

The four men dismounted and began walking over the uneven ground towards where they had last seen movement. Many stumbled in the darkness, and the moon had disappeared behind a layer of clouds. Without their torches, it was blindingly dark.

Suddenly, the two men watching from the path let out a shout, and the four men ran from the trees, panting and out of breath. The two lookouts had already mounted and were pointing down the path. In a moment, all six horses were racing down the path at full speed, and all six torches were held up, lighting the way ahead. The black figure, running on foot, darted left and right across the path, looking back frequently, and sometimes disappearing alongside the path, but then appearing a few seconds later in the middle of the path further on. Corbin kept his eyes trained straight ahead, his gaze menacing and determined.

The path soon went downwards, and rocky crevices lined the path. Between and among the rocks, the runner continued to conceal himself, only seen occasionally darting among them, or running along the path briefly, only to disappear into the darkness again.

The rocks slowly closed around them, and Corbin pulled his horse to a halt when they were cut off entirely by a rock wall, nearly twenty feet high. He jumped angrily from his horse and looked around with scorn. "It is as if he is mocking us, leaping in and out of view," he said with rage.

He looked up to the top of the rock, and then on either side. Huge boulders stood, blocking their vision into the woods to the left or to the right. The only way out of this enclosure of rock was by the path they had entered. The forest was dark and quiet, with only the sounds of heavy breathing filling the air.

Corbin frowned suspiciously and walked back to his horse, peering between the dark boulders scrutinizingly. He felt a strange feeling rising inside him. "Is this prince more cunning than I thought? Is this some sort of trap?" he thought warily.

The moon crept out from behind a cloud, offering a small, eerie light to surround them.

Another man dismounted and stood near Corbin.

"He must have led us into this closure as a way of escape. He is no doubt running through the woods, getting as far away from here as he can," he said, frustrated.

"Either that," Corbin said in a low, quiet voice. "Or he is still very near, watching and listening."

He took slow, steady steps towards one of the boulders that lined the enclosure. His men also dismounted and drew their bows and swords, prepared in case there was a sudden attack. All found themselves filled with the same feeling of dread and wariness, surrounded by a shroud of mist and darkness. Not even the light of the moon was able to reach them through the heavy covering of branches above them. Silence reigned the woods. Not a breath of wind blew through the trees, not a creature made any noise. It was complete, unbroken silence. Corbin took slow, deep breaths, listening, and peering out into the darkness.

Without warning, the silence was suddenly broken by a twang and a whizzing sound, followed by a shout. The horses screamed, and one ran down the path, away from the enclosure, his hoofbeats dying away in the still air. Corbin whirled around to see one of his men lying on the ground, an arrow struck through his neck. He dropped his torch and grabbed his bow and quiver of arrows from his back.

But before he had fitted his arrow, another man yelled out and fell to the ground in a heap. An arrow had struck him in the head. The four men looked at one another, all with bows at the ready. Corbin saw fear and trepidation in the eyes of the other three men, and held up his hand.

Then with his eyes, he scoured the rocks surrounding them, holding the bow steadily, looking and listening. With a suddenness that caused him to start, another arrow whistled through the air very near him. It sailed past him and struck one of his three remaining men, and a few seconds later, another fell with an ear splitting cry. Only Corbin and one man remained.

"Run, Your Highness!" the man yelled frantically, motioning towards his horse. But no sooner had he spoken than he was struck from behind and fell facedown with a groan.

Corbin looked at the fallen men all around him, frozen with fear. He stared frantically looking into the darkness, tense and still, bracing himself and waiting to be struck down by an arrow. Nothing happened. Only the horses' deep breaths broke the silence.

Among the five men lying on the ground, pierced by deadly arrows, Corbin stood, bow and arrow in hand, staring into the darkness. He listened, waiting to hear or see something that would give him a clue to where this man was concealed, trying to shake away the tremors of fear that were causing his hands to shake slightly. He began to feel sweat drip down his forehead, and he heaved slow, heavy breaths.

Suddenly, there was a noise. He whirled around to his left and trained his arrow towards where the rustling had come from. Then, with slow, fluid movements, a figure stepped from behind a tall boulder. He was dressed all in black, and a mask covered his face. He stood, a shadow against the black night, facing Corbin defiantly. Then, slowly and stealthily, he crept forward towards him. A bow and quiver was slung over his back and a dagger was at his side, but his hands were empty. Each step was slow and deliberate, and each foot fell with such care that the grass did not even rustle under his feet. A horse whinnied nervously.

"Make one move to your weapons and you are a dead man, Julius," Corbin said harshly, his hands tightening around his bow.

The man gave no response and kept walking forward, his pace neither slowing nor increasing, staring straight at the arrow pointed directly between his eyes.

"Stop where you are!" Corbin said sharply. "If you get any closer, you won't live to see another second."

The figure continued approaching, not speaking, or making a sound. Corbin's eyes narrowed. "I know it is you, Julius," he said harshly. "There is no trying to hide it. Show yourself and give up!"

The figure was only five feet away now. He stopped and stood, staring at Corbin through his mask. Not a muscle of his body moved as he stood, surrounded by the men he had slain, and Corbin faced him with equal stillness, filled with an intense rigidness, ready to let his arrow loose if the man so much as flinched.

"Give up, Julius," Corbin growled in a low voice.

Suddenly, the sound of shouts echoed through the woods and the sounds of running horses began to grow near.

"It is too late now," Corbin said. "Throw down your weapons and surrender!"

The shouting grew nearer. The band of men would reach the enclosure in less than a minute.

Suddenly, the figure made a quick move and darted away, dodging behind the boulder. Corbin ran after him, but when he reached the wall of boulders, not a sight of the man or a sound of his presence could he detect, and he threw himself against the boulder, panting and seething with anger.

At that moment, seven men on horseback ran into sight, and seeing the slain men on the ground, drew their weapons.

"This way!" Corbin shouted, running to his horse and mounting. He led the men out of the enclosure and onto the path, pressing his horse forward at a full gallop. "He must be near, he can't disappear into thin air! He is wearing all black and armed with arrows and a dagger."

The men thundered behind, all lighting the path with torches, looking left and right. The trees became less thick above them, letting in gleams of light from above. After nearly ten minutes of running, Corbin pulled his horse to a halt, and those behind did so as well.

"This is madness, how could he have escaped? He stood five feet from me, and yet he escaped!" He spoke with hard, severe words.

He stared off into the darkness for a long time, thinking and sometimes muttering under his breath.

"Let's retrace our steps at a slower pace. Alert me if you see or hear even the slightest thing." They had barely been walking for five minutes when one of the men let out a gruff exclamation. "Look!" he said urgently. Corbin followed his gaze as he pulled his horse to a halt. Hidden far off the path, sheltered behind a cluster of trees, the roof of a shack could be seen, almost completely hidden from view.

Corbin held up a hand for silence and dismounted. The other men dismounted as well. Corbin indicated for two men to stay and watch, and beckoned the other two to continue with him. Noiselessly, they crept off the path, pushing into the forest. As each step brought them nearer, they were able to better see the crude shack, concealed in a grove of trees. Just as they reached it, one of the men leaned close to Corbin and said, "Perhaps a few of us should go inside and you should remain, for safety."

But Corbin shook his head. "We will all go in."

Leading the way, he climbed up a small wooden step and looked at the door. He looked around him at the men standing, their weapons at the ready, their faces set with determination. Then, with a quick, sudden movement, he threw the door open and six men spilled inside, their weapons held at the ready. The cabin was only one room, with only a broken window to let in any sounds and sights from beyond the four walls. Huddled in the far corner, a man was leaning against a bundle, a dagger lying at his side. He leaped to his feet as they entered, and stood frozen in the gleam of the torchlight. Corbin lifted his torch, and in the light of the flame, saw the features of the man who had struck him with such anger only the day before, and whose face had not left his memory since, looking back at him.

"Julius," he said with seething tones. "At last." He strode forward. Julius looked around at all the men and his arms fell limp with defeat. He looked down, not meeting Corbin's hard stare.

"Take him back to the castle," Corbin ordered.

Three men surrounded him and dragged Julius from the shack. His head was hanging and he did not resist, but allowed himself to be pulled roughly from the small building. Corbin watched him from the doorway, crossing his arms with satisfaction.

"I must ask one question, Your Highness," one of the men said. "Why is he not dressed all in black, as you said?"

"Bring his bag of possessions back to the castle," Corbin said with a wry smile, without taking his eyes from the back of the departing figure. "No doubt you will find his black guise among them, as well as a quiver with five arrows missing."

Then he strode through the woods away from the shack with a strong step of satisfaction.

Chapter 19 - Corbin Confronts Ellyn

That night, Ellyn tossed and turned fitfully in her bed. The curtains in front of her windows had been closed, so the little moonlight that crept behind the clouds did not find its way into her room. The impenetrable darkness pressed in around her, and occasionally the wind hummed and whistled through the pane. She often awoke with a start, as if something had scared her from her sleep, and sat up in bed, staring into the darkness. When awake, she felt sick with regret, but even in her dreams, she was haunted by her guilt and could not escape the feeling of remorse, even in the unconsciousness of sleep.

She woke just after the sun had risen. She felt heavy and empty, and moaned as she lifted her head. Alys was standing at her bedside watching her. Ellyn fell back onto the pillows and pressed her palm upon her aching forehead.

"I learned everything that happened," Alys said in a quiet voice full of sympathy. Ellyn did not move, or seem to regard her words.

"Is there anything I can do for you?"

Pushing the blankets away, Ellyn shook her head and slowly sat up. Her golden hair hung around her so that it almost touched the bed on which she was sitting. The bright rays of the morning sun streamed into the room between the partially opened curtains. The sunlight fell on her, illuminating her hair. She edged to the side of her bed and slipped her legs over the side. There she sat, shoulders bent and head downward, while Alys stood at her side, at loss for what to say.

"There is nothing that can be done. I have ruined everything," Ellyn said forlornly.

Alys hesitated, trying to think of words that would encourage the distraught girl. "I don't think that is true," she said at last. "Even though you were involved, it was Maerynn's plot and she who should pay."

Ellyn shook her head. "No, I am the one to blame. If it were not for my agreement, Julius would not have been brought here. I will forever have to live with my grief and shame."

Alys hesitated, then said, "Time will pass, and it will be forgotten."

"You don't understand, Alys," Ellyn insisted, tears beginning to fall from her eyes. "It is not as simple as you seem to think. Soon enough, everyone in the castle will know, and then everyone in the kingdom. The honor of this family will be ruined, and it will all be because of me. The guilt I feel seems to be eating away at me. The more time passes, the more distraught I feel. Before Julius came, things had changed. It was different than when I first arrived. When I first came here, I did nothing more than drown in my sorrows, and was nearly paralyzed with grief. But as time went on, I felt more hopeful and less despairing. But now, my happiness and reputation are forever ruined. This is not an error that time will make right. My life is worse, so much worse than before, and it will never improve. He hates me now, and I do not blame him. I hate myself."

Then she fell to her knees on the floor and began to weep, covering her face with her hands.

Alys knelt beside her, placing a hand on her shoulder, and sat in silence.

When Ellyn had at last calmed herself, she looked up, and took deep, heaving breaths.

"It was clear from our last conversation that I will never be reconciled in his mind. I have gone too far. Why did I ever trust Maerynn? I blame myself for trusting her. It was foolish. Can you believe that she offered to take me to see him again? She said he was hiding in a place he could never be found, and could safely let me see him. He must be far from Lyntirith now."

Alys hesitated. "Then Corbin did not speak to you when he returned late last night." Ellyn shook her head. "Why, what would he have said?"

Alys dropped her voice. "I don't know if I should be saying this, because I have heard very little. But I do know that Julius is… Well, he is here in Lyntirith."

Ellyn frowned, confused. "He was captured."

Ellyn stared at Alys in disbelief. "They found him," she murmured. "And now, because of my actions, someone else must suffer."

"His actions as well, though. It is not as if you dragged him here against his own will," Alys said. "You are not the only one to be blamed."

"Don't try to comfort me, or make me feel I am not to blame; it is no use. I understand the gravity of what I did."

She sighed and was silent for several minutes. Then she said, "Did you hear anything else?"

Alys averted her eyes and looked at the floor. "Perhaps it would be better if you heard from someone besides me," she said.

"No, tell me," Ellyn said hastily.

"Very well. I don't know any details, but I heard rumors that he may be tried for murder, or something of the sort, but I am not certain why, or what for."

"Murder?" Ellyn gasped with astonishment.

"I really don't know any more than this," Alys said. "I am sure you will find out in due time. Until then, I will dress you and fix your hair. Then you should eat something. It will make you feel refreshed."

Almost before she had finished speaking, a firm step was heard, echoing in the hallway beyond the closed door. Ellyn stood from the floor and looked towards the door. The step was all too familiar to her. She sat on the edge of her bed again and pulled her legs up, crossing them, and looked at the door with distressed anticipation. "Here he comes," she said under her breath. "I don't want to speak to him, I'm too ashamed. Tell him I am ill, or still sleeping."

There was a sharp knock at the door and she started at the sound, even though she was expecting it.

"Are you sure?" Alys asked.

Ellyn sighed. "I'll have to see him again eventually. Let him in."

She closed her eyes and pressed her lips together, then stared into her lap as Alys went to the door. Corbin stepped slowly into the room. Alys slipped out behind him.

Still in her nightgown, Ellyn was sitting on the edge of her bed, her legs crossed and her head down.

Corbin strode slowly into the room, each step falling with a soft thud on the floor. He pulled a chair from under the window closer to the bed and then sat in it, crossing his arms. For several long moments, he looked at Ellyn silently. Neither moved nor spoke until, at last, Corbin cleared his throat.

"Many things have happened since we last talked," he said calmly. "Some things I'm sure you are aware of, others you are not, and some things you still conceal, and I wish to know them."

Ellyn lifted her eyes for a moment, then dropped them quickly, fiddling anxiously with her hands in her lap.

"First of all, no doubt you received word that he was captured." Ellyn nodded. "I heard, but I received no other details."

"I led several bands of men last night on a search, and, for many hours, our attempts were fruitless. We looked for many hours in the forests surrounding Lyntirith without a trace to be found, until we were nearly ready to give up. He was seen far into the western woods, miles from here, and he was able to elude us for a while, but it was not until after several of my men were shot by arrows that he was finally captured. He is now kept under close guard in the dungeons, probably soon to be sentenced to death for murder, and attempted murder."

He paused, waiting to see if Ellyn would react, but she stared at her bedspread expressionless. "There is one thing that has left us baffled," he continued, speaking gravely, in quieter tones. "I saw him very clearly in the woods; he stood only a few feet away from me, and he was disguised entirely in black. Even a black mask covered his face. But when he was found later in the woods, his black clothes were gone, and his quiver of arrows was full. As we speak, the forest near where he was found is being closely searched for his black garments. But they have been looking for several hours with nothing to show as a result. Somehow, he was able to carefully hide these items before he was found; that is the only way."

"The only way?" Ellyn looked up. "What if it was not him?"

"Impossible. I pondered that for only a moment, then immediately dispelled it. Who else would it have been? Even dressed in black, I could tell it was him. His build was the same. One man was seen running loose in the woods, and one was found that night. I cannot see how the man dressed in black could have been any other besides Julius."

"I don't want to defend him," Ellyn said slowly. "But I don't think he would have killed anyone."

"Are you really sure of what you are saying? How can you know for certain? He is a clever man. Clever enough to elude us for hours in the forest. Clever enough to enter and escape from this castle without being seen. And," he paused and looked directly at her, "clever enough to pose as a kindhearted, gentle man when, underneath, he is a liar and a killer."

Ellyn frowned and shook her head. "But that would not make sense," she said, feeling overwhelmed with confusion.

"How long did you know him, Ellyn?" She looked down uncomfortably. "How long?"

"About four months," she said quietly.

"There, see, that is far from enough time you need to know someone. How can you really say you don't think he would kill someone when you only knew him for four months? All the while you were in love with someone who was putting on a facade to fool you and make you think he was someone he wasn't. Last night, it was he who let the arrows fly from his bow to kill my men, and his black attire will be found; there is no question in my mind."

Ellyn's heart was heavy, and she stared at the floor blankly.

"I may have only known him for a short time," she said slowly, "But if he had wanted to harm me, he would have had so many opportunities. But he aided our family so much in our final days in Lyntirith. When the Northmen attacked, he did not hesitate to help my father and brother fend them off, and helped us when we were in danger. It was because of his quick actions that my life was spared when the Northmen first attacked. He saved my life that day. I can't understand how he could be the man you speak of."

"How does the saving of a few lives justify his current actions? Even an evil person is capable of doing good deeds, but it does not make them less wicked."

"I don't mean to justify him," Ellyn said with frustration. "I am not saying he is guiltless. I can't speak for his lapse of judgement on the point of which you are speaking, but you must at least know that it was not entirely of his own planning and choice that he was brought here. I elicited his coming here."

She looked down, ashamed.

After a short silence, Corbin said, "That still does not free him from guilt."

"I know." Ellyn nodded, taking a deep breath to calm herself. A feeling of guilt and confusion had been rising inside her, this combination of emotions beginning to frustrate and irritate her.

"I know you did not tell me everything when we last spoke," Corbin continued. "Some of the things you left hidden, I have since found out. I spoke to Maerynn yesterday, and her actions in this ordeal are clear. But there are other things I don't understand, and I think you may have the answers to some of my questions. First of all, have you spoken to Maerynn since Julius left?"

Ellyn hesitated, then nodded.

"Before he left, did Julius convey anything whatsoever to you, even the smallest detail, about how he planned to leave the castle?"

"He only said Maerynn was waiting for him nearby."

Corbin nodded. "That is what I thought," he said under his breath, as if to himself. "And did Maerynn speak to you at all concerning how he escaped?"

Ellyn hesitated.

"I have already spoken to her," Corbin said with an edge of annoyance. "Don't refrain from answering my questions only because you are worried she might try to get revenge for you revealing her plans."

"She did not tell me everything," Ellyn said slowly. "Then tell me what she did say."

Ellyn took a deep breath. "She was able to keep him hidden by dressing him as a guard when he came to the room after leaving mine. And he was able to leave the castle without being noticed."

Corbin stared at Ellyn for a few moments, then chuckled wryly. His brows were knit together, and he shook his head.

"That woman!" he muttered. "Did she say anything else at all?"

"Only that he was hiding in the woods until she gave him the signal that it was safe to leave the country."

Corbin nodded thoughtfully, then stood up and walked to the window. He leaned against the frame and stared out. He was frowning, deep in thought, and was silent for several minutes. Ellyn waited in anxious silence, not daring to speak, but also dreading the silence.

The remorse and guilt she was feeling was urging her to speak, to tell him the sincerity of her regret and penitence. "It would not make any difference, though," she thought to herself. "I have already gone too far, so that he is indifferent to my feelings. It would not change anything." So she kept silent, waiting for him to speak.

"One more question," he said slowly, still staring out the window. "Be perfectly truthful. Did Julius say anything, or hint in any way, that he wanted to take action in… taking you from Lyntirith or something of a similar nature?"

Ellyn opened her mouth to speak when, suddenly, she remembered part of the conversation she had had with him. She remembered his words as if he were speaking them at this moment: 'I know it is very wrong of me, Ellyn, but I often try to think of a way to reverse this situation.' He had said those very words to her less than a day ago. And he had said something about a marriage being broken if 'unusual circumstances' were to arise. She shuddered. She had been confused by his words, and now felt frantic. What had he meant by them? Did he intend to take action? Had he perhaps attempted to do so? She looked up. Corbin was watching her darkly.

"I … I don't know," she finally said, shaking her head.

Corbin looked at her for a long time, then finally sighed audibly and leaned against the wall. "As soon as the black garments are found, his sentence will be decided," he said gravely. "And they will be found. Until then, without obvious proof, I will not make a decision. He will stay imprisoned until then."

"And if they are not found?"

"They will be."

"How can you feel so sure?" Ellyn pressed. "It may be that I knew him for a very short time, but at least it was longer than you have."

"And what would that matter?" he asked sharply, turning from the window to look at her. "What reason would I have to trust you on this matter, or in fact any matter, after what you have done?"

Ellyn's face fell with shame, and she looked down into her lap. Corbin stood rooted to the spot for a few moments, then sighed and turned to leave the room. Ellyn felt numb. As the sound of the door closing echoed in the room, her eyes began growing blurred with tears, and she fell back onto her bed.

Chapter 20 - In the Dungeon

Three days passed.

Each morning, several men were sent to the forest near where Julius had been found to look for a bundle of black clothes. They looked in and around the shack, on the ground in a large radius around, and even in the trees and bushes. Each day, they came back empty-handed. On the third day, one of the men went to the cabinet on the lower floor, where the king spent many of his hours. Corbin was seated across from his father at a table, leaning back in his chair. He sat up when the door opened.

"Is there anything to report?" he asked anxiously. "No, Your Highness," he replied slowly.

Corbin frowned and slumped back into his chair. He ran his fingers through his hair contemplatively.

"I don't understand it," he muttered to himself. "And you searched in a radius of at least half of a mile?"

"Yes, Your Highness. We searched very thoroughly, and not a trace was found."

Corbin rested his forehead on his hand. "You don't need to go out to the woods again tomorrow," he said at last. "After three days of thorough searching with no results, it seems it may be useless. But I have other methods of investigating."

The man bowed and closed the door. Corbin sat back in his chair and stared blankly at the table. King Evander had watched this conversation in silence. When the door closed, he said, "I think it's time you told me about this ordeal, Corbin."

His son looked up at him, brows furrowed.

"I don't understand it," he said. "I thought for sure that black tunic and mask would be found hidden near the shack."

"I am weary of being left in the dark," the king said shortly.

"You keep making allusions to a strange event and are sending search parties into the woods. But you haven't said a word of explanation to me. Why is that?"

Looking up at his father, Corbin said. "It is because I can't tell you all. Part of it is something I wish to keep private for the time being. The rest is hard to explain without the background story. But I will tell you what I can.”

Corbin began a detailed explanation of the events in the woods three nights before, how he had chased the black-clad man all in the dark of the forest until finding him hidden in a shack deep in the recesses of the forest, and had him imprisoned. The king listened, leaning forward intently.

“You should have stayed at the castle instead of putting yourself in harm’s way that night in the woods,” he said admonishingly.

“I would have killed him before he had the chance to draw a weapon,” Corbin said confidently.

The king raised his eyebrows skeptically. “So you are certain that the man in black is the same as the one you found in the shack?” he asked.

“I have trouble understanding how he could have been anyone else, but it is beginning to seem like there was someone else involved as well.”

“How do you mean?”

“Maybe there was someone else in the woods that night, helping him escape. Someone who could stay very well hidden and out of sight, and who could have taken his black disguise sometime between when I saw him and when we found him in the shack, so that it would not be found.”

“Are you sure that the man dressed in black was the same as the man you found hidden in the shack? Or could it have been several similarly dressed men you were chasing, who looked the same?”

Corbin shook his head. “Only one, I think.”

“Who is this man? I think I should know who is prisoner in my own dungeon,” the king said with annoyance.

“His name is Julius,” Corbin said. “That is all I will say for now. I wish I did not have to be secretive. But for now, I am not letting a word of this out to anyone. I don’t want news of his crime spreading.”

“What was the severity of his crime? What is the gravity of the punishment he will receive?”

“Originally, his punishment would have been a very lengthy imprisonment at the least. But now that he has killed several men, of course now he is deserving of death.” The king was silent, stroking his beard thoughtfully.

"This is what I think," he said at last, looking at Corbin. "I think that you are so convinced that Julius was the same man you saw dressed in black that you are unable to see it, or refuse to see it, any other way. Perhaps you could consider alternatives. It is certainly very likely that they are in fact one and the same person, but from what I can gather, there is also a possibility that he was not."

Corbin was silent, thinking.

"I see the reason behind what you are saying," he said slowly. "But there are several things that made me think he was the same person. For one, he was able to elusively escape from the castle almost under the guards' eyes. In the same way, he was able to avoid us in the woods for hours. Few other men could be as agile and elusive as he. It was almost as if he disappeared, and reappeared at another place. His build, also, was the same; he had broad shoulders, and was almost my exact height. Besides, he had a reason for fleeing. He had done something wrong and was trying to escape justice. Who else would be running from us, and why? And why would they be in the woods the exact time we were, running from us as if he had done something wrong? The coincidence seems to be too great. That is why I came to the hypothesis that there could have been another person aiding him. There are a few others I know of who were aware of his presence here, so it is a possibility."

"It is a serious penalty, death is," the king said. "I would investigate very thoroughly to be sure that my decision was right and that I was not condemning an innocent man to death."

"He is certainly not innocent," Corbin said with a dry laugh. "But I intend to do what you say and investigate thoroughly. I think it is time I had a conversation with the prisoner."

The king raised an eyebrow. "Has he not been interrogated yet?"

"He has been informed of his accusations, and denies being the killer. I have not spoken to him myself yet, though."

"I wouldn't expect to get anything truthful from him."

"Perhaps not," Corbin said. "But I may be able to get him to confess or answer some of my questions. He has nothing to lose, at any rate."

He stood up from his chair and rested his palms on the edge of the table, looking down.

"I don't know what all has happened, Corbin. But I hope you will not keep it from me forever. Whatever the case, we will have to be sure the castle grounds are under closer surveillance, and more careful security. It disturbs me that this man was able to enter and exit the castle without being caught."

Corbin nodded. He went to the door and opened it. But he stopped short in the doorway, and frowned darkly. Corineus was standing in the hallway, and made a sudden movement when the door opened.

"What are you doing here?' Corbin asked sharply.

"I'm just passing through the hall," Corineus said defensively.

Corbin squinted his eyes suspiciously as he closed the door behind him. "Well, what are you standing here for? Move along."

Corineus shrugged and turned, slinking down the hallway. Standing in front of the door, Corbin watched him until he was out of sight. Then, he turned and went down the hall in the opposite direction, towards the entrance to the castle dungeon.

The door down to the dungeon was guarded at all times by an armed man. He stood from his chair by the door when Corbin approached and, at his command, unlocked the door and lit a torch. Walking slowly down the dark, narrow stairway, Corbin followed a guard down to the dungeon. The stone ground was wet, and a musty smell filled the air. The guard held up a torch to light the way as they reached the bottom of the stairs and turned left, following the low corridor past rows of barred doors, hiding empty cells. A rat scuttled out of view as they walked through the passage, their footsteps echoing through the passageway.

They at last reached the end of the long gallery, where two guards stood on either side of the door, the enclosure lit with two torches casting flickering shadows on the walls around them. They stood at attention as Corbin approached.

"Let me speak to the prisoner," Corbin said.

One of the guards placed a key inside the lock, turning it with a loud grating sound. Then he pulled open the thick wooden door. On the other side was another door, this one constructed of thick iron bars. The cell was small and dark. There was no window, so the only light came from the guard's torch as he held it up to illumine the cell. Julius was sitting in the corner. His clothes were torn and smeared with dirt and grime. His head was lowered and his shoulder slumped. He lifted his head as the door opened. His expression was filled with pain. Not a physical pain, but an inward pain, surfacing from torment of the spirit.

Corbin took the torch and nodded at the guard, who stepped away, standing a few yards back.

Then he leaned closer and grasped one of the bars with his free hand. "Come closer," he said harshly. "I want to speak to you."

The silence was filled with the clashing and clamoring of chains as Julius slowly pulled himself to his feet, leaning against the wall once he had stood. His skin was white and sallow. With slow, weak steps, he shuffled to the door and stopped, inches away from Corbin's face. The two men stared at each other in silence for several moments, separated by a wall of iron bars.

"I have been told, Julius, that you refuse to confess that you are guilty of murder, and say you deny being the killer of my men the night you were found."

"That is true," Julius said slowly. "But what difference does it make now?"

"It may make a difference in whether or not you get to keep your head," Corbin said dryly. "I have not decided whether or not I am going to believe your claims, but of course I am inclined to reject them."

Julius nodded, then looked down.

"But I have some questions I want to ask you," Corbin continued. "Tell me what happened the night you arrived here. Tell me every single detail, including Maerynn's involvement."

"What do you already know?" Julius asked.

"What does it matter? Just tell me everything, from when you first set foot in Lyntirith until the moment you were captured."

Julius took a deep breath, then began. "We arrived in horse and carriage sometime in the afternoon, I don't know when exactly. Maerynn had given me clothes to look like one of her servants, and we were not hindered in getting in. She led me down to the servants' quarters where I was able to hide while she visited Helena, and planned our next move. She came back and said that Ellyn was out, so she took me upstairs. There was a hallway of empty guest rooms, apparently, and I waited there for many hours. It was just after nightfall that she finally told me it was safe, so she led the way…" Here his voice trailed off.

"Go on," Corbin said coldly.

Julius coughed and cleared his throat before continuing. "She showed me to her room, where I was for a few moments before I made a quick escape, as you already know. I ran back to the room I had been hiding in. Maerynn was waiting and hid me in the closet where she had prepared the attire of one of your guards if I should need it. I put it on, and in that way, was able to make my escape. I went out to the stables and was able to hide without being seen. There was no way out of the kingdom, since it is surrounded by a wall, and all of the exits were guarded. But Maerynn found me the next morning; we had designated the place beforehand as a place I could hide, and helped me past the castle walls."

"How did she do that?" Corbin asked incredulously.

"She hid me in her carriage and had her driver take me to the edge of the woods. By that time, there were already a few men searching through the woods, so she told me the location of a small shack in the woods, and told me she would come and alert me when it was safe to leave the boundaries of the kingdom. There I waited all day, until I was found that night."

Julius let his words trail slowly away. Neither spoke for a long time. Corbin was standing stiff and straight, his fists clenched at his sides.

"Do you have any sense of morality whatsoever?" he finally asked, his voice rising.

"I know, it was wrong of me," Julius said, his voice shaking. "I realize that now. I was so overcome with thoughts of her that it blinded me of my senses. I acted thoughtlessly."

"Thoughtless is putting it lightly," Corbin said severely.

"Did you not even think about what the consequences of such an act could be, not for yourself, but for others?"

"I know," Julius said, wiping his forehead with the palm of his hand.

There was a long silence. Then Corbin said. "So you were in the shack all day until you were found, and never left it once?"

"Yes."

"Not once?" he asked harshly.

"I never once left that building!" Julius said forcefully, lifting his head and looking straight at Corbin. "I know I have given you no reason to believe my word, but it is the truth."

"Very well," Corbin said in a low voice. He looked at the bent, weary form of Julius for a moment longer, then turned to leave.

"Wait," Julius said urgently. Corbin stopped, but did not turn around.

"Please," Julius said, his voice faltering. "Tell her I am sorry. Because I am. It is my fault, and I regret it. She may have agreed to Maerynn's plot, but she is not to blame."

Corbin turned slowly and looked at Julius. "If you really cared for her," he said bitterly. "You would not have come here and risked her honor."

Julius lowered his head, and Corbin turned, walking swiftly down the dark corridor. The sound of the dungeon door slamming shut echoed in the passage.

Once upstairs, he winced in the brightness and strode down the hall, staring at the floor in deep thought. He went down several hallways until he reached a winding staircase. Reaching the top of the stairs, he turned the corner and lifted his head. Corineus had just rounded the corner at the other end of the hallway and was walking towards him. Corbin stopped and stood in the hallway, watching him approach, his arms crossed. Just as Corineus was about to walk past, Corbin stepped away from the wall and stood in front of him.

"You weren't just passing by the door earlier," he said in a low voice. Corineus glanced up at him furtively and tried to pass.

"Wait," Corbin said firmly. "Corineus, what do you know about this?"

"About what?" he asked, looking bewildered.

"You know what I'm talking about. You know more than you are saying."

"And if I do," Corineus said, looking him in the eyes. "Why would I tell you?"

Corbin raised his chin, without taking his eyes off Corineus.

"If you do know more than you are saying," Corbin said slowly. "Don't breathe a word of it to anyone. If you do, you will regret it."

Chapter 21 - Ellyn's Letter

Ellyn stood in her bedroom, staring vacantly out her window. For almost an hour she had been in the same position. Alys was busying herself in the room, trying to initiate conversation with Ellyn, hoping to distract her from her troubles. Ellyn occasionally answered Alys with a distracted mumble, but was mostly silent. Alys finally abandoned her attempts, and hummed to herself softly as she dusted the mantlepiece.

Grey clouds rolled across the sky, and a stiff wind blew through the bare trees. Autumn was waning, and winter was setting in. The grass was brown and stiff, and a few brown leaves swirled in the breeze. Ellyn's eyes were glazed over dazedly, and she stared into nothingness. A single tear rolled slowly down her face, leaving a trail on her cheek, and falling to the floor.

"Ellyn," Alys said softly, her voice echoing hollowly in the room.

Blinking, Ellyn lifted her head and reached her hand up to her face. She looked at her fingers and stared at them blankly.

"Ellyn," Alys said again.

Ellyn turned from the window. Her face was pale and her blue eyes surrounded by dark circles.

Deprivation of sleep and food had quickly left her weak and her complexion blanched.

"You have not left your room for days," Alys said. "You should try to breathe in some fresh air; it might revive you."

"He might be there, though," she said, leaning her back against the wall.

"No, he is gone for the day," Alys said. "You won't encounter him there."

Ellyn sighed and left her place from the window. She walked slowly across the room, her shoulders bent as if a weight was bearing them down. Alys watched her as she left the room, her face set in an expression of anxiety.

The corridor was empty, and Ellyn shivered in the draft, away from the warmth of her own room. She was just turning a corner in the hallway when she caught a glimpse of movement out of her peripheral vision. She glanced quickly towards it and saw Helena leaning against the wall only a few yards away. Stopping, Ellyn looked anxiously at the young girl. She was taking deep breaths, and her face was ashen.

"Are you well?" she asked, taking a step toward Helena.

Holding up her hand, Helena took a step back. Then her body began to shake, and she coughed violently, her frame sinking under the wracking coughs. Ellyn winced.

When the coughing fit had passed, Helena leaned her back against the wall and pressed her palm to her chest, inhaling deeply.

"It has passed," she said in a weak voice, looking at Ellyn. She stood up and cleared her throat.

"It is nothing. It happens every day."

Ellyn's brows furrowed and she looked at Helena with sympathy. "Have you always been ill?" Helena nodded. "I was born too early as a child and almost did not live past infancy.

Sometimes I wish I hadn't," she said, dropping her eyes. "I have always been so ill, and wasn't able to live a life like other children: always in my room, often alone, without the strength to venture very far."

"You must have been lonely."

"Loneliness is a part of who I am. I have grown accustomed to it."

Ellyn's eyes lowered with sympathy. "I can keep you company for a while, if you wish."

"You don't look very well yourself; are you sure you don't want to rest?"

"I feel well enough."

"Alright, you can come to my room for a while if you'd like."

Helena led Ellyn down the hall and opened a door about halfway to the end. A large bed with green coverings and tapestries stood at the back of the room and a large gold and blue rug covered the hard floor. Ellyn stepped inside and relaxed, the warmth of the room pushing at the chill air from the hallway. Helena indicated two chairs at the edge of the room, and Ellyn sat in one of them as Helena softly closed the door and took the other chair. She leaned her head back and heaved a sigh, relaxing into the chair.

There was silence for several moments. Helena had closed her eyes and Ellyn did not want to disturb her. She studied her face, wondering if she had fallen asleep. But she lifted her head and opened her eyes, looking at Ellyn.

"I'm just a bit tired," she said, smiling weakly.

"Is this how you always feel?" Ellyn asked. "Or do you have days that are better than others?"

"As a girl, I was always weak and sickly. Sometimes, I spent months in my room, because I didn't have the strength to leave it. But, as I got older, I grew somewhat stronger, and was able to walk around the castle for brief intervals. A few years ago, I thought I was nearly healthy, and even went riding sometimes with my brothers. I couldn't exert myself very much, but it was better than before. But then… the incident ruined that."

Ellyn's brows furrowed. Helena had said "the incident" as if she assumed Ellyn knew what she was talking about, but instead, she stared at Helena, puzzled.

"What are you talking about?" she asked slowly. "If I may ask." Helena looked at her quickly. "You don't know?" she asked.

Ellyn shook her head.

"I suppose you wouldn't," she said, leaning her head back again. "It was… well, an event that changed my life, as well as the rest of my family's, forever." Then she dropped her voice and almost whispered, "Especially Corbin's."

"Corbin's?"

Helena nodded. "It hardened him. Not that he wasn't a quiet, solemn person before, but this made him bitter. Even though it has been years, the effects are still plain, and probably will be for many years to come, if not for eternity."

Ellyn listened to Helena's words with increasing bewilderment. "I … don't understand," she said.

Helena dropped her eyes. "I really can't speak of it," she said slowly. "It pains me to talk about it. It has only been just two years, and the horror is still fresh in my mind."

"I'm sorry," Ellyn murmured. She was studying the young girl's face with incredulity, as if she were trying to read her thoughts, or reap through her memories.

"You don't need to speak of it, of course not; it is just that I didn't know that anything of such gravity had happened to your family before. No one breathed a word of it to me."

"We keep it very secret. I only thought you might know, since you're now a part of our family, but I should have realized no one would mention anything to you. The subject is rarely dwelt upon."

An expression of pain was now etched on Helena's face, and she was wringing her hands in her lap.

"I shouldn't have pressed the subject; I see it is painful to you," Ellyn said. She was suddenly struck with a strange feeling she could not interpret, and, before Helena could reply, she stood up. "I will let you rest now," she said.

She stood quickly from her chair, and she left the room, closing the door quietly behind her. She took a few steps, then stopped in the middle of the hallway and leaned stiffly against the wall. What incident could have happened to so alter the lives of this family, to cause the health of Helena to falter, and Corbin to grow hardened, as she had said?

"Maybe that is why they are all so withdrawn," she thought. She felt numb and breathless. She walked slowly down the hall back to her room.

"How do you feel? Did the fresh air help? Ellyn are you alright?" Alys asked as she entered.

Ellyn looked at her, her expression troubled. "Do you know of anything that happened in the past about two years ago, something that heavily affected the family?"

Alys frowned. "I don't know what you are talking about," she said.

"Helena alluded to something that happened a few years ago to her family, but she didn't say what it was. I can't figure out what it could have been, but it must have been grave, by the way she spoke of it."

"No, I am not aware of anything of the sort happening," Alys said thoughtfully.

Ellyn went to the window at the end of her room and sat, crossing her arms and looking blankly at the floor. Light in the room was dimming, and Alys got up and lit the fire, closing the curtains to keep out the chill draft.

"Whatever happened, it causes Helena great pain to speak of, but apparently Corbin was directly affected. She said he never speaks of it though." There was a heavy, empty feeling in her heart, but she did not know why.

"Perhaps we will never know," Alys said. "But then again, you may find out someday. It is no use speculating though. That rarely leads to the right answer."

Ellyn sat silently for a few moments, then said, "Alys, please get me some parchment with a quill and ink. There is a note I want to write."

On the second floor of the Wyndham castle, Maerynn was sitting in her boudoir. A square of embroidery was in her lap, but it had been neglected long before. Her hands were idly clasped together, and she was staring ahead in thought, her expression set in its usual smirk.

Maerynn had grown up in her father's palace her whole life, but without the guidance of either of her parents. Her mother had died before she was old enough to remember her. Her father, grieved by the loss of his wife, closed himself in his room where he drowned in his misery. The sight of his three children caused him such painful reminiscence that he rarely let them in his presence and, when he did, was distant and cold. Thus, Maerynn and her two older brothers were left without the nurture of either parent, and left to the care of the nursemaids and governesses who were designated to raise them.

All three children had received a rigid and thorough education. As a young girl, Maerynn was taught to sing, dance, read, sew, speak fluently in foreign languages, and was rigorously taught in every subject necessary for her to learn. She lived comfortably and luxuriously. But Maerynn was discontent. She saw her brothers treated with respect and kindness, especially her oldest brother, the future king of the country. Meanwhile, she was treated with indifference, and sometimes mistreatment. This planted seeds of bitterness in the young girl's heart, and caused her to grow willful and stubborn. Her nursemaids often threw their hands up in exasperation at her acts of rebellion. These reactions pushed her to continue her behavior, until she was sent away from Wyndham at age eleven to study abroad in the hopes she would return a better child.

No one ever knew what happened those years when she was away because she never spoke of them, but she left angry and willful, and returned bitter and haughty. She had been malicious and stubborn, and returned resentful and sullen. She kept all of her thoughts bottled inside her. Occasionally, something would enrage her, and she would spew forth the anger she had kept concealed, and it was a frightening thing to behold. No one would stand in her way when she was angry, and she sought revenge on anyone she thought deserved it. Rarely did she show her hidden emotions, but deep in her heart, the dark experiences of her childhood boiled into black and malicious webs, and a hatred welled inside of her.

On this day, she had sat alone nearly all day with little to do, as many other days, when there was a knock on her door.

"Princess Maerynn," a servant said, entering with a bow. "Prince Corbin of Lyntirith is here and requests your presence."

"Oh, is he," Maerynn said, her eyes darkening. "He is down in the foyer."

Maerynn stood as the servant left. She went to the mirror above her dresser and looked at her reflexion. She twisted her hair between her fingers, laying it carefully over her shoulder, then raised her arched eyebrows before gliding from the room.

She walked resolutely from the room and down the winding stairwell. At the bottom of the stairs and around the corner was the door to the foyer. She pressed her lips together and opened the door.

Corbin was standing at the end of the room leaning against the mantel above the fireplace. Maerynn was not easily disturbed, but the expression on his face made her shudder. It was not anger or indignation that she saw. Instead, he was calm and imperturbed, but austere, and his uncompromising gaze did not leave her as she entered the room and closed the door behind her. She locked eyes with him and stepped into the room, raising her chin defiantly.

"I did not expect you to come so soon," she said coolly.

"I know, that is why I came," he replied with equal evenness.

Maerynn squinted and continued to approach him and crossed her arms, standing in front of the table which stood between them.

"Your journey was in vain," she said. "I already know that Julius was captured, so you can't have the pleasure of breaking the news to me and watching my horrified reaction, and gloating over your success."

"That is not why I came," Corbin said wryly. "Why don't you just be silent and listen to what I have to say."

Maerynn smirked but said nothing.

"Your involvement in the plot to bring Julius to Lyntirith was obvious to me, but an assistant? This is something new, hiring someone to carry out your plots."

Maerynn scrutinized his face, her eyes narrowing. "Your accusations arise from mere speculation. Besides, my business is my own to keep, not yours."

"It is your own, until you make it mine as well."

Maerynn walked slowly around the table, brushing her fingertips across its surface. "You are trying to figure out exactly what happened, aren't you? You don't know, and you're trying to find out," she said mockingly.

"There is no need to discover what is already known. I already know there was another man you used to help you in bringing Julius to Lyntirith."

By this time, Maerynn had reached the other side of the table. She stood in front of him and looked up defiantly at him.

"I know you don't know all of the answers, and I'm afraid it must stay that way," she said haughtily. "You are wasting your time here, Corbin."

"In my few conversations lately, you have denied having any part of this situation, but everything you say and do leaks with guilt, and you might as well be giving me a confession. Even though you have not spoken your words of confession, your guilt is clear to me, but I think that is what you intend. Your mock innocence and coy remarks are intentional. You are mocking me, because you know that I know you are not revealing everything, and you want me to keep pressing you for answers. So why don't you just answer them? I already know you were involved, and you are aware of it. So why continue to keep everything hidden?"

"So you came for a confession; is that why you're here? Of course I know you are aware of my involvement in bringing Julius, but what would the pleasure in it be if you knew all the details, and the extent of my involvement? All you know is that I was involved. Does that mean Julius made me bring him to Lyntirith, or that I dragged him from his home to see her? And how exactly was Julius able to escape the castle, and where did his black clothes go? Do you really think I would answer your question?"

"You seem to forget I have the advantage. You may know more than I know, but I may also know more than you think I know. And by knowing more than you think I do, I know when you are deceiving me, and when you are twisting the truth, and when you are not."

Maerynn scoffed. "You can't really know anything, Corbin. You did not witness anything. All of the information you have would have had to come from those who were involved in the plot. You have Julius, yes, but would he really tell you the truth? Or would anyone who knew the answers really tell you the truth? You are getting your information secondhand. Is that really reliable?"

"You don't have to witness something to find out the truth," Corbin said shortly. "The truth is not always clear, but it does not mean it cannot be revealed."

Crossing her arms, Maerynn stepped back. Her back was held stiffly upright, and her eyes dark and menacing.

"You still don't know what information you have is true, and what is false."

"That is not true. For example, I know that there was someone else in the woods that night, the black-clad man, and I know you were involved with his presence there."

Maerynn's eyes narrowed. "You are trying to trap me," she said with a short laugh. "You really think it is that easy? How can you really know there was a second man that night, and that it was not Julius? Clothes are easy to conceal, or dispose of."

Corbin took a breath and strode from his place by the mantel, which he had not left since she entered. He walked to the window, then turned and looked at her again.

"Don't pretend I don't understand your motives," Corbin said. "Because I do. I know what you want, and you were foiled not once, but twice. Give it up, Maerynn."

Maerynn's expression was livid. "You think you understand my motives? You know nothing about me, Corbin. And don't think you do, or pretend to. You think I am predictable; that is far from the truth, as I will show you."

"There is no need. The only way you are predictable is in your unpredictability. It is not that I think I can predict your actions, but I know you are bitter and I know why. And I warn you that any further actions to try to secure what you are aiming for could not only damage others, but bring on your own destruction."

"Don't think that you can order me about," Maerynn said forcefully. "I'll make my own decisions; there is no one to stop me."

Corbin stepped closer to her and looked down into her eyes, full of fury.

"Just remember," he said calmly. "When you find your plans ruined, and all your hopes and aspirations fallen into pieces at your feet, and your life has fallen apart, that it was by your own deeds that you were ruined."

Then before she could say a word, Corbin brushed past her and was walking out the door. Maerynn's hands tightened into fists at her sides, and she glared at the door, seething. She began pacing the room, walking in long, swift strides and muttering under her breath.

It was just after dark by the time Corbin reached the Lyntirith castle. He walked wearily from the stables and into the castle. He went to his room and pulled his riding coat off, draping it over the side of his bed. His manservant was hanging clothes in a closet, and looked up as he entered.

"There is a note for you on the dresser," he said nonchalantly. Corbin nodded but gave no reply. He sat on the edge of his bed and scratched the back of his neck, staring at the floor. His face was troubled and full of anxiety. He stood and walked to the end of his room, and back to his bed again, taking slow, heavy steps. When he reached the other end of the room, he rested his hands on the edge of his desk. He sighed heavily.

Standing up, he was about to turn away when a flash of white caught his eye. He looked quickly at the top of his dresser and saw a piece of paper, folded and sealed. He frowned and picked it up. His name was spelled in black, flowing letters on the front. He broke the seal and unfolded it, and began to read its contents.

This is what he read: "Corbin: I know that you have been very upsetted over the ordeal with Julius coming to Lyntirith and what transpired because of that, and with good cause. I realize that my thoughtless act caused others trouble and strife, and that is one the many reasons I regret my actions. First of all, I know it was very wrong of me. Even though I knew it was time to forget my life in Eurasia, and my life there had ended, I refused to let go of it entirely, for which I paid a price. I am truly sorry and regret all the trouble I have caused. I am not saying these things to quell your anger, or make you sympathetic, but because I must tell you the depth of my guilt. I don't need a reply from you, or even a word, as long as I know you are aware of my penitence. Ellyn."

Corbin read the words, then re-read them, then stared at the page long after he had finished. He stood, frozen in place, staring at the blank wall in front of him. Then with a sudden movement, he dropped the page onto the desk in front of him and strode from the room. Swiftly, he walked through the hall and down the stairwell. Down hallways, through corridors and down small stairwells he went until he reached the door that led down to the dungeons. A guard was sitting on a chair and sprung to his feet as Corbin came around the corner.

"Light that torch," Corbin ordered.

The man fumbled with the flint and struck a flame into being. Then he lit the torch, which Corbin pulled from his hands and held up as he walked down the stairs. His heavy, determined step echoed in the narrow passageway until he reached the cell where Julius was kept.

Without a word, he took the keys from the wall and, handing his torch to one of the startled guards, he twisted it in the lock and threw the door opened. Julius lifted his head and blinked in the light.

"Give me the keys for his shackles," Corbin said shortly. "Your Highness, what are you…"

"I said give them to me," Corbin interrupted.

The guard pulled the ring from his pocket from which a single key hung. Corbin took it and roughly loosed the cuffs and shackles from his hands and feet. Then he grabbed Julius by the shoulders and pulled him to his feet and looked directly at him.

Julius lowered his head, streaked with mud and filth.

"I want you to leave Lyntirith," Corbin said in a low voice. Lifting his head, Julius looked at him blankly.

"To another prison, then?"

"No, don't you understand? I just released you from your bonds."

Julius stared at Corbin for a moment, then he opened his mouth. "You aren't setting me free are you?"

"You'll no longer be held under lock and key. I am going to have you taken to your uncle's kingdom in Brystol where you belong."

"I don't understand," Julius said falteringly.

"Why should you want to? Just accept your freedom without question," Corbin said roughly.

He let go of Julius, who staggered back against the wall and looked back at Corbin with disbelief.

"Don't think I am doing this as a mercy on your part. My reasons for releasing you are my own. But know this: if you ever set foot in Lyntirith again, your life will be in danger, and I will not be so merciful the second time. But as long as you are far from here, you are free."

Julius took deep heavy breaths, his amazement growing with every word.

Corbin turned to the guards. "Take him up and have him driven to Brystol this very moment," he commanded.

"But, Your Highness, has your father given this order?"

Corbin sighed with irritation. "He was my prisoner, captured and imprisoned by me, and thus I have the right to release him at my own will. Now take him away."

The guard motioned for him to leave, and with slow, staggering steps, Julius walked past Corbin and through the doorway to the cell that had kept him captive for more than a week. He glanced at Corbin as he walked past and was met with his steady, even glare. His face was full of amazement, and he stood up straighter as he passed from the dungeon into the corridor and followed the two guards away from the cell. Corbin stood behind with his arms crossed, watching him leave.

Chapter 22 - Secrets Revealed

Ellyn sat in front of a mirror in her room while Alys brushed her long, golden hair. The sun had just set, and the horizon still glowed with its rays. The moon was already shining in the clear blue sky, the silvery crescent shedding a dim light on the earth below.

Alys twisted Ellyn's hair into a long braid, then let it fall gently over her shoulder.

Ellyn lifted her eyes and looked at Alys's reflection through the mirror. Her downcast eyes shone in the dim light.

"I hoped he might reply to my note," she said. "But I am not surprised that he didn't. I know he thinks me a corrupted, immoral person, and I'm sure he wants to avoid me as much as possible. He probably did not even read it."

"You only gave it to him last night. I would not despair yet," Alys said, setting the brush down on the table. "You may receive a reply from him yet tomorrow."

Ellyn sighed and folded her arms together, looking into the mirror dejectedly. "I wonder why I care so much that I am reconciled in his mind. I have treated him with such indifference, and even spite, but now I can hardly recognize the feeling and opinion I have of him. I might have loved him, if I had only tried. But now it is too late." She stared into the flickering flame of the candle, sitting in front of her. "It is too late," she murmured again. "And it is all my own fault."

Alys took a deep breath. "I probably shouldn't be saying this. I was going to wait, and see if you would receive word of it today, but evidently, you have not."

Ellyn turned in her chair and looked at Alys uneasily. "What are you talking about?"

"This morning, I was told that Julius was released from prison," she said with a whisper. "Apparently Corbin released him last night and had him sent to Brystol. But the reasons for his actions have not been confirmed, and King Evander has criticized him for taking action before all the evidence was collected."

Ellyn stared at Alys, bewildered.

"Julius, released?" she said with disbelief.

Alys nodded. "That is all that I know. Hildegarde told me. I don't know how she gets her information, but it is usually accurate."

Ellyn stood up and walked a few paces into the room.

"But it doesn't make sense," she said. "Why would he release him without evidence? In Corbin's mind he was guilty of at least one offence, which was trespassing into the castle, and of what transpired after that. But he seemed so sure that Julius had killed those men in the forest that night. Why would he release him, after only a week to consider the evidence?"

She walked to the window and looked up, gazing into the clear night sky. Then she turned and looked at Alys. She took a deep breath and said in a quiet voice, "I wonder if he is in the castle. I think I might want to speak to him." Even as she spoke these words, she felt a twinge of nervousness.

"But do you think I should?" she asked with uncertainty. Alys shrugged and gave no reply.

Ellyn pressed her lips together, frowning thoughtfully.

Then, without speaking, she crossed her room. She opened her bedroom door, and without looking back, slipped out into the hallway and closed the door behind her. Corbin's door, just across from hers, was closed, and she stopped in the middle of the hallway. The air around her was chill, and no sound came from within the room. She took a few steps until she stood just in front of it. For a few moments, she stood, biting her lip, trying to decide if she should knock. Meanwhile, she could still hear no sound beyond the door. Finally, she lifted her hand and gently knocked. Even though the sound was quiet, it reverberated in the empty hallway. She stood waiting, listening, wondering if it would open, and yet hoping it wouldn't.

Just as she was about to turn away, the sound of the lock being unfastened reached her ears, and she inhaled sharply. Her heart leaped. The door creaked open, and from the shadows within, Corbin emerged, holding a small candle. His features were dark and obscured in the low light, but his eyes reflected the glow of the candle.

Ellyn felt tense and her hands began to tremble. "I'm sorry, I only wanted to speak with you for a few moments. But I can leave, if you would rather." With these last few words, her voice trailed off.

Without speaking, Corbin pulled the door opened and stepped aside. Ellyn lowered her head and stepped quickly past him, slipping into the room. The door closed behind her.

Two other candles were lit in the room, one placed in front of a mirror on a table, the light reflecting into the room. Warm embers were glowing in the fireplace, and the room was filled with warmth.

Ellyn turned and faced Corbin, who was watching her in solemn silence.

She hesitated; realized she had not thought about what she was going to say. She took a breath, then her words came out in a nervous rush. "I just heard from my maidservant, well, that is, I heard you freed Julius. I wondered if it was true."

"Yes, that is true," he said slowly, without releasing her from his steady gaze. "Then… did you find evidence by which you could free him?"

She took another breath and held it, waiting for his response. He was silent for a moment, unmoved. Then, he cleared his throat and walked over to a table along the wall and set the candle down on it. Then he turned to her and, crossing his arms, leaned against the wall behind him.

"No," he said in a calculated tone. "I did not find any physical evidence."

Ellyn was silent, waiting for an explanation. He did not speak for a few moments, then sighed and raised his eyes towards the ceiling for a moment. "You should sit down," he said, and nodded towards a chair in front of the fireplace.

Walking softly across the room, Ellyn went to the chair and sat down.

Corbin walked to the fireplace and picked up the poker. Staring into the flames, he pressed it into the embers, stirring up the flames. Sparks rose up into the air and faded away. After a moment, he put it back in the stand, and then rested his arm on the mantel. He lowered his eyes, then finally began to speak.

"No, I did not find any evidence with which to uphold him. There were a few things that led me to believe that he was not the man in the woods, but I was not sure. There is still a slight possibility it was him, but I don't think so." He paused for a moment. Then he said, "The truth of it is, I think Maerynn is more to blame than any other. She had her own reasons for wanting to bring Julius here. While I blame him for accepting her offer, Maerynn is coy, and has a way of twisting words and meanings, and making things sound enticing, even if they are wrong. Julius was a man in love, and that is enough to drive some people to act irrationally. I am not trying to justify what he did, I am only trying to rationalize this unreasonable behavior."

He fell silent. Ellyn was staring into her lap, frowning with contemplation. "Then you felt that he did not hold enough blame?"

Corbin hesitated. He ran his hand through his hair and cleared his throat. "It's complicated," he said slowly. "I felt that his imprisonment was enough to keep him from coming here again, and trust that he will not return." His words trailed off. He was silent for a moment, then seemed to want to speak again, but then closed his mouth. His jaw was clenched tightly, and he was looking down at the floor.

Ellyn shifted in the chair, and stared into the flames in the fireplace. There was a quick pop from below the depths of the coals, but everything else in the room was silent.

"Why do you not blame me?" Ellyn asked in a small voice, breaking the tense silence. He looked up at her quickly.

"You knew that Maerynn asked if she could bring him. I know my decision upset you, with good cause because I was wrong, but you have never said a word of blame."

He took a deep breath. "I do not hold you responsible. I think Maerynn asked you so that she could turn to someone on whom she could point the blame if she were found out. She would have brought him without asking you otherwise." He paused and sighed. "I know you were lonely, you were brought here against your will, no doubt. You left the familiarity of your home and came here to what? A family who resented you, and treated you with bitterness. And you were forced to marry a man who treated you with indifference. You never stopped thinking about your family, because the treatment you received here drove you to do little else."

"That is true," Ellyn said, standing suddenly from her chair. "I did think about my family, every single day, and Julius too. I was practically living in my memory. But that was wrong of me. I was never mistreated here, or felt threatened by anyone. Yet I refused to separate myself from the life I left behind and accept my new one. Instead of striving to make the best of my situation, I worsened it by withdrawing from it and living in the shadows of my past, instead of facing what lay ahead. It was wrong of me. I knew my life as it was before was over, and I could never go back, but my actions, the way I lived, the way I treated everyone and the decisions I made reflected the opposite. I was holding onto false hopes that I would see them again, trying to forget my fate instead of accepting it."

"Your fate," Corbin scoffed with frustration. "It was not your fate to marry me in the first place."

Ellyn stared at him, confused.

With an abrupt movement that startled Ellyn, Corbin took a step away from the fireplace, standing with his back to her. For several moments, he was silent. Then he turned to her and said, "I might as well tell you." His tones were agitated, and an expression of pain was etched on his face.

"None of this should ever have happened. It is not your own fate that determined you would come here and marry me, but my own. I was never meant to marry you. I was never even meant to be king."

"Yes I know, but—"

"No, you don't know," he cut her off. He stared down at the floor for a few moments, then lifted his eyes and looked at her again. "A few years ago, something happened that changed the course of my family, and our future." He wiped his brow, then said slowly. "A few years ago, I had an older brother."

Ellyn gasped quietly.

"My brother Conrad was to inherit the throne. And he was so much greater of a man than I am. He was born to lead, and treated with respect. But he was not only respected because he was to be the king one day. He earned his respect through his genuine acts of courage, honor, truthfulness, wisdom, kindness, humility. He would have been a great king. This kingdom would have flourished under his rule. But instead, because of his absence, I must rule, though I was never prepared, and never desired to, and was never meant to. It was Conrad who should have ruled, not me. But that is not the worst part." He paused and sighed deeply. "It was my own actions, or lack of them, that resulted in his life being lost.

"A few years ago, I was riding on horseback with him and our younger sister Helena. There was a man in the woods near the castle. We have never found out why he was there, or what he intended to accomplish. All that we know was that he was a man that had gone insane. He charged at us with no reason, no warning. We were walking at a slow pace when he just darted from the trees and pulled Helena from her horse and began to drag her away into the woods. There was hardly time to react or think about what had happened, and no doubt calamity and great harm would have quickly befallen Helena, but Conrad dismounted immediately and threw himself on top of the man with his dagger. They struggled for a few moments. The man, crazed with rage, pulled out his own dagger. They had only been struggling for a few moments when his weapon was thrust into Conrad's heart, and he fell back onto the ground. We were only a few paces into the woods, and Helena's cries had been heard. There were already men running to our aid, and the man was surrounded and captured on the spot. But it was too late. Conrad was dying, and there was no one to save him. I was at his side when he died, only a few moments later. He could not speak. He only stared at me, and was holding tightly to my arm. He could barely breathe, and the dagger was still stuck in his chest."

Corbin was now pacing, his face filled with anguish. "My brother died with no one to save him, even though I was only a few feet away. Instead of jumping to his aid, I watched from my horse, too cowardly to know what to do. I have brought my own fate on myself, and there is no way to escape."

He stopped pacing and looked at Ellyn. She was watching him with horrified amazement. He took a few strides and stood in front of her. He grabbed her shoulders and looked into her eyes.

"I'm sorry, Ellyn," he said, his voice broken with emotion. "You have been forced to marry a worthless, bitter, uncaring man who has been the cause of all your unhappiness."

Shaking with emotion, Ellyn felt tears gathering in her eyes. She was at loss for words, and looked back at his face, full of distress.

"He would have made such a better husband than I have. He would have treated you with the kindness that you deserve."

"Don't say that," Ellyn said, struggling to hold back her tears. Corbin dropped his eyes, but his grip on her shoulders did not lessen. Pressing her lips together, she pushed his hands from her shoulders and threw her arms around him, burying her face against him. He held her tightly, and rested the side of his face on the top of her head. Ellyn squeezed her eyes tightly, and tears spilled down her face.

After a few moments, Corbin relaxed and pulled her in front of him, looking down at her. She pressed her hand to her lips, her eyes filled with unfallen tears, and her cheeks were stained with wetness.

Ellyn looked up and took deep breaths. "You have nothing to apologize for," she said, then paused and closed her eyes, pressing her lips together. "You say that you were never meant to be king, and that I was never meant to marry you. Well, if that was true, then it would not have happened. Things do not happen that are not meant to. I am the one who has been in the wrong. My reasons for treating you distantly and with coldness were much less justifiable than yours. It is you who must forgive me."

"Of course, I forgive you. I did long before now."

Ellyn sighed. "You think of yourself with too much doubt and belittlement. I have seen your actions, how others treat you and think of you. The only person who thinks you are unfit for kingship is yourself. I believe you when you say your brother would have made a great king, and when you praise him so highly. But you have the potential to be just as great a king as he would have been. You may feel defeated with where the past has brought you, and where former events have led you, but if they had turned out otherwise, then I would not have you."

He raised his eyebrows and looked at her.

"I did not mean that in a way that implied…" Ellyn's voice trailed off.

"I know how you meant it," he said tenderly. "I have little to boast of when I speak of the hardships that brought me to where I am now, but if you are the reason I had to endure them, you are worth every single one."

Then he drew her towards him and wrapped her in a tight embrace, and there they stood in silence for a long time.

Ellyn stirred beneath the covers. She opened her eyes and stared into the blank darkness, wondering why she had awoken. She raised her head slightly and looked into the room. Instead of the window of her own room and the fireplace on the far wall, the fireplace stood on another wall, and a strange table stood next to the bed. The unfamiliarity of her surroundings roused her, and she turned quickly, looking on the other side of her. Corbin was sleeping soundly, and stirred slightly as she moved. Then she remembered the night before, and why she was not in her own room and fell back onto the pillows with relief.

She closed her eyes. At that moment, a muffled grating sound came from the end of the room, interrupting the silence. Ellyn tensed and opened her eyes widely, staring up at the ceiling. From her peripheral vision, she saw a dim light growing from the corner of the room. She slowly turned her head and saw, through the shadows of the darkness, a small flickering candle moving about at the end of the room. She laid frozen for a moment with fear. Then, making as small movements as possible, she reached over the side of her bed and groped around for the rope, which would alert someone with the ring of the bell. But, no matter how far she leaned from the bed, she could not find it. Then she realized with horror that the rope had been cut. A coil lay on the floor just below her. She covered her mouth with her hand and looked to the end of the room again. The light had been extinguished, and no sound came from the corner of the room.

She sat up slowly, the blanket slipping from her shoulders. Wearing only her nightgown, she shivered without the warmth of the blankets. But it was not only the air that chilled her. The ominous silence of the room reverberated in her ears and made her tremble with uneasiness. She glanced over at Corbin, who had not stirred, then back into the darkness of the room, trying to see through the darkness, listening. She pulled her hand out from under the blankets and reached towards Corbin to wake him. But before her hand reached him, a cold hand snatched at her from the darkness and covered her mouth. She felt two strong arms twist around her body and secure her from behind. She was pulled from the bed with one swift yank, and the hand pressed tighter against her mouth.

Chapter 23 - The Assassin

Ellyn was dragged across the room, spun around, and thrown roughly against the wall. She struggled against the strong arms that were holding her, but in vain.

"Do not make a noise," a voice hissed next to her ear. "If you do, you will immediately regret it." Then the fingers slowly lowered from her mouth. With eyes wide open, Ellyn stared into the blackness, trying to glimpse the dark form, but without a light in the room, all she saw were vague movements. The grip tightened around her arms, and the voice whispered, "Stay right here. Don't move, and don't make a noise."

The ironlike hold on her arms was finally released, and the figure faded into the darkness. Ellyn reached her hands to her neck and took deep breaths, trying to calm herself. She pressed her palm against her chest. Her heart pounded against the pressure of her hand.

There was a shuffling sound just next to her, and she froze. She cringed as the groping fingers found their way to her arm in the dark. She soon became aware that a rope was being wrapped around her wrists. When her hands were tightly secured, she was roughly pushed away from the wall and shoved into a chair.

"If you make one little noise, you will pay, and so will he." Then, once again, the form faded into the darkness.

Ellyn was trembling, and pressed her lips together to keep from crying out with fear. Silence fell over the room, and she felt cold with terror.

Then, out of the dark void of the room, a light was suddenly struck into being, and shadows were cast against the walls. Ellyn took a quick breath and held it as the figure stepped from behind her and held the light up to her face.

It was a man; she could tell by the broad stature and large, rough hands, but his face was hidden by a black scarf that covered his features. The rest of his clothing was black as well, and he stood in front of Ellyn, staring at her. Just above the scarf, she was able to see his dark, piercing eyes, gleaming in the candlelight. He blinked, then narrowed his eyes, leaning towards her. Ellyn dropped her eyes and stared into her lap, trying to suppress a rising feeling of panic.

Then, he slowly backed away from her, and Ellyn followed him with her eyes as he slunk across the room to the door. He examined the lock, leaned his ear against the door, then picked up a torch that was lying on the floor in front of it. Using the candle, he set it ablaze, then, with slow, noiseless steps, he snuck over to the bed and peered at Corbin, who was still in a deep sleep. Ellyn's eyes widened and she opened her mouth to cry out. But the man made a sudden movement and jerked his head towards her, and she snapped her mouth shut.

The man moved away from the bed and went to the corner of the room where there was a pile of cloth, and Ellyn watched in horror as he picked them up and put them against the back wall. Then, with his candle, he lit the torch, and a tall flame burst into being. He stood and lifted the torch, watching the flame flicker. Then, slowly, he lowered it towards the pile and set them ablaze. Immediately, a black smoke began billowing from the pile, and flames licked upwards. Then, he went across the room and collected another similar pile of cloth, and threw it on the floor on the other side of the room and promptly set it ablaze as well. Ellyn began blinking, her throat narrowing as she began breathing in the dense smoke.

Her eyes began to water, but she struggled to keep them open as she watched the black-clad figure pick up the candle and move once again towards the bed. He glanced furtively towards it as he set the candle on the bedside table, just next to where Corbin lay. He leaned close to him for a moment, staring at him through his mask.

With a suddenness that startled Ellyn, Corbin leapt from the bed and leaped at the black figure, throwing his arms over him, and shoved him to the floor. The man, caught by surprise, twisted his body around just as Corbin dealt a harsh blow on his head.

The man tried to stagger to his feet but was immediately overpowered and thrown back onto the floor. Just then, a black cloud of smoke blocked Ellyn's vision, and the figures were shrouded from view. She coughed and tried to loose the bonds from her wrists, but they did not slacken. The flames were growing in height, and the black smoke billowed into the room. Through the sound of crackling, licking flames, Ellyn heard shouts and pounding from the other side of the door. The noises and smoke from the room had begun to seep out into the hallway, alerting the guards posted nearby.

The smoke momentarily cleared, and Ellyn saw a violent struggle taking place across the room. Corbin in his nightclothes, and the man, dressed all in black, were striking each other with blows, each trying to overcome the strength and fortitude of the other.

Ellyn's eyes were now filled with a stinging pain and she gasped for air, coughing violently. The light in the room was dimming, obscured from the thick smoke, and the room was filled with a hazy color. Ellyn strained her eyes, but could only see the vague shadows of the two figures fighting across the room.

Her breathing became more difficult, and she was taking deep, heaving breaths. The room seemed to be fading, and sounds became less distinct. She struggled to stay alert, but could feel her consciousness slipping.

Suddenly, she felt two hands grab her arms and pull her from the chair. She forced her eyes opened, and could see Corbin through the smoke, leaning over her. She stood and swayed, trying to remain steady, though she felt faint and lightheaded. Her surroundings became grey and faded, and she lurched forward with a cry. Reaching out quickly, Corbin steadied her, then he lifted her off the ground. He stumbled through layers of smoke and leaned against the door, coughing in the thick smoke. With shaking fingers, he unlocked the door and pulled it open. Then they fell through the doorway onto the floor. Smoke billowed into the hallway, and there was suddenly a flurry of noise around them. Ellyn felt someone helping her from the floor. She could hear a voice, but could not distinguish the words through the haze of her confusion. She felt a sharp utensil slip between her wrists, and the ropes were freed from her hands.

At last, she found she was standing in the middle of the hallway, supported by the strong arms of a guard at her side. Through the smoke, she saw Corbin leaning against the wall, grasping his throat, and pointing frantically into the room, trying to speak between violent coughs.

"Quick, in here," the guard said, pulling a door open.

Ellyn stumbled inside and found she was in her own room, and rubbed her eyes, trying to erase the sting and pain from them. The guard hurried her to the window and opened it. She took gasps of the fresh air, and leaned against the frame with exhaustion. Shouts and heavy footsteps echoed through the hallway just past the open door behind her.

"Are you recovered, Your Highness?" the guard asked as her breathing became less labored. She nodded.

"Then I will need to take you to another room where it is safer, away from the danger of the flames. Follow me."

Ellyn saw her robe lying across her bed and grabbed it as she ran by, wrapping it quickly around herself. Then she was hurried from the room, and the guard led her into the hallway, through a swarm of noise and confusion. Buckets of water were already being carried into the room. Servants were flurrying past, and guards stomped among them. Ellyn followed the guard through the milling people and around the corner. More servants ran past her, carrying more buckets of water. Ellyn saw a glimpse of King Evander storming through the halls towards the disarray and commotion.

"Stay here," he said as they at last escaped the tumult and reached Corbin's cabinet. "I will alert your maidservant that you are here, and you may have to move if the fire spreads."

Then the door closed and Ellyn was alone. She sank into a chair against the wall and stared at the ceiling blankly. Through the walls, shouts, footsteps and voices echoed through the hallway and blended together into frantic uproar.

"Ellyn, are you alright?" Alys asked as she threw the door opened and ran to her side.

"Yes," Ellyn said in a hoarse whisper. She coughed, and winced as a sharp pain shot through her chest.

"What happened?"

"I… I don't know. There was a man trying to kill us. He was trying to burn us alive." Ellyn's voice was trembling, and her words came out in a confused jumble. Alys stared at her with horror.

"I woke up suddenly—he must have made a sound that roused me—when he pulled me from the bed and tied me up. I don't even remember much of what happened except there was so much smoke and I felt sick. Then somehow Corbin woke up, and I don't know what happened, but he carried me out of the room and then I could breathe again. But it's all so muddled in my mind. It could have lasted for ten seconds or half an hour. I just don't know."

She pressed her fingers to her aching temples and leaned her head back against the wall. "How awful," Alys said. "Do you need anything? A drink of water? A blanket?"

"Water, please."

Alys hurried from the room and soon returned with a glass of cold water, and a wet cloth with which she cleaned the black streaks from Ellyn's face. Then she let down her braid, which had become frazzled and disarrayed, and tied it up into a knot. She wrapped a blanket around Ellyn's shoulders.

"There," she said. "You look more refreshed."

Ellyn smiled wearily. Her heart was no longer pounding, and she was breathing steadily once again. "But I'm curious as to what is going on now. There is not so much noise as there was before."

"I don't know. I would try to find out, but I don't want to leave you alone after the scare you have had."

At that moment, there was a loud commotion from the hallway. Ellyn started and looked at the door with concern. It was the sound of a man yelling wildly, and other voices mumbling gruffly. Alys went to the door and slowly turned the knob. Then she opened it slightly and looked through the narrow opening. The shouts became louder and more distinct.

"Murderer!" the voice yelled. Ellyn frowned and rose from the chair. She went to the door and, standing on her toes, peered out over Alys's head. Alys stepped aside from the doorway so that Ellyn could observe what was happening.

A group of men had congregated in the middle of the hall at the top of the stairs. From the doorway, Ellyn was able to clearly observe all that was happening, but the shadows of the hallway kept her concealed. The hall was aglow with torchlight, illuminating the excited faces of the men. They were milling around a figure that seemed to be the focus of their attention. But Ellyn was unable to see him, surrounded by so many people.

"You deserve to die!" the man was shouting. "You are a murderer!"

"Cease your shouting." Ellyn heard King Evander's voice rise above the tumult.

At last, there was an opening in the crowd, and Ellyn saw the king, facing a bent figure, who was constrained by a guard on either side.

"You deserve to be punished, and the family line obliterated," the man yelled, ignoring his command.

"Silence," a guard said, roughly striking him on the side of the head.

Corbin walked around the corner and stood next to his father, staring down at the man in front of him. He said a few words to his father in undertones, and the king frowned and shook his head in response.

Up until this point, Ellyn had only been able to catch glimpses of the man being held captive. Flashes of his hair and dark clothing would catch her eye, but suddenly, he turned his head in such a way that she was able to see his full profile. A glimmer of light struck his face, and she gasped. She turned and looked quickly at Alys.

"What is it?" Alys asked. "Look at him!" Ellyn said.

Alys stepped forward and looked out into the hallway again. Then she looked at Ellyn with the same blank expression.

"I don't understand," she said slowly.

Ellyn stepped past her and wrapped her fingers around the door and its frame, opening the gap to see better. There were now several men standing in her way once again, hiding the man from her sight, but she strained her ears, trying to listen.

"If you won't identify yourself, you'll be forced to later," the king was saying harshly.

"I already told you who I am," the man said loudly. "I am your enemy, seeking justice and revenge on your head, and your sons', so that the family line will be broken. You do not deserve to rule, and neither do your heirs."

"Take him away," the king said with fury. The guards dragged the man down the stairs. Ellyn turned and looked at Alys.

"I've seen him before," she said. "Where?"

"I don't know." Ellyn frowned. "But I know I've seen him. Didn't he look familiar to you?" Alys shook her head slowly.

"I need to see him again, closer. Then maybe I would remember," she said. She looked out the door again. The guards had dispersed and only a few were in the hallway. Servants were carrying empty buckets of water down the stairs. Most of them had black streaks on their faces and clothes. King Evander and Corbin were still standing in the middle of the hallway, in serious conversation. Both looked troubled. Ellyn watched them converse for a few moments, then turned again to Alys and closed the door softly.

"Are you sure you recognize him?" Alys asked.

"Yes. It has been a long time, I think. But his features are so distinctive. He has a sharp jawline and such dark eyes, and the sides of his face seem to sink in. And there is that jagged scar running down his face. He almost looks more like a wild animal than a person."

She walked slowly back to the chair and sat down slowly, staring pensively at the floor.

There was a knock at the door. She stood up again as Alys opened the door, letting Corbin into the room.

Ellyn gasped softly as the candlelight fell on his face. It was bruised, and still tarnished with black streaks.

"He hurt you," she said with sympathy.

"I harmed him more than he did me," he said grimly. "But you are not injured, are you?"

"He only frightened me, nothing more," she said. "I was afraid you wouldn't wake up, and we would both be killed."

"I knew he was there," Corbin said. "But I waited because I wanted to see who I would be challenging, and if there was more than one person. I hoped to surprise him, and not announce my awareness of his presence."

"Who was he, though? And what possessed him to do such a thing?"

Corbin frowned. "I don't know," he said, lowering his voice. "He obviously has a want of revenge on our family, but I don't know why. I have never seen him before. My father is as clueless as I."

He fell silent, thinking.

"I think I may have seen him before," Ellyn said. Corbin looked up at her quickly.

"I don't know for certain, but he looks familiar. I think if I saw him closer I might be able to identify him."

Walking slowly across the room with his arms crossed, Corbin sighed. He leaned against the table in the room.

"Another thing that baffles me is how he was able to break into the room," he said. "The guards are not blind, and the castle has been under even closer watch since the attack in the woods."

"The woods," Ellyn said thoughtfully. "Do you think he is the same man as the one in the woods?"

"I don't know; I wondered that as well," he said. "It could be. It seems likely, even."

"Since he was able to break into the castle, and into your room, it would seem someone was helping him. Someone who had access to the castle, and whom the guards trusted."

Corbin nodded slowly, staring at the ceiling. "That seems likely as well. But I have learned not to assume something that has not been confirmed, because things can seem one way when they are another. But the truth will be discovered. That is certain. And there will be consequences."

"There is something else I am reminded of though," she said slowly. "Many months ago, soon after I arrived here, someone broke into my room. He was dressed all in black, but that is all I know. I ran from the room before he saw me."

"And then what happened?" Corbin asked.

"Corineus was in the hallway. He went in and looked around, then told me it was safe to go in. That was all. I went back, and the room was empty. Everything seemed untouched."

"Corineus," Corbin mused. "I might have a word with him later."

There was a sudden and heavy knock at the door. Corbin strode across the room and opened it.

"Something unexpected has happened." Ellyn heard the king's solemn voice from the other side of the door.

"What is it?"

"I received word only a few minutes ago that we are needed immediately in Eurasia. Spies have been observing the Northmen and reported they have been rallying all of their forces. They plan to attack very soon, and no doubt it will be a final assault, and they need all the men they can."

"How soon do we need to leave?"

"This very night. I have already given the command for our forces to organize and prepare for departure. They are doing it now."

Corbin sighed heavily and wiped his brow with his palm. "Do you still intend to speak to the prisoner, or will you wait until we return?"

"I was going to give him some time to calm himself, but there is no time for that. I want to speak with him before we leave and try to prod some answers from him. I am going there now."

"I will join you," Corbin said.

He turned from the doorway and looked at Ellyn. He raised his eyebrows and reached around for the handle.

"Wait," Ellyn said quickly. "Let me come."

He looked down at her apprehensively.

"I think I might have seen him before, and I may be able to identify him, if I can see him once more."

"He is probably still very agitated," he said. "But you can come. Just prepare yourself for shouting and uncouth speech."

Ellyn descended the dank stairs to the dungeon. Corbin was just in front of her, and King Evander in the lead. Two guards escorted them. The sound of their footsteps pierced through the heavy silence.

When they reached the guarded cell, the king stepped up to the small barred window near the top of the thick wooden door and looked inside with a scowl.

Ellyn shuddered when a hideous face suddenly appeared on the other side of the bars, only a few inches from the king's face. It was marked with scars and stained with blood. His expression was filled with a wild fury.

"What have you disturbed me for? To try to make me spill out a confession?" he asked in a sneering, hateful voice.

King Evander ignored his question and said in a voice of authority, "You were able to gain entrance into this well-guarded castle and onto the upper floor, to which only my family and select people have entrance. How?"

The man laughed, a malicious, dry laugh. "I can make myself vanish from view when I want to."

The king rolled his eyes upwards. "If you will not give me an explanation of any kind, at least tell me this: What are your reasons for a want of revenge? I think I should at least know what the accusations you are claiming against me are."

"You know very well. You ordered an unjust murder a few years ago. You cannot be trusted as king of this country, and neither can your sons. I was doing my duty and sparing the inhabitants of this country by killing your sons, and then you, so that neither you nor your family would remain rulers."

King Evander scoffed with indignation. "Did you really think you could complete such an ambitious thing? Impossible."

"You are not telling the truth," Corbin said, stepping forward. "If you wanted to kill me, you could have. You had the advantage in the woods that night. You had a quiver full of arrows, but you only killed my men, and not me. And tonight, you could have thrust a dagger through my heart, and I would have never woken. But instead, you set the room ablaze. If you just wanted revenge, you wouldn't go to all the trouble that you have been to. I would be dead now if revenge was all you wanted."

The man stared at Corbin through the bars. "Revenge is all I want," he said slowly. His voice was simmering with anger, an outburst of fury growing beneath his calculated tones.

"Then why didn't you take it when you had the chance?"

"Why should I?" the man shouted. "My reasons are my own."

"Or are they?" Corbin said, walking slowly towards him. "Are you really making your own decisions?"

The man began sputtering and yelling with rage, and shook the bars with his hands. The door squeaked and groaned.

"Silence!" Corbin shouted, raising his voice above the man's violent fury. "We are trying to communicate with you."

The man fell silent. He looked slowly and threateningly from the cell, and his gaze fell on Ellyn. His eyes narrowed, and he stared at her. "If it were not for you, my plan might have been carried out," he said with disdain. His intense glare made Ellyn shudder, but she stared back at him, until Corbin stepped in front of her, blocking the man's view of her. She relaxed, but could not erase his face from her mind. It was so familiar, but in a strange, distant way.

"It's that long scar on the side of his face," she muttered to herself. "Why is it so familiar?"

"Now, I think it is time for you to explain your threats and reason for revenge," the king said. "This is my last question before I leave you. If you won't explain now, maybe a few weeks rotting in here will bring you to your senses."

The man stared at him, his head lowered and his beady eyes glaring from below his thick brows.

"You murdered my brother," he said slowly, without altering his gaze. The muscles and lines on his face were purple, and with each breath, he emitted a thin wheezing sound. There was no reply. But King Evander and Corbin stared back at him. "You murdered my brother!" the man repeated, this time with more force. "Go on," the king said with impatience.

"My brother was poor. He was a good man. He had a wife and two children whom he loved."

"Don't tire us with the long, heart-wrenching tale," the king interrupted impatiently. "Just tell us what we need to know."

The man's scowl deepened, but he continued. "His whole family grew deathly ill. His wife and children all died, but he recovered and lived. He was alone, and left to grieve over the loss of his family. It did not take long before he grew mad. The loss of his family turned him into a bitter and angry soul, and it drove him to do something drastic. It was not something that was in my brother's nature. He was a good man at heart, but he was alone, and his madness drove him to do unnatural things. He saw your daughter riding in the woods one day. He didn't know who she was, or what he was doing. He just…"

"I know who your brother was," the king interrupted. His face reddened with rage. "Your brother killed the heir to this kingdom, my oldest son, who was protecting his sister. I did not commit an unjust murder. I justly executed a vile murderer, who deserved to die."

"He had gone mad! You did not consider his situation. You should have had a little more compassion."

"Compassion?" the king spat angrily, grabbing the iron bars and shaking them violently. "I give compassion only when it is warranted. I will not listen to any more of this madness."

He turned away, his face darkened with fury. Corbin turned also, and Ellyn caught a last glimpse of the man when Corbin stepped aside. He was staring after the king with a wild expression and yelled, "You deserve death! Curses on you and your family!"

"Come," Corbin said in a hushed voice. His face was grim and troubled.

"Wait." Ellyn grabbed his arm and stared back at the pitiful creature behind the bars. "I know where I saw him. I remember now."

The man was still yelling threats and angry remarks after the king. "Tell me once we are out of this place."

Ellyn turned and went towards the stairs. Corbin soon passed her, striding with long steps up the stairs, staring at the floor deep in troubled thought. Ellyn quickened her steps trying to keep up.

When they reached the top of the stairs, the king had already disappeared from view. Corbin turned to Ellyn and walked a few paces away from the door and beckoned her to follow him.

"Who is he?" he asked in a low voice, once they were out of earshot of the guards in front of the dungeon entrance.

"He was on the ship that brought me here," Ellyn whispered. Corbin frowned. "As a sailor?"

Ellyn nodded. "It was such a long time ago, and he looks so different now that it is like a memory of a memory. But it was the scar on the side of his face."

"Did he say his name?"

Ellyn pressed her palm to her forehead and mumbled to herself for a few moments. "I don't remember," she said at last.

"We will discover it eventually," he said.

He sighed and looked down the hall. "I have to prepare to leave now," he said.

Ellyn looked down. "You must go? Aren't there already enough men to fight them?"

Corbin looked down at her. "Yes, I must. I am the future king; it is my duty. This will probably be our last encounter with the Northmen. They are gathering all of their forces, and are many. But we are even more, and our numbers and strategies will defeat them."

"Do you think I will be safe?"

"Of course, I would not leave you if I doubted it. But stay in your room as much as you can, and don't remain alone. It was me he was after. You just happened to be in the way tonight."

He ran his fingers through his hair. "I really must go now," he said. "We will probably leave within the hour. Try to get some sleep if you can."

He gently held her face in his hands and kissed the top of her head. Then he turned and strode quickly down the hallway. Ellyn watched him until he disappeared from sight.

Chapter 24 - Dark Schemes

Ellyn stood in front of her window, looking out between the curtains. The moon was full and shining on patches of glimmering snow below. The Lyntirith soldiers had left for Eurasia earlier that morning, marching from the castle with swiftness and determination, prepared to defeat the enemy that had been pestering the eastern borders of the country for so long. They were filled with confidence that this final battle would mean the end of all their encounters with the barbaric and warlike tribes.

Standing from within the castle, Ellyn had watched them leave, King Evander and Corbin leading them. She felt weary and empty as she watched Corbin depart, as if she was losing him, even though his absence would likely be less than a few weeks. She had spent the day trying to sleep, exhausted from the events of the night before, and pacing the room restlessly. Now that the sun had set, she felt unsettled and perturbed.

The night was cold, and frost was already creeping up the panes, and Alys had given her the warmest garments to sleep in to keep out the cold. But she still felt a chill as she stood in front of the window, where the winter air was seeping from under the panes.

"You should close the curtains. The room would stay warm longer," Alys said from the corner of the room, where she was sitting in a chair waiting for Ellyn to settle. "You hardly slept at all today; you should go to bed."

"I know I should," Ellyn said, turning from the window and letting the curtain fall over the glass. "But I know I would just lie awake for hours, staring at the ceiling, waiting for sleep to come. I can't sleep yet."

Alys sighed and folded her hands together in her lap.

"But don't stay awake on my account," Ellyn said. "You need rest too."

"Are you sure?"

"Yes of course. I want to go to the room at the end of the hallway. It always gives me a feeling of peace somehow, and there is a clear, refreshing view from the window. It might help to calm me."

"I would feel uneasy if you went alone. Shouldn't I come? There have been so many strange things happening here lately."

"No, just rest. I won't be very long, and this place is well guarded. I will be perfectly fine." Alys looked at her uneasily, but did not reply.

Ellyn went to the door and opened it, stepping into the hallway. She walked slowly and noiselessly over the wooden floor. Flickering candles, lining the walls, lit her way, and she crossed her arms tightly around her.

As she turned the corner, three guards standing in the hallway looked up quickly and one reached for his hilt, then let his hand fall slowly as she stepped into the candlelight.

"Shouldn't you be sleeping, Your Highness?" one of them said.

"I will only be a few moments. I want to step into the room down the hall."

They nodded and Ellyn walked past them. She looked at the guard posted at the top of the stairs, and against the wall of the stairwell were the shadows of more guards standing on the steps below.

She turned the corner again and went down an empty hall, lit with much fewer candles. It was colder and darker, and she wrapped her robe tightly around her. At last, she reached the door at the end of the hall. She stepped inside and relaxed as she looked around.

Moonlight streamed through the window and onto the floor. She closed the door quietly and went over to the desk in the corner of the room. She picked up a feather pen and twisted it between her fingers, studying it thoughtfully. Then she set it down and walked across the room to the window. She saw a glimpse of the moonlit garden below, the plants shining with snow and frost. Just beyond, a small stream wound over the land and into the forest beyond. It was a calm and serene sight, and she began to suddenly feel tired. She sat down on the chair next to the window and leaned her head back and closed her eyes.

Suddenly, there was a shuffling in the hallway. She opened her eyes and sat frozen, listening. She looked toward the door, wondering if she had locked it, and saw it had not been closed all the way. She sat up and listened.

Again, a slight noise, almost imperceptible, came from just outside the door. Then, she saw a shadow against the wall. A figure was walking in the hallway, and appeared to be nearing the room.

Acting quickly, she jumped from the chair. There was a small chest placed against the wall nearby. She grasped the sides and pulled it away from the wall. Then she leapt behind it and crouched against the wall, pressing herself into the shadows.

Peering out over the top of the chest, she watched as, slowly and steadily, the door was pushed open, and candlelight crept into the room. Ellyn ducked her head, trying to keep herself fully concealed behind the small piece of furniture. She heard footsteps tread slowly into the room. It sounded as if more than one person was now entering, and light was being cast against the wall above her. She laid on the hard floor and peered around the side of the chest as the door was closed, the sound echoing in the silent room.

"I feel uneasy in this room. No one is allowed here," a voice said in a hoarse whisper. Ellyn gasped silently, recognizing the voice as Corineus's.

"That is all the better, then," a smooth, low voice replied. "That means we will not be discovered here."

"That sounds like Maerynn," Ellyn thought with amazement. Just then, the form of the princess stepped into view as she walked to the window and closed the curtain. The light from the moon now blocked, the only light came from the candles, offering spare light in the dark room.

"It makes me feel… uncomfortable," Corineus said slowly.

"Oh, be quiet, Corineus," Maerynn said impatiently. "Just sit down and don't make any noise. We need to be able to talk without you whining and complaining. The only reason I brought you into this was because I knew you would be able to help me get in and out of the castle easily and into select rooms. It was certainly not for your bravery. Now be silent, or leave."

Ellyn saw Corineus as he walked to the window and sat down, crossing his arms. "Now, on to business," Maerynn said.

"Yes, about that," a thick, husky voice said. Ellyn frowned, unable to recognize the man's surly voice. "You guaranteed us that the last plan would be successful. But it was our third failed attempt. And we have gotten further from our goal instead of closer, and only made the king more suspicious and aware of danger."

"Patience, patience," Maerynn said coolly. "This is not a plan that is easily carried out. Each step must be taken carefully. Sometimes, not everything happens according to plan. We just have to keep trying until it does.”

“Things are becoming more desperate though,” another strange voice said. “You said no lives would be lost. But the further things progress, the more I begin to doubt that. I thought our plan was to capture Prince Corbin, not kill him.”

“Well, that is what I have been trying to do,” Maerynn said angrily. “But Corbin is not a man easily captured.”

“Well one more attempt, that is all. If it fails, I give up,” the first man said.

“Oh no, you will do as I say,” Maerynn said threateningly. “You know what information I have against you, and what will happen if you don’t follow my orders.”

The man made a defeated grunting noise and sank down into a chair.

“However, one more attempt is all you will have to stay for, because it will be the last one we are going to plan,” Maerynn continued calmly. “Without Cadwallo, we are one less, and with only five originally, one man is a significant loss. If we are unable to complete this next step, I will go to the most extreme measures.”

“Cadwallo!” Ellyn muttered to herself. “The man on the ship. The one who was captured and is now in prison!”

Corineus interrupted her thoughts by saying, “You don’t mean… Maerynn, you can’t do that. Corbin and I may not be on the best terms but I certainly do not want him… killed.”

“Corineus, you are so shallow. You can leave us, and expose my plans if you would like. But imagine your family’s response to your involvement.”

“But I didn’t know it would be so drastic!” Corineus said defensively. “At first, all you needed was my help getting that man Julius inside the castle. And then, it was helping you get into the castle secretly. And now I’m suddenly embroiled in this complicated scheme that I have never agreed to.”

“You know they won’t believe a word of your excuses,” Maerynn laughed. She walked over to him and knelt next to him, resting her arms on the arm of the chair. She now began to speak in smooth, mellow tones.

“You are my last hope, Corineus, to get what is owed to me. I have been vying to be queen of Lyntirith for years, and I would have been, if it had not been for that idiotic madman. But I am not the only one who would benefit. You are well aware of the position you would be in if Corbin was removed as the future king. Lyntirith is one of the largest kingdoms of this country. Don't you see what we could do if we were leaders of the whole country and how we could expand it?"

Corineus sighed and crossed his ankle over his knee. "It all sounded so enticing at first. But now I don't think it would be such a good plan. Maybe we should just let Corbin rule after all…"

"Corineus," Maerynn interrupted harshly, grabbing his collar and leaning close to his face. His eyes widened and he stared back at her.

"Alright, never mind then," he said irritably. "Do what you would like." She let go and stood again, eyeing him severely.

"Now, onto our plans," she said icily. Corineus sank back into his chair when she turned away and wiped his brow.

"We already know that trying to get her to elope, or something of the sort, will not work," the second man said. "And trying to capture him seems to be improbable too."

"Not if it is done the right way," Maerynn said grimly. "I haven't given up yet."

He heaved a heavy sigh. "You are insane. Do you know what would happen if you were discovered?"

"I won't be," she said with an edge of anger. "Corbin suspects I have something to do with Julius's visit to the castle, but that is all. For all he knows, Cadwallo was truly a madman who wanted revenge for his brother's death. That is partly true, but not entirely. As clever as Corbin is, he won't figure anything else out, until it is too late." She chuckled to herself and paced slowly across the room.

"Since no one suspects you yet, this might be an opportune time to put this madness to an end," the first man said slowly. "Are you really this desperate to be queen of Lyntirith? After all, it is only one kingdom, and Corineus will be the ruler, not you."

"Corineus will rule, but he'll need someone to rule him," Maerynn hissed slyly. "It may only be one kingdom in a country of kingdoms, but it will someday be a large kingdom, uniting all of them into one."

"Very well then," he said wearily. "Just as long as you remember your promises to keep my involvement secret, and the rewards that you owe me."

"We have already been over all of that," Maerynn said impatiently. "Now let's discuss our next move. I already have several plans. First…"

"Wait," the first man said urgently. "Is that a foot sticking out from behind the trunk?"

Ellyn's eyes grew wide with panic and she clasped her hand over her mouth, beginning to tremble.

"Don't be ridiculous," Maerynn said. But she began to walk towards the chest behind which Ellyn was concealed. Her heart pounding, Ellyn shrunk against the wall with horror.

Just as Maerynn was approaching she leapt to her feet, facing the astonished young woman. "Stop," she said forcefully. "If you make one move, I am screaming. The halls are filled with guards. They will hear me, and you will be found."

Ellyn glanced into the room and saw Corineus, staring at her in amazement, and two strange men whom she had never seen, watching her with mouths agape.

Maerynn's eyes narrowed, and she took a breath, raising her chin.

"You won't live another moment, if you do," she said lividly, raising her hand, which was wrapped around a long, sharp dagger.

"They will still find you," Ellyn said, her voice trembling. "You will be found out, and you will pay."

She stared at Maerynn, who glared back at her. Neither of them flinched. Then Maerynn's mouth stretched into a thin, evil smile. Her face, darkened in the shadows, was filled with a wild rage. Then, she slowly lowered her arm and smirked wickedly.

"If you cry out, not only will you pay, but Corbin will as well. Do you think I haven't thought I might be discovered here? I already have a plan of escape. They won't catch me. You will only do yourself harm by crying out."

Ellyn looked quickly at the locked door across the room, knowing it would be fruitless to try to escape. It was hopeless. There was no way for her to escape.

"Don't hurt me," she said, her voice trembling. "I won't cry out, just don't do anything." Maerynn smiled with evil satisfaction.

"Take her to the room just down the hall on the right, Bardolph. It locks from the outside and she won't be able to get out. I'll decide what to do with her later."

The man stood from his chair and dragged Ellyn from behind the chest. He covered her mouth to keep her from crying out. Then he pushed her from the room and down the hall. He opened the door to the room Maerynn had ordered and pushed her inside.

As he closed the door, Ellyn grabbed it before he closed it and whispered with desperation, "Please, help me."

He looked down at her with sympathy and said. "I'm sorry. I can't."

Then he closed the door quietly, and Ellyn heard the sound of the lock sliding into the place.

She leaned her back against the door and covered her face with her hands helplessly. She was trapped. There was no way out, and no one would find her until it was too late.

For a long time, Ellyn sat alone in the dark room. It was too dark to see anything, so she remained sitting against the door, listening and waiting, too terrified to even draw open the curtain. All was silent and dark, her slow breaths the only sound that filled the depressing silence of the room. Several times, she considered calling out for help, but her fear of Maerynn and her threats would seize her, and she could not find the courage.

A long time passed before Ellyn finally heard a sound from beyond the walls of her imprisonment. It was a shuffling sound from somewhere beyond the door. It lasted only a few seconds, then all was silent. Then from another corner of the room, she heard it again. She stared into the darkness, and realized with horror that the sound was no longer coming from the hallway but from the room on the other side of the wall. There was a scraping sound, and if someone was scratching against the wall. Then Ellyn watched in fearful amazement as a small light began to glow from the direction of the noise. Then, she could see the outline of a desk as it began to move across the floor. She gasped and sank to the floor, paralyzed with fear. Then, through a hole in the wall, someone stepped into the room and held up a candle, looking into the room. It was Corineus.

As soon as he saw Ellyn, he hurried across the room and knelt next to her. "You need to get out of here," he whispered urgently.

Ellyn stared up at him with disbelief. "What do you mean?"

"You need to go into hiding, or leave the castle, now that you know everything. Your life is in danger."

Ellyn gasped and looked at him in horror. "Do you really think she would…"

"She would do anything. You are no use to her, so she will not give a second thought to dispose of you. There is no time to lose. You need to leave."

"Why are you helping me?" Ellyn asked.

Corineus shrugged. "She is insane. I don't want to be a part of her schemes anymore, and I certainly don't want to be stuck with her for the rest of my life. It doesn't matter if she finds out and does something to me. I would deserve it. I was a fool to listen to her. So it is the least I can do to keep her from hurting you. It might appease my father and brother's anger against me if I succeed."

"Thank you," Ellyn said, grasping his arm.

"It will be dangerous, and the guards on the stairs were posted by her, so we can't just walk down them. It won't be long before she figures out what I am doing, so we have to hurry."

He stood and helped her to her feet.

"What are we going to do, then?" Ellyn asked, her voice trembling. "You need to get out of the castle. You are not safe otherwise."

"But where will I go and how will I get out?"

"Where you will go, I don't know. But you seem to forget you are in a castle, filled with passageways and tunnels."

He hurried across the room and set the candle on a table. Ellyn watched as he knelt to the floor and began feeling the rug. Ellyn looked nervously towards the door, beyond which was complete and ominous silence.

At last, Corineus began fiddling with a latch and pulled up a small door, covered with a square of the rug. He jumped inside and looked up at Ellyn motioning for her to follow. She handed him the candle which he had set on the table then lowered herself through the trapdoor. Corineus slowly lowered the door behind her.

The space was small and cramped, so that she could not even sit up straight. Corineus placed the candle on the floor and began sliding on his stomach on the floor, pushing the candle ahead of him.

Suddenly, there was the distinct sound of a door opening just above them, and he froze. Ellyn looked up at the trapdoor and edged silently from underneath it. Then she sat, breathing heavily and listening tensely.

The sound of footsteps just above them echoed in the passageway and made her shudder, and she looked desperately at Corineus. He pressed his finger to his lips and looked upwards. The floor squeaked as the step found a loose board, and Ellyn pressed her hand against her mouth, trembling. The footsteps stopped just above her, and she waited, looking up with dread. Then, after only a moment of silence, the footsteps receded from the room, and the door closed. Ellyn closed her eyes and breathed a sigh of relief.

Corineus pressed on, and Ellyn followed just behind. The small space was cold, and full of wet musty air, and she pressed her lips together to keep from coughing.

The narrow passageway lasted for about twenty feet until they reached the end. Then they encountered a small door, and Corineus looked at Ellyn. He pressed his finger to his lips, then pointed above him. Ellyn nodded.

Corineus reached for the latch to the door and grasped it tightly. Then, he took a deep breath and pulled slowly and firmly. The latch broke open, and he cringed, looking up at the ceiling of their crawlspace. There was only silence above. Then, he slowly pulled the door opened and crawled forward, peering to the left and right down a corridor tall enough to stand in. Then, he slid out of the crawlspace and reached back in, pulling the candle through. Ellyn crawled out after him and stood in the narrow space.

"We're almost there," Corineus said, leaning close and talking in a faint whisper. "But Maerynn is on the other side of this wall."

Ellyn nodded, and crept after him through the narrow enclosement, looking at the door, expecting to see Maerynn crawling through in pursuit.

They had only taken a few steps when a voice, just in front of them, stopped them both in their tracks.

"You were gone for too long," Maerynn's cool voice said.

Ellyn grabbed Corineus's arms and looked over his shoulder. The passageway was empty.

Corineus pointed to the wall next to them.

"I didn't see him," the faint voice of Bardolph replied from the room on the other side of the wall. Ellyn let her breath out, and leaned weakly against the wall.

"He must have gone to bed, the coward," Maerynn said. "Did you look in on her?"

"No, but how could she have gotten out?"

Maerynn sighed loudly, and her voice became more distant as she moved away from the wall. Corineus wrapped his fingers around Ellyn's wrist and walked slowly through the passageway, holding the candle up ahead of them.

Only a few more yards and they reached another door, which opened to a steep, rock stairway, which was rough and crumbling. He began to descend, and Ellyn stepped into the stairwell, closing the door behind them.

"She will realize you are gone soon," Corineus said in a low voice. "She'll probably figure out I helped you."

"Then you should leave as well," Ellyn said.

"No, I will stay. I will try to make it back up to my room, which will throw suspicion off of me.

Then I will try to keep her from following your trail."

"I don't want to leave alone, though."

"You won't," he said. "I will find someone to accompany you."

At last, they reached the bottom of the stairway, and Corineus opened the door and stepped out into a small kitchen. Ellyn looked at the small room as she stepped out, closing the door behind her. Wooden utensils and dishes were displayed on shelves and hooks on the walls, and herbs and other plants hung in clusters on the ceiling. An iron kettle hung above the fire pit, and baskets lined the walls. Even though the room was empty, a small candle was burning in the middle of the table.

Footsteps echoed in the hallway leading to the kitchen, and a servant girl stepped through the open doorway. She froze in amazement when she saw Corineus and Ellyn standing in the corner.

"Listen, we are in danger," Corineus said, stepping towards her. She started and looked up at him, astonished.

"We need your help, and you must not say a word about this." She nodded, her eyes wide.

"Alys would be able to help too," Ellyn said. She turned to the servant girl and said, "Go up to my room and bring my maidservant here."

"Yes… Your Highness," the girl stammered. Then she turned and hastened from the room.

A few moments later, she reappeared, followed by Alys, who looked at Ellyn with disbelief as she entered the kitchen.

"I need to leave the castle," Ellyn said. "I am in danger. Maerynn has reason to find and harm me and, without Corbin or the king here to turn to, I have to escape."

"Are you sure? Why can't you alert some of the guards so that they can arrest her?"

"We cannot trust all of the guards. Some of them have been posted by Maerynn, but I don't know which ones. Besides, it would be a task to be able to catch her. She would probably escape, and then do great damage before she could be stopped," Corineus said.

"You could hide," Alys suggested.

"I don't want to stay," Ellyn said. "I feel unsafe here. Even if Maerynn was captured, I would feel in danger. Too many frightening things have happened, and without Corbin here, I feel so susceptible and exposed."

"Where will you go, then?"

"I don't know," Ellyn said slowly. "But I want to be able to go to Eurasia if I can."

"Eurasia? But Ellyn, it is so cold, and such a far journey," said Alys.

"But I will be safe there. And where else could I go?"

"I don't know that it is safe. There is a war underway," Corineus said slowly. "Corbin is there," Ellyn said. "And I won't go alone."

"Then we need to get you beyond these castle walls, and quickly," Corineus said. "This door leads us straight to the stables. Maerynn may have posted a few guards in the premises, but the castle gates will be guarded by our own soldiers. They will let me through."

"Who will go with her though? Shall I?" Alys asked.

"No, you should stay. Only one person should go with her, to avoid being noticed. As soon as Maerynn realizes Ellyn is gone, she will certainly have her pursued. We need a trustworthy man to go with her, who is skilled with the bow and arrow."

"I know someone," Alys said quickly. "He used to be a soldier, but now he is one of the king's messengers, and has taken many journeys to and from Eurasia. Thus, he can be trusted to know the way very well. He is a brave man, and skilled with weapons."

"Do you know how to find him quickly? We need to go to the stables and saddle some horses so that Ellyn can depart in the next few minutes."

“Maude, go find Hamlin and send him to the stables,” Alys said quickly. The servant girl, still awestruck, hurried from the room.

“Now I need to go up to your room and get some warmer clothes,” Alys said. “You can’t travel to Eurasia in the snow wearing only your nightclothes and a robe.”

“Go on, then,” Corineus said, looking quickly towards the doorway. “Make haste, though. It may only be minutes before Maerynn realizes you are gone, and she must be as far away as possible when she does.”

Chapter 25 - Moonlight Escape

Ellyn stood next to the horse Hamlin had chosen for her, dressed in thick, warm riding clothes. Alys was loading the horses with satchels of provision and Corineus was pacing back and forth, giving instructions to Ellyn and peering out of the door of the stables, looking with anxiety towards the castle.

"Do you have any skill with the bow and arrow, Your Highness?" Hamlin asked her. "Yes, my father trained me in the skill of archery."

He handed her a long bow and a quiver of arrows, which she slung over her back.

"Travel as far as you can tonight and do not rest until you are sure it is safe," Corineus said. "I will do my best to keep Maerynn from guessing your direction, although it is likely she will discover the path you will be taking."

"I have trodden many different paths and byways to reach Eurasia," Hamlin said. "I have confidence that I will be able to elude any pursuers."

Corineus looked again out into the cold night. Large flakes were now falling softly to the ground in the moonlight.

"Please stay warm," Alys said, tightening the tie on Ellyn's cape.

"Don't worry about me," Ellyn said. She grasped her maidservant's cold fingers with her own and smiled reassuringly.

"I think everything is ready," Corineus said.

"Yes, we can depart now," Hamlin said, slinging his bow and arrows over his head onto his back. A sword and dagger were sheathed at his side.

Ellyn approached Corineus. "Thank you," she said quietly.

He shrugged, and the corners of his mouth turned up crookedly. Then he glanced quickly out of the open door again and his face fell.

"I see some movement near the castle," he said slowly. "It may be someone looking for you. You should hurry and leave now,"

Mounting her horse with ease, Ellyn shivered beneath her thick cloak. Whether the chills came from the cold winter air or anxiety, she could not tell. Snowflakes were still falling steadily from the sky, and Ellyn's breath came from her mouth as clouds of vapor that evaporated into the air. Following Hamlin's lead, she urged her horse into a slow walk, and they left the stables through a small door at the rear of the building where any eyes that could be watching from the castle could not reach.

Following the castle wall behind the stables and outbuildings, the two horses and their riders traced the shadows, keeping a close watch on their surroundings.

The castle wall had a main gate at the front of the castle, but it also had one other entrance, situated behind the castle. It was a small, guarded door, used primarily by the servants, messengers, or traders who needed access to the castle's grounds. A narrow dirt path trailed from the iron, barred door to the outbuildings within. It was to this exit that Hamlin and Ellyn aimed, hoping to stay undetected by using this route.

At last, the door was within sight. Through the gently falling flakes, Ellyn could see the silhouettes of two guards, standing within the walls. One was looking out between the bars of the door and the other faced the castle, standing tall and menacing with the helm of his sword glinting in the moonlight. Ellyn shuddered anxiously.

Both guards looked up with a start as the two riders escaped the shadows and stepped out into the dim moonlight.

"Halt!" one of them ordered sharply. Both pulled their horses to a stand, and Hamlin said with boldness, "I am with the princess Ellyn, wife of the future king of Lyntirith. We have been given leave to escape the walls of the castle."

"By whom?"

"By a member of the royal family."

"Who are you, and who gave you permission to leave? Furthermore, what is your purpose in leaving so secretly?"

"My name is Hamlin, former messenger to King Evander, but now working on the castle grounds. The details of this escape are not to be spoken of, not by me, but it is of utmost safety and importance that we leave the boundaries of these walls. The safety of the princess is in jeopardy here."

"How do I know you speak the truth? You may be taking the princess under force."

"He is not," Ellyn said. "I am leaving at my own will to avoid a danger that we cannot speak of at this time. You must let us leave, lest you want the harm that would otherwise become me to be at your own doing."

The two guards looked at one another. They spoke in low tones that Ellyn could not hear. Then one of them stepped forward and looked at them with skepticism. He stared at them in silence for several moments, then said, "If we let you pass through these gates, we are taking a great chance in letting you leave, and possibly putting ourselves at the blame of others, namely King Evander. It is not under his orders that you are leaving."

"It is because he is absent that we must leave," Ellyn said. "You must trust me." Both guards were silent.

"Is there a third member to your party?" one of them asked at last. "Why do you ask?" Hamlin said slowly.

The guard pointed past him, and both he and Ellyn looked behind them to see a dark figure standing just outside the shadows beyond, watching them. When they turned, he stepped aside and disappeared into the darkness.

Hamlin swiftly dismounted and stared face to face with one of the guards. "Let us pass," he said in low, even tones. "In the name of His Majesty, King Evander, let us through."

"By naming the king," the guard said, "You are holding yourself responsible that this deed was approved by the king, and ascertain that, if he finds out, he will also hear that you did this in his name."

"Let it be so."

At last, the door was opened, and Hamlin mounted once again. He looked back at Ellyn, looking out from beneath the hood of her cloak. He nodded, and rode through the gates. Ellyn followed, and at last they were past the castle walls.

"Surely they will not let anyone else past," Ellyn said softly once they were out of earshot. "Maerynn and the others who work for her must be imprisoned within now."

Before Hamlin could respond, a sharp cry rang out through the forest. Both looked quickly over their shoulder, looking toward where the sound had come from.

"What was that?" Ellyn asked, trembling.

"I don't know," he replied. His hand was gripped tightly around the sword at his side. "It sounded as if it came from the castle gates. I should go back and look. If we are in danger, I want to be prepared for what we must face."

"Then let me come too," Ellyn said quickly. "I don't want to be left alone."

"No, stay with the horses," he said.

He climbed down from the horse and unsheathed his sword. Then, with swift agility, he leaped along the path and into the shadows.

Alone in the woods, Ellyn looked all around her into the blackness. The moonlight was kept hidden by the roof of branches, and no light found her, hiding in the grove of trees. One of the horses nickered quietly, causing her to start uneasily. She bit her lower lip nervously and fingered the dagger at her side. Distant cracking and twittering noises occasionally pierced the silence of the forest as the nighttime creatures of the woods patrolled their hunting trails.

Each second she was alone, Ellyn grew more anxious. "What if he doesn't come back?" she thought to herself. "Where will I go? What will I do?"

She coiled her fingers through the mane of her horse and shuddered.

"Who could have made that noise?" she thought. "Was it someone within the castle walls, or were we wrong in thinking we were alone in the forest? Or what if it was a trap? Someone could have meant for me to be left alone so they could more easily target me. One of the men in league with Maerynn."

The sound of running footsteps caught her ears and she jumped, gasping slightly. Her horse, sensing her anxiety, whinnied and tossed his head. Hamlin's horse stomped his hoof on the ground. Ellyn looked down the path, listening to the footsteps as they grew closer. She swallowed nervously and, with cold, trembling fingers, pulled the dagger from her belt and held the cold blade beneath the folds of her cloak.

A flurry of black, Hamlin sprinted from the shadows, running towards her. "Run!" he gasped.

Ellyn put the blade back in its sheath and fumbled for her horse's reins, her heart pounding.

With a deft leap, Hamlin was in the saddle again and, in the same moment, urged his horse into a run, yelling for Ellyn to follow. She leaned forward in the saddle as her horse began racing through the woods in pursuit of Hamlin. Branches struck Ellyn's face as they raced along the path, and she winced as they streaked through the woods. She watched the path ahead of her, hoping her horse would not find a loose stone or hole and stumble. His powerful body lunged forward, each leap seeming longer than the last. The sides of his body heaved with heavy breaths as he raced along the path.

Even as the pounding of the horse's hooves and the air rushing past her filled Ellyn's ears, she heard a shout from behind. They were not alone in the dark woods.

The woodlands were unfamiliar to Ellyn, and she narrowed her eyes as she tried to see the path ahead and guide her horse behind Hamlin's. His familiarity with the forest paths allowed him to maneuver through them with ease. At last, she let her grip on the reins lengthen, and she trusted her horse to follow. With sickening speeds, they raced through the peaceful forest, stirring the silence with sounds of charging horses' hooves. Ellyn's mind was racing with fear, but her body was controlled and was matching the horse's every stride with composure.

The snowflakes grew larger and heavier as they fell from the roof of branches above. The cold air that struck Ellyn's face from the flying steed made tears gather in her eyes, and her face felt numb with cold.

At last, Hamlin slowed his pace, and Ellyn's horse lifted his neck as he slowed to a sudden walk. Ellyn fumbled with stiff fingers for control of the reins again and looked down the path from where they had come, listening.

"I think we lost them," Hamlin said, taking deep heavy breaths.

"But they must not be far behind," Ellyn said breathlessly. "I don't think they will give up.

How will we stay concealed tonight?"

"Follow me," Hamlin replied in a low voice.

The two horses and their riders walked stealthily over the forest path. Both Hamlin and Ellyn often turned their heads, listening and peering into the silent darkness. Then, Hamlin led his horse off of the path and into the black woods.

Several long strides into the woods, he pulled his horse to a halt and dismounted. Ellyn did likewise and stood next to her horse, looking around at the darkness. She shivered against the chill air and pulled her long cloak around her.

"I think we'll be safe here," Hamlin said.

"I wasn't sure I would be able to keep up," Ellyn said. "Thankfully, he knew he was supposed to follow," she said, resting her hand on the horses' back.

"It's she," Hamlin smiled. "Her name is Raven."

Ellyn ran her fingers through Raven's black mane and leaned against her warm body. "What do you plan to do after this?" Ellyn asked.

"We can't stay here for long," he said. "But we can rest for a few hours. Then, we'll get as far as we can before daybreak. Once the sun rises, we'll have to be even more careful, if your enemies are as determined as they seem. To what extremes do you think they will go to find and harm you?"

"I don't know," Ellyn said slowly. "But I overheard something that would ruin the princess of Wyndham, Maerynn, and I have learned that she is not easily opposed. I think she will keep looking until I am found, or until it is too late."

"Hm." Hamlin grunted thoughtfully and scratched his brow. "But didn't the king leave someone to take charge in his place? Couldn't you just tell someone about her, and get protection from the guards?"

"I don't think I was safe within the walls of Lyntirith," Ellyn replied. "It would seem that Maerynn has perfected the art of getting past the guards in some way or another. I don't know to whom I could have turned, and I know I couldn't have rested peacefully as long as I remained in the castle."

"Princess Maerynn sounds like a desperate woman," Hamlin said, shaking his head.

Ellyn nodded thoughtfully, but did not reply. Hamlin took a rope out of the saddlebag and attached it to his horse's bridle, looping it over a branch. Then, he pulled an identical rope from the satchel hanging from Raven's side and secured her to another tree.

"I'm sure this will be far from the comfort you are used to," he said. "There should be blankets in your knapsack if you need them." Then he heaved himself down on the ground and leaned against a tree, crossing his arms.

Ellyn found the knapsack and pulled a pile of blankets out. She spread one out on the cold, hard ground and laid on it. Then, she pulled the other one up to her chin. Knots and clumps of dirt pressed into her back as she lay, and snowflakes fell gently onto her face. The forest was still and quiet, the dark veil of night concealing those within.

Waking with a start, Ellyn sat up slowly, wincing at the pain in her back. It was still dark, but the snow had ceased to fall, and now a chill wind was blowing through the trees.

"We need to go now," Hamlin said. She looked up to see him standing over her, his thick hair tousled. The horses had already been prepared to continue the trek through the woodland paths. Standing up, Ellyn rolled her blankets up and stuffed them in the satchel. She picked her bow and quiver from the ground where she had left them the night before and hung them over her shoulder. Then she pulled herself into Raven's saddle and wrapped her cold hands around the reins.

"How far is Eurasia?" she asked, shivering in the cold and pulling the hood of her cloak over her head.

Hamlin laughed wryly as he mounted into his saddle and urged his horse into a walk. "It's still a bit of a distance. But if we can cover the ground I hope to tonight and tomorrow, we should arrive by daybreak after tomorrow."

Ellyn nodded, though her body groaned as she thought about two more nights in the cold, with only a few layers to shield her from the persistent winter air.

"How much more of the journey will be in this forest?" she asked.

"I chose a path that takes us mostly through the forest," he replied. "We'll travel over open fields and plains for a short time and then through a sparsely wooded area. But we'll be in these woods until dawn, no doubt."

Looking around her, Ellyn perceived the tall trunks in the pale moonlight, which had found a few gaps to glimmer through the canopy of branches above. Every tree looked the same, and every branch identical to the others, and every stone the same, and continued in a never-ending void as far as she could see.

She stared straight ahead of her, moving methodically with the movements of her horse and keeping her eyes trained on Hamlin, who often turned his head and asked if she was doing alright. Even though she was not alone and both she and her companion were armed with weapons, she felt susceptible, surrounded by the pressing darkness and eerie silence of the forest. She knew that Maerynn's future and fate were now in her hands, and that she would be sought after with determination. It was still many miles to Eurasia, and anything could happen before they reached the country, and if some harm befell her, it could be months, if not longer, before anyone discovered it. She shuddered. Her mind filled with these thoughts of worry and dread, she fell into a subdued and exhausted subconsciousness.

"How are you doing, Ellyn?"

Ellyn started and looked up quickly. Blinking with confusion, she was surprised to see a dim light shining between the trees, and the regularity of the trees was lessening.

"We are nearly out of the woods," she murmured. Her head was throbbing, and she felt a dull aching in her back. Her hands and feet were numb, but she felt a wave of relief in seeing the edge of the forest.

Hamlin nodded. "It is almost daybreak now. We have left the borders of the kingdom Lyntirith safely. But we will have to be careful because now we do not have the safety of the trees to hide us. The next part of our journey will be along plains and fields. We will probably reach the edge of Eurasia before the sun has set, and then we will be in a wooded area once again. But for today, just keep your dagger and arrow ready at hand, in case we need to use them."

Ellyn nodded and bit her chapped lip. She looked up at the pale sky as they left the confines of the forest and stepped out onto the frosty moss, imbedded with a sprinkling of snowflakes. The sky was a white, and the wispy clouds seemed to be frozen in place above. As far as the eye could see ahead, and to the left and right, the terrain was flat, with only a few rolling hills breaking the flatness. They walked for more than half an hour before Ellyn broke the silence saying, "Since we are just east of Lyntirith, we must be in the kingdom Carlisle, which separates Eurasia from Lyntirith."

Hamlin grunted, staring off to the right. Following his gaze, Ellyn scrutinized the horizon and could barely distinguish a small band of horses, far off in the distance. They were so far, she could not tell if they were running, or walking at a slow pace. She looked back at Hamlin and saw his eyes were narrowed.

"Who are they," she asked, an edge of worry in her voice.

"I don't know." Hamlin shook his head slowly. "We should go with greater haste, though. If we had been given more time before we left Lyntirith, I would have sent someone to scout this country to see if it was safe before travelling this way. But since there was no time, I don't know whether or not any danger lurks here."

Ellyn spurred Raven to a gallop. "Then let's hurry," she said. Hamlin urged his own horse to meet Ellyn's speed, and soon they were riding at full gallop over the cold plains of Carlisle, the brisk wind blowing in their faces. Constantly turning her head toward the possible threat, Ellyn noticed that they seemed to have altered their path and were also riding in a westerly direction. They seemed to be aiming towards Hamlin and Ellyn, and as the minutes passed, Ellyn could gradually make out more details about them. She was first able to distinguish that there were five horses with riders. Then, she could make out the color of the horses as they grew closer. Looking over her shoulder at Hamlin, she saw his brows were furrowed, and his eyes darted constantly towards the horses.

"What are they?" Ellyn shouted above the sound of wind rushing past her ears.

"Northmen," Hamlin said shortly. At the dreaded word, both spurred their horses into a run, streaking across the frozen meadows.

Ellyn focused on the ground ahead and leaned forward in the saddle, clutching the reins between her stiff fingers. Suddenly, there was a whizzing sound, and Hamlin shouted as an arrow sailed past, missing him by inches. He pulled his horse to a halt and swung to the ground, grasping his weapons in a defensive position.

Ellyn dragged Raven to a halt and reached for the bow and arrows. In a moment, she had aimed the arrow, fitted to the string, towards the approaching riders. The Northman, all with weapons drawn, slowed to a halt, then stood ten yards away. For a few moments, no one from either side spoke, or moved a muscle. Each one stared in front of them at their opponents, grasping their weapons, and breathing heavily. The clouds of air that rose from their mouths was all that moved on the vast frozen plains in the middle of the wilderness.

Chapter 26 - Captured

Memories of her encounter with the Northmen in the woods of Eurasia flooding into her mind, Ellyn inwardly quaked with fear, facing the hostile warriors once again. Her hands trembled slightly, and she struggled to keep the bow and arrow trained steadily on the Northman in front of the group.

"Who are you, and why are you travelling through this land?" one of the Northmen asked, his voice thick with a heavy accent.

"You do not own this land, so what right do you have to ask such a question?" Hamlin asked boldly.

"It is not ours, but it will be," he responded angrily. "Why are you travelling alone, as if in hiding, and where have you come from?"

"If you wish to live, leave us, and let us continue on our way," Hamlin said harshly. Ellyn glanced at him and saw his face was flushed with anger, and his temples pulsed quickly.

"You think you have dominance over us," the Northman scoffed. "But you seem to forget it is you and the small lass against the five of us. You will not survive trying to defend yourselves."

Hamlin stared at him without speaking.

"Where are you going, girl?" he asked, turning to Ellyn.

"You will glean no more information from me than you already have," Ellyn said. "You seem to forget that you are about to lose this war with Eurasia," she added callously.

"Since you will give us no information, we have no need of you," the leader of the pack said. He turned to a warrior behind him, "You know what to do," he said.

One of the Northman urged his horse forward towards Ellyn and raised his spear towards her. "If you injure this young woman in any way, you will pay," Hamlin shouted, jumping in front of Ellyn. "She is the daughter of royalty, and if any harm befalls her, you will answer to the king."

The leader looked at Hamlin, and his brows furrowed darkly. "To what kingdom does she belong?" he asked.

"She lives in a nearby kingdom," Hamlin replied vaguely.

The leader dismounted from his horse and stood only a few yards away from the two arrows that were pointed towards his head.

"If any of my men dies, you will lose your life, but the girl will live. Release your arrows and you both die."

"What do you want from us?" Hamlin asked. "Nothing from you. Only the girl."

"No, absolutely not," Hamlin said firmly.

"Do not fear, no harm will befall her. If she refuses, it will be easy for us to overpower you and force her to come with us."

"I have been placed in charge of her safety and will fight to defend her no matter what may become of me," Hamlin said with angry passion.

The leader narrowed his eyes and made a motion to the men sitting on their horses behind. They dismounted and stood behind their leader. He took a step towards Hamlin, whose grip on the bow tightened. Then, with a flash, the broad-shouldered leader grabbed the bow and pushed Hamlin's arms up. An arrow sailed into the sky above, and Hamlin was wrestled to the ground, yelling threats. Before Ellyn could react, she was surrounded by the three other Northmen and was stripped of her weapons.

"What are you doing?" she asked with indignant fear.

The leader stood up and pulled Hamlin to his feet. "Count it not violence that we take this royalty, but mercy that we let you live."

Ellyn shuddered as he stepped towards her and stared down at her. His clothing reeked of his uncleanliness, and his beard was tousled and tangled with briars and burrs. He grinned cruelly, displaying two rows of brown, crooked teeth.

"Don't look so frightened," he said mockingly. "All we need from you is some information. One never knows when it may be helpful to have someone your enemy considers valuable. It is my belief we may be able to use you for our advantage. If not, we can easily dispose of you."

"If so, you will never live long enough to regret your actions," Hamlin shouted.

"We have no need of your words," the Northman said harshly. Then he mounted his horse. Ellyn was pulled roughly into one of the saddles of the Northman, and he pulled himself into the saddle behind her. Then, with a shout from the leader, the horses were urged into a trot, and Ellyn found herself being carried away through an unknown land to an unknown place. Her stomach sank with a sickening feeling of dread.

After hours of riding over long plains and fields, Ellyn saw smoke rising in the distance over a rolling hill in the terrain. As they reached the peak of the hill, she saw tents set up below in a circle, guarded by armed watchmen. It was the camp of the Northmen.

As they approached, the guards stood aside and let them pass, looking at Ellyn threateningly as she passed between their ranks.

"Our ruler will be pleased to see you," the warrior behind Ellyn smirked. "He will have many questions, and there will be consequences that I dread to imagine if you do not do as he bids you."

Past armed Northmen lying in front of their tents, small fires surrounded by small stones and lines of tents, the four horses went. Then, they stopped in front of a tent larger than all the others, surrounded by many guards. The leader of the band of Northmen spoke to one in their native tongue, words that Ellyn could not fully understand. However, she was able to understand his last sentence as he said, "She is the daughter of the Eurasian king."

The guard entered the tent, then emerged a few moments later. He approached Ellyn and said gruffly, "You are to go inside alone."

The guard behind her dismounted, and she slid down from the saddle. Towering above her, the barbaric warriors stared down at her as she walked among their ranks. The door of the tent was pulled aside and she stepped within.

A black curtain hung in front of her, concealing what hid beyond, but she saw a shadow flickering on the fabric, cast from the dim light of a torch. She lifted her fingers and pulled the curtain aside, peering around into the inner chambers.

At the end of the enclosure sat a man large and menacing. His face was gouged with scars, and his black hair fell over his shoulders. His nose was large and red, and his eyes glared with fury into her own. In his palm he clutched a sword, and both guards that stood on either side of him stood stiffly, scrutinizing Ellyn as she stepped from behind the curtain.

"Your name," the ruler said gruffly. His voice made Ellyn's heart leap. It was so filled with hatred and bitterness. It sounded as though a fit of rage was barely contained below his even voice and unrelenting expression.

"I am Ellyn," she said timidly, clenching her hands into fists.

"Step forward," he said. She obeyed, and took a few steps closer to him. "Who is your father?"

"King Wulfred of Eurasia," Ellyn said fearfully.

His eyes narrowed, and he gave a low rumble of disapproval. "Are you married?"

"Yes, to the future king of Lyntirith."

The king glared at her without moving for many long minutes. Then a light seemed to blaze in his eyes, and his lips stretched into a thin line.

"You come from the two kingdoms that are united against my people," he said wryly. "I do not think I am wrong in that you must have sealed the treaty between the two kingdoms' alliance. Your marriage assured the cooperation of both sides. Am I not correct?"

Ellyn nodded her head slowly, clasping her hands behind her back.

Then, a slow grin curled over the ruler's lips. "You are the hope I have been waiting for. These many months, the combined forces of Eurasia and Lyntirith have been draining my forces and warriors. But that will end tomorrow at the meeting of our forces. When they see the asset I now have in my hands, they may be more willing to listen to what I have to say."

"The fate of this whole country rests in their hands. I am but a minor princess. They will not risk the welfare or future of this kingdom merely to save my life," Ellyn said in a quavering tone.

"We will see," the king laughed. Then he made a gesture for her to leave, and leaned his head back satisfactorily. "When the strings that bind a treaty together are taken away, what is left to keep them bound?"

Ivor, the oldest son of King Wulfred, stood in the middle of a tent, securing the plates of steel over his mail in preparation for battle.

"Your Highness, the armies have been stationed in their assigned locations, just out of sight from the battlefield."

The king nodded towards the knight who stood in the doorway of the tent, who turned and mounted his horse at the king's gesture.

"I highly doubt they will attempt an attack," Ivor said. "No doubt we will all spend countless hours in this council with them, which will end in surrender once they realize how far outnumbered they are."

"The Northmen are a fierce and determined people. They have so much honor bound in their cause, to the point that they are so unpredictable. There are many times I have thought they saw their defeat was imminent, when they make a startling move that seems to put them at an advantage. They cannot see themselves defeated in this long-lasting battle, which I think may be their downfall. It may push them to make unwise decisions that will prove their destruction. But no one can tell what this day may hold, so strap on your bow and arrow, sheath your sword and always stand at the ready."

"I still don't understand why we don't refuse their request for a council and engage in battle," Ivor said, pulling his helmet over his dark blonde hair.

"You understand because I have explained it to you, you just do not agree with me," the king said wryly. "You know how all of our battles have ended these past weeks. Though we have the advantage of numbers, they find a way to surprise us, and force us to retreat. This request for a council, however… This is something they have never done before. If it is a trap, now that our new forces have arrived, we will be able to crush them so that they will never have a second chance. But I think this council may be the way to prove to them that we are just as determined as they, and that we have the upper hand."

"But you know it could be dangerous."

"In the life on the battlefield, we are always in danger."

With these words, King Wulfred stepped from the tent and squinted in the blaze from the hot sun. He looked up to see King Evander riding towards him, with his son just behind. Both were fully suited in armor.

"Shall we bring cups of tea to enjoy while we exchange pleasantries with our enemies?" King Evander said dryly.

"I know you don't approve of my plan to meet face-to-face with the Northmen," King Wulfred replied. "But you know we are fully prepared to engage in battle. But what does your son think of my plan? I am curious."

"This is your war, not ours," Corbin replied shortly, pulling the visor of his helmet over his eyes.

As he spoke, Ivor emerged from the tent and mounted his warhorse. King Wulfred looked around him at the mounted knights, waiting for his command. "We are ready," he said. "Ride forth."

At a quick, steady pace, the band set out from the camp. Sounds of trotting hooves and metal clapping against itself filled the air and sailed away with the hot breeze. Over the dried, brown grass, they rode to meet their enemies. Though the face of each was set into an expression of determination, each gripped the hilt of his sword tightly between his gloved fingers.

Only a few minutes passed before the riders climbed to the top of a hill and, looking down, saw the whole of the Northmen army that remained after their months of fighting. Rows and rows of the warriors stood at attention, facing them with raised heads, watching them as they appeared over the crest. In the front stood three men and, in the center, the leader of the Northmen. Their faces were solemn as King Wulfred and his men approached and stopped thirty yards in front of them. Several hundred of the combined forces of Eurasia and Lyntirith took their posts beside the kings and stared back at their foes.

"You come for a council, yet it appears you have come ready for war," the Northmen leader said, stepping forward.

"As do you, Halldorr," King Wulfred replied, dismounting. He stepped forward as well, his son and several knights following only a few paces behind. Behind his helmet, Ivor stared with menace towards the Northmen leader, and his breaths came thick and heavy beneath his armor.

"In the message you sent," King Wulfred continued, "you claimed there have been developments that you believe will change the course of this battle, and requested a meeting between us. What made you believe I would agree to your request when I could smash you and all of your men within an hour?"

"So you say," Halldorr said with a scoff, his heavy, accented voice seeping with hatred. "But that has not been the result of our recent encounters, has it? I think we have proved to be more mighty than you think. I knew because of our recent successes that you would comply. And I am glad for your sake that you did. Otherwise, the result would not have been so pleasant for a certain person."

"If you mean myself," King Wulfred began. But Halldorr cut him short. "I was not referring to you," he said. "This is who I was referring to."

He turned his head, and the lines of warriors parted. Two Northmen stepped from the ranks, both holding the arms of a small, dirt-stained frame. King Wulfred watched as the prisoner was dragged forward, her head bowed so that he could not see her face. She was bound at the wrists, but her ankles left free. He noticed that she did not use her legs, however, as if she was unable to. She was dropped onto the ground where she fell in a heap. One of the men reached and grabbed her hair and pulled her up to face them.

A rope was wrapped tightly around her mouth so that she could not speak and her face was stained with blood. Her eyes, filled with desperation, spoke words that she could not through her mouth. It was then that King Wulfred realized it was his own daughter, and choked with shock and anger.

But, sitting horseback behind him, the prince of Lyntirith had recognized the prisoner even before her father and was staring in disbelief at Ellyn, helpless and at the disposal of Eurasia's most vile enemies.

For many moments, no one from either side stirred, and the valley was filled with an ominous silence. Then the king turned his horse and turned back to his men, all watching to see what his reaction would be.

Halldorr laughed loudly and sneered with approval.

"I cannot believe this," King Wulfred said under his breath. "How can this be?" His face was red with anger, and sweat dripped down his face.

"How, indeed? Could it be the Northmen have attacked Lyntirith and captured her?" King Evander said, his brows furrowed.

"What does it matter?" Corbin said angrily. "We need to decide how to spare her."

"Calm yourself, son; don't think irrationally. We can't go charging against them because we are angry; we need to organize our forces and attack strategically."

"We can't attack now, or she will be killed," Ivor said quickly.

King Wulfred ripped his helmet off and ran his hand over his face with distress. "It may be that we will have to put her life in danger in order to become victors over the Northmen. They are expecting us not to attack because we want to spare her life, but it may be that the option of saving her will prove our defeat."

"Father—"

"Ivor, do you see any other way?" the king asked with impatient distress. All of them fell silent.

"One thing is for sure," King Evander said slowly, "They wouldn't take us for such fools that we would exchange this country for her life, but what do they want in return for her? They must have some plan."

King Wulfred sighed and pulled his helmet over his head once again. Then he turned and led his horse several steps towards the Northmen once again.

"What is it you want so that her life may be saved?" he asked weakly.

"I have one request," the smug leader said slowly. "That to end the encounters between ourselves, we duel one against another, you and I. If you are victor, you may have your daughter, and we will admit defeat. If I win, everything will be lost to you."

"This is not acceptable," the king shouted. "I refuse to agree to these terms. Though the life of my daughter is precious, I will not risk the possibility of losing my kingdom to you and your tribe."

King Wulfred, exhausted from days and days of battle, weakened from wounds, heaved with weariness. The heat of the sun glared down, his hands shook, and he began to feel a weight pressing down on his shoulders.

"Then do you surrender?"

"Never!"

As he unloosed his hands from the reins and prepared to meet his enemy, King Wulfred heard the step of someone approaching from behind. He turned his head to see Corbin approaching.

"I will fight him," he said resolutely.

"You cannot. He is a warrior of many years of experience; you cannot defeat him," King Wulfred said sorrowfully. "And I fear I will not be able to either. But it is my only choice."

"No, it is not!" Corbin insisted. "It is a risk we must take. The wound you received only days ago has weakened you, and months of combat has made you weary. But I have never felt more invigorated. Let me have the honor, Your Highness."

The king sighed and looked down at the prince. Even through the helmet, he could see Corbin's eyes gleaming with anger, ferocity and determination. He stared at him for a moment, then looked back at his enemy. Lying on the grass, Ellyn was motionless, her face turned, hidden from his view. Then, he turned back to Corbin and nodded.

"The fate of our country is in your hands."

Chapter 27 - The Duel

Corbin stepped forward on the plot of ground that had been marked off for the duel that was about to take place – the duel that would decide the future of Eurasia. He stared across from him at his opponent, fastening the plates of steel armor. Sweat was already dripping down his face and back as the sun beat down relentlessly on the battlefield. His armor was heavy and he felt the weight of many weapons at his side. But he did not feel the discomforts or heat of the day. He only saw the leader of the Northmen, preparing to meet him in combat, and he only felt the determination to defeat him, and not only declare Eurasia the victory, but secure the safety of Ellyn. He glanced towards the place where she lay on the ground, only twenty yards away, and felt a surge of determination, even in the face of such a threat. The Northman king was broad in stature and towered above Corbin as he stepped forward. His many battle scars were a tribute to his years of experience on the battlefield.

Unsheathing his sword, Corbin held it upwards in front of his face and gripped his shield with the other hand and watched as Halldorr drew his own. The entire valley was silent, and everyone felt the numbness of anticipation surround them.

With one swift movement, Halldorr raised his sword above his head. Glinting in the sunlight, it was brought down with a terrific crash on Corbin's shield, held over his head in anticipation of the blow. Then Corbin lifted his sword and met the next slice of the weapon with the blade of his own. The sound of metal scraping metal reverberated through the valley as the swordfight began. In and out, the swords weaved around each other, sometimes colliding with a crash, other times, a dull clang.

Countless times, Halldorr took advantage of his height and stood above Corbin, raining blows from above. But the small opponent had the advantage of agility, and with every blow that threatened to prove his defeat, he met it with the edge of his sword, or the face of his shield. His eyes trained steadily on his adversary. Preparing for every advancement of the Northman, he watched the eyes of his opponent under his heavy helmet. Forward, backward, he stepped and dodged in the dry grass, smashing it under his step.

Sitting on the ground, watching with dread, Ellyn gripped the rope tightly between her teeth. Nearly paralyzed with fear, she winced every time a blow struck Corbin's armor, and clenched the ropes that bound her hands as the adversaries dealt blow upon blow on each other. But with every strike, the other seemed to retaliate with even greater strength and determination.

A deafening crash resounded through the valley as Halldorr's sword found its mark on Corbin's shoulder, throwing him to the ground. Corbin's sword spun upwards into the air, then fell to the ground with a thud. Halldorr stood, watching his opponent as he lay motionless on the ground, waiting for his admittance of defeat. Corbin rolled slowly to his side and raised his head, staring back at his opponent. Then, he leapt to his feet, pulling a dagger from his belt and, with a yell, leapt towards the king, sinking the dagger into the flesh of his shoulder.

With a shout of anger, Halldorr knocked him onto the ground, as if brushing a bug from his arm. He raised his sword above his head, but it stuck the ground as Corbin rolled to the side.

As Halldorr struggled to pull the blade from the ground, Corbin leapt to his feet and stood ready to face his foe once again. The two stared at one another, taking deep, heaving breaths, sweat dripping down their bodies.

Then Halldorr brought his sword down to be warded off by Corbin's shield. Now without his sword in hand, armed with just a dagger, Corbin could now only defend himself, unable to make a move against Halldorr. Over and over, and jabbed his dagger forward, or tried to strike him with the short weapon. But it never found its mark, and every time was met with the shield of Halldorr, and answered with a sharp blow from the sword blade.

Weariness began to clutch him. He dodged and warded off blow after blow as Halldorr tried to wear him down. He gasped for breath. Even though his body was weary, his steps did not slow, nor did his attention waver, until the sword heaved down heavily on his helmet, unprotected by his shield. With a groan, he fell to the ground. The sun glared into his eyes from above, and he squinted in the light. He tried to lift himself from the ground, feeling around for his shield, but fell back in exhaustion. Then, a shadowed figure blocked the sun from his eyes and Halldorr stood, towering over him, and pulled the helmet from his head. He looked down at Corbin with contempt.

Then, he raised his sword above his head to crush the blade between the plates of steel.

But before the blade found its mark, an arrow whizzed through the air and stuck him between the eyes. His expression changed from malicious victory to the frozen expression of death, and he fell to the ground with a terrible crash. Sitting atop his horse in front of the Eurasian army, King Evander was now holding an empty bow, from where the arrow had been sent.

A tremendous roar of anger resounded from the ranks of the Northmen, as the warriors raced into the battle.

King Wulfred scrambled for his sword and raised it in the air as a command for his own men to attack. But already, the armies that had been hidden, waiting to attack, were already running towards the attacking Northmen, and the knights and soldiers were already running into battle against the advancing Northmen. Their forces met with a great roar.

Ellyn found herself helpless, lying on the ground as Northmen ran past her and horses trampled next to her, some leaping over her just before crushing her. She looked around her frantically, but all she could see were the flashes of metal and running horses. She tried to stand, but a pain shot through her legs and she fell to the ground.

Just as she was about to give up hope, there was a shout next to her, and a Northman fell as he raced past her. She found herself surrounded by Eurasian men, and one leaned from his saddle and pulled her from the ground onto the back of the horse behind him.

She felt a blade slip between her wrists as the bonds were cut by another soldier sitting astride a horse next to her, and she wrapped her numb arms tightly around her rescuer. Now surrounded by fighting on all sides, the rider of the horse heaved his sword left and right, hewing Northmen from their horses and off their feet, making his way toward the edge of the fighting, sounded by his own men. Arrows ricocheted off of his helmet, and Ellyn winced every time one whistled past her head.

"Hold tight, Your Highness," she heard someone shout.

She turned and saw a Northman raising his sword to strike her, but it was warded off by the sword of her allies. A group of Eurasians now surrounded her, shielding off attacks from all sides, and warding off blows from those that attempted to kill her.

At last, the group broke from the lines of battle and the horses began running from the fighting, toward the camp. Ellyn looked back, but all she could see were arrows flying through the air and swords glinting in the sunlight as men fought against each other for the ultimate victory.

In only a few minutes, she reached the Eurasian camp, and the men dismounted and helped her from the horse. She tried to stand, but her bruised feet could not hold her. The rope was cut from her face, and a cup of water offered to her. She breathed deeply and gulped the water hungrily.

"We will take you to one of the tents where someone will tend to your wounds," one of the soldiers said. He lifted her and carried her to a tent nearby, guarded by several armed men.

She was laid on a mat and a servant appeared to make her comfortable.

"Thank you," she said in a hoarse voice to the soldier as he turned to leave. He nodded as he left the tent, then mounted his horse and went with several others back to the battlefield.

"I am a physician who will be tending you," a man said as he knelt by her side. "Tell me where you feel pain."

"What is happening out there? Shouldn't you go tend to the soldiers?"

"There are none to tend to yet," he replied. "Let me help you until they arrive." Ellyn nodded and sank back onto the mat.

It was several hours before the Eurasian camp finally began to rustle with the weary voices of men, the whinnying of horses and clanging of metal as the soldiers returned and began removing their heavy armor. Though exhausted from hours of battling under the afternoon sun, it was with jubilance and a light heart that they returned.

The Northmen had been defeated.

From the camp, Ellyn listened to the sounds of jesting and laughter between the soldiers, and sat up, listening.

"Please, find out for me what happened. I want to know how the soldiers fared."

"I am sure we will receive word very soon, but I have been instructed to remain here, Your Highness," the servant said.

Ellyn fell back impatiently and waited. The camp grew louder as more and more soldiers returned and filled the camp with their exclamations of victory. The battle had ended, and the next morning they would be able to go back to their homes and their families after months and months of fighting.

There was a rustling at the tent door, and King Wulfred stepped into view. His expression relaxed from anxiety to relief as he strode towards the mat where his daughter sat.

"Ellyn," he said gently, resting his hand against her face. She grasped his large, rough hand between her own small fingers and pressed it against her lips.

"Father," she said, smiling. "What happened?"

"The Northmen have been defeated," he replied. His careworn face was now full of exhilaration. "I never thought we would spend almost eleven months waging battles against this persistent tribe, but now, it is over."

"So they won't try to reassemble and attack once again?"

He shook his head. "Their forces are so diminished they would be unable to even think of trying for a very long time. Besides, if they have learned anything from this long and trying ordeal, it is that Eurasia is not a country easily conquered. This bitter defeat will not be easy for them to forget."

"Were any of your men injured or killed?"

"Very few. I am just now going to assess the number of men we lost and receive reports regarding the battle. I may see you again before you depart from this camp, but if not, God bless you, my child."

He leaned forward and kissed her forehead, then stood to leave. As he did so, Ivor stepped into the tent. His hair was wet and dishevelled and he was covered with dirt and filth, but his face was radiating with an expression of happiness.

"Ellyn, dear sister, I have missed you," he said, smiling jovially. He sat on the ground next to her and rested his arms on his knees.

"I have missed you as well," she smiled.

"You aren't in pain, are you? Did the Northmen do any serious harm?"

"Only my legs are sore and it is hard for me to stand. They bruised my legs to keep me from being able to run away."

Ivor's face clouded with an expression of anger.

"But other than that, I have recovered," she said quickly.

"And have you been treated well in Lyntirith? Are you happy?" She smiled and nodded. "Yes," she said.

Sighing, Ivor looked around the tent and said thoughtfully, "It is a shame Julius left Eurasia. He could have seen you one last time before going back to Brystol. But I suppose it may have made matters worse. It was just as well he isn't here, I suppose."

Ellyn pressed her lips together and looked at the ground.

"He was so upset when you left, as I'm sure you imagined. A few months after you left, he disappeared from Eurasia and we had no idea where he had gone. It was more than a week before he returned. I suppose he must have just wanted to get away for a while and spend time alone. Anyway, when he got back, he said he was going to spend some time in Brystol with his uncle, and then he planned to try to begin the process of building up an army so that he could reclaim his throne in Veridell."

When he had finished, he looked at Ellyn. "Are you alright? You look pale suddenly."

"Yes, I am fine," she said quickly. "I am only a little tired. Do you know how Mother and the others are?"

"Ready to come back home, I have no doubt, which we will now be able to do in a few short weeks at the most."

He paused and ran his fingers through his hair. "It won't be the same without you, though, Ellyn. I miss the days when we played and rode together through the woods as children, without anything to trouble us."

"So do I," she replied. "But when you think of me, don't think about my absence. Just remember all of the memories we share, and know that I am happy in Lyntirith."

At that moment, the opening to the tent was pulled aside and Corbin stepped in. He looked down at Ellyn sitting next to her brother and stood, frozen in place. His face was still stained with dirt and blood, and white bandages had been wrapped around both of his arms. Forgetting the pain she had been suffering, Ellyn jumped to her feet when she saw him. The next thing she knew, she was lifted from the ground in his arms, and she held him tightly with her own. She buried her face into his shoulder.

At last, his grip lessened and he lowered her gently to the ground. She winced when her feet touched the ground.

"What is it?" Corbin asked quickly.

She shook her head, "Just my ankles, it's alright."

He carried her to the mat and sat down next to her once she was comfortable. She looked around and noticed that Ivor had left the tent, although she could not remember when.

"Tell me honestly," Corbin said, looking into her eyes. "How did they hurt you? What did they do while you were prisoner?"

"I am alright; really I am. I wasn't fed very much, and they kept me in bonds the entire time, and beat my ankles to keep me from running away. But the doctor said they were not broken and they would heal quickly if I rest them. But I am feeling much better now, especially since I know you are well."

"How did you get here?" Corbin asked, lowering his voice. "How did they capture you?"

Ellyn sighed. "I will need some time to explain everything in full."

"We have the time," Corbin replied.

"Well, Maerynn is the reason I fled from Lyntirith. Her plans against the kingdom are more elaborate and dastardly than anyone realized."

"Maerynn?" Corbin asked in astonishment. "I know she has taken offense against me, but I did not expect her to make a move to place anyone in danger."

"She has done more than that. The attempts on your life in the past few months were at her doing. She is desperate to do anything to control the kingdom. When she realized her attempts to rule through you were in vain, she looked to Corineus, and planned to remove you and become his wife, and thus queen of Lynitirth. There are men who have either been bribed or threatened by her, whom she is using to try to harm her victims. One of those men has already been imprisoned. The one I remembered from the ship. His name is Cadwallo."

"She is not only desperate, she is mad," Corbin said in disbelief. "Are you sure all of this is true?"

"Yes, I overheard her making plans a few nights ago, and I was found. I only escaped with the help of Corineus, who realized the depth of insanity Maerynn has fallen into."

She then gave a descriptive tale of all that had taken place since his departure, her flight from Lyntirith, and capture by the Northmen. When she had finished, Corbin shook his head in disbelief.

"If I had known you would be in such danger, I would never have left you. But there were others there who could have protected you; why did you not turn to them?"

"Maerynn has been able to find a way to avoid the guards at the castle because she is so familiar with the methods of the kingdom. I felt unsafe there and wanted to be as far away from the walls as possible. Perhaps it was not the best decision, but I thought it was at the time."

"It does not matter now; it is all past, and I thank God you are safe. But we should return to Lyntirith as soon as possible. Who knows what we will find there when we arrive. I will inform my father of what you have told me, and he will decide what our next step will be."

Chapter 28 - At Home in Lyntirith

A small caravan of mounted horses walked briskly through the forest surrounding Lyntirith, approaching the castle walls. King Evander was in the lead, surrounded on both sides by knights, who kept a close watch on their surroundings. Just behind him rode Corbin, and sitting in the saddle behind him was Ellyn, her arms encircling his waist. Behind them, five armed soldiers followed, their hands resting on the hilts of their swords.

It was two days after the Northmen had been defeated, and King Evander had left promptly when he learned of the situation at Lyntirith. They had ridden ahead of the army in order to make as much haste as possible, and they had ridden with only one brief rest where they slept for a few hours.

Now, weary and careworn from the battle, they emerged from the woods and approached the gates of the castle. The guards standing inside the gates unlocked the latch and stood at attention as the king and his band passed between them. Stable boys appeared and took their horses as they dismounted.

King Evander immediately strode towards the entrance of the castle, just after two armored knights, who had gone ahead to assess the danger. Corbin stepped in just behind them and held his hand up for Ellyn to stay back. She looked around the grounds of the castle. Everything seemed as it always had. The stable boys were leisurely leading the horses to the stables, and the guards stood in their usual posts. She saw a servant walk past one of the windows, carrying a pile of cloths. Nothing seemed tense or abnormal. It was strange to feel so comfortable in a place that had felt so threatening only days before.

"You have returned!" Ellyn heard an exclamation from inside. She looked up and Corbin motioned for her to step inside. The door closed as the soldiers entered and shut it behind them. Queen Guinevere had appeared in the hallway and was looking with relief at her husband. "I expected to receive a message from you. Is everything well?"

King Evander hesitated and looked over her shoulder. Servants bustled about the halls going about their daily tasks.

"Yes, is everything well here?" he asked.

"It couldn't be further from well," she said in rushed tones. "Corineus has disappeared! It was only just this morning, and I have been worried and fretting all morning, wondering where he is."

"And that is all?"

"What are you talking about?" the queen asked with a hint of indignance. "Heaven knows what happened to our son. He is being searched for now with no success."

"Of course, I am very worried, but I will need to explain a few things to you. Let us step into the hall," he said, indicating a door next to them.

He opened it and stepped inside, followed immediately by Queen Guinevere. Corbin turned to follow them, then looked back at Ellyn. She had paused in the corridor, and was watching them retreat into the room.

"Come in," he said, beckoning her forward. She slipped into the room just as King Wulfred began to give the account to his wife which he had heard.

"There are murderers living amongst us?" she gasped when he had finished his brief summary. "There were, or that is they could have been if their plans were successful. Thankfully they were not."

"I refuse to believe that Corineus was involved," the queen insisted. She looked at Ellyn with scrutiny. "How can we know you are telling the truth?"

"She is, Mother," Corbin broke in. "I think our first step should be to find Corineus and Maerynn."

"Most certainly," his father agreed. "Then this whole ordeal can be sorted out in full. I will take some men to search for them at Wyndham, and I will have a word with Arnos. Most likely he knows nothing of what has transpired here."

"I will come with you," Corbin said quickly.

The king nodded, then said, "If neither of them are found there, we will have to find out which of the surrounding areas have been searched today in an attempt to find Corineus. But for now, let us go to Wyndham."

"Are you sure you don't want to change first, and perhaps rest for a few moments? You look exhausted," the queen said.

"If they are escaping the country, we can't spare a second," Corbin replied.

"We won't be too long, I hope," King Evander said to his wife. "I have every expectation that we will find Maerynn and perhaps Corineus at Wyndham, and this will all be figured out."

He turned and went to the door. Upon opening it, he stopped short and stared into the corridor. Corineus stood across from him, sallow, his eyes fallen with shame.

Queen Guinevere gasped. "My son," she said quickly, hurrying to her husband's side. Corineus held up his hands before she could embrace him.

"Where have you been?" she asked gently. "Please tell me what I have heard is not true, that you have been involved with Maerynn in such wicked plans. It cannot be true."

Corineus did not reply, but his eyes trained to his father, who was glaring at him with uncompromising severity.

Then, he stepped forward and into the room. He glanced up at Corbin and Ellyn for a moment, then looked down quickly at the floor. The sound of the door echoed from the room as King Evander closed it and turned to face his son.

"It is true," Corineus said in a low voice. He looked up quickly, then his eyes skirted away and he ran his fingers through his hair.

"Before you begin," King Evander said. "Where is Princess Maerynn?"

"I don't know," he replied candidly. "I have been looking for her, but I have not seen her since yesterday. She left the castle in such a state of anger and fury, it was frightening. But that's…" His voice trailed off and he pressed his palms to his forehead.

"I think you should tell us everything, from the beginning, son," the king said solemnly. Corineus sighed and crossed his arms, nodding slowly.

"First, I would like to acknowledge my own foolishness and blindness in all of this. I was blinded by Maerynn's promises of gain and prosperity if I followed her. It started out with very small requests. Such as showing her Ellyn's room, and helping her enter and leave the castle unnoticed. She had reasonable excuses for them, and I didn't want to question her, so I didn't. It wasn't until one night when she crept into Ellyn's room that I realized her aims may not have been as innocent as she claimed."

Ellyn recalled the night many months ago when the dark-clad figure had crept into her room, and she had narrowly escaped and encountered Corineus afterward.

"But when I began to question her motives, she was so cunning with her responses and wording, it seemed I had no choice but to continue helping her. She kept promising, only one more favor, then that would be all. Before I realized it, the favors had so accumulated and become so drastic that I felt trapped. I felt ashamed for helping her arrange men to murder my brother, although she did not admit that was her scheme at the time, and I did not know that was her plan. She kept all of her true plans to herself, and used me to carry out what she could not as easily, such as helping herself and others enter the castle without notice. It was not until I was so deeply entwined in her schemes that I realized what were her aims. One night, she clearly said it was her intent to harm Corbin, which she had not admitted to me before, and I was desperate to cease my involvement. She was desperate to keep me following her every whim, threatened me, bribed me, promised me with the honor of becoming king of Lyntirith, and so on. At last, realizing her desperation, I told her I would continue only a few days longer, but would not be any part of harming Corbin, Ellyn, or anyone else. That seemed to satisfy her.

"But everything changed when Ellyn was discovered listening to our conversation. Maerynn had her trapped, and locked her into a room. She then made it clear that there was no way Ellyn could be allowed to live, after everything she had heard. It would be death to allow her to live, and possibly have someone else find out, and thus our plans be ruined. It was then I realized I had to make a choice. I could either join Maerynn, in which there was no turning back, or I could stop following her commands and free Ellyn before she was killed. Clearly, I chose the latter. I was able to secretly help Ellyn escape, and Maerynn believed me when I told her Ellyn had escaped on her own. She did not know I had assisted her. If she had, I do not believe I would be standing here now.

"As soon as she realized Ellyn had escaped, she chased after her with several of her cohorts. But they were unsuccessful. She returned, livid and mad with despair. She paced the room for hours, not saying a word. Then, she left, before the first light of morning showed itself. I only saw her briefly the next day when I went to Wyndham. She was lying around, in despair. All of the men who had been helping her had scattered, and left her when they realized the danger of being caught. She said it was only a matter of time. I asked her what she was going to do and she did not reply. I came home and have not seen her since. I went to Wyndham every day since, but was not allowed to see her, and then I decided to ride around the surrounding areas to see if I could find her, but to no avail."

Corineus now stopped talking and took quick sharp breaths, looking around at those to whom he had told his tale.

After several moments of silence, the king finally spoke. "There is much I want to say to you on this subject, Corineus, but it will have to wait until later. For the time being, Corbin and I will go to Wyndham and speak with King Arnos, and try to find out what happened to Maerynn. I trust you will stay here and wait for my return."

Corineus nodded.

"Very well, let us go," the king said, turning to Corbin. The two of them left the room. Ellyn followed, but instead of going out to the stable, she went towards the stairs to go up to her room. It had been many days since she had felt any comforts, and though her steps were heavy with weariness, it was with relief that she ascended the stairs.

"Ellyn!" Alys hurried towards her as soon as she reached the top of the stairs and clasped her hands. "I have been so worried. Are you alright?"

"Yes, but I will be much better once I have had a bath and changed from these filthy clothes," Ellyn said with a smile. "It is so good to see you, Alys. I will relate to you everything that happened to me after I left Lyntirith, and I think you will find it a harrowing story."

Ellyn sat on her bed, refreshed, looking contentedly out the window. The sky was painted with orange and pink as the day dwindled into evening. Many thoughts raced through her head, but they were thoughts that caused a gentle smile to flit occasionally across her lips.

There was a knock at the door and Alys went to open it. Corbin stepped in. His face had finally been washed clean and only a few cuts and bruises remained. He was no longer in the dirt-stained clothes that he had been wearing for the past few days. He smiled as their eyes met, and walked towards her with slow, even steps.

"Can you walk easily now?" he asked, sitting on the edge of the bed.

Ellyn nodded. "There is no pain now; I think passing hours without walking must have healed them."

He smiled wearily, then looked down into his lap.

"Did you find Maerynn?" Ellyn asked after a moment of silence. He nodded, then slowly lifted his head and looked at her.

"She is dead."

Ellyn raised her eyebrows. "How?" she asked in disbelief.

"She killed herself," he replied. "She was found in her boudoir, lying on the floor, holding a dagger through her heart." Ellyn gasped slightly.

"No one else knew, except apparently one of the housemaids whom Maerynn had confided in before she inflicted the fatal blow. It was a scene of grief when we left."

He sighed, staring blankly into the room.

"And what are your thoughts? Does it grieve you as well?"

Corbin did not answer immediately, but sighed heavily. "Yes, it does," he said at last. "But not in the same way that I imagine it does her family. Their grief is in the loss of their daughter, and the princess of Wyndham. It is a different grief I feel. That someone so young threw away the chance of a long and happy life, and instead lived a short one of misery. Even though I don't miss her as a friend, I can only imagine how different her life would have been if, instead of craving more, she had been content. But that was what drove her: the desire for more. More power, and more honor to herself."

Ellyn nodded thoughtfully.

"But I also cannot help thinking about what would have happened if she had continued in her evil ways." He looked up at Ellyn and gently rested his hand on hers.

She looked down at the hand that covered her own and was struck with a sense of awe. His face had always seemed to her so stern, so mysterious, so uncompromising, as if there was anger kindled behind his dark eyes. The hand that now lay on her own had been used to smite and slay both men and beasts, but his touch as she had known it was so gentle and kind. Those hands, full of strength that were capable of so much damage, were resting with gentle firmness on her own.

She lifted her eyes to see he was watching her. His expression was set with solemnity, but behind it, she saw peace, calmness and contentment. He pulled himself up next to her and wrapped his strong arms around her.

"I am so glad to be home now, safe, with nothing to worry about," Ellyn said thoughtfully. "It feels like the end of a long and harrowing journey."

"The end?" said Corbin. "I feel that we are just at the beginning."

Rachel was born in Indianapolis, Indiana in 1996, the first of eight children. She loved hearing, reading, and sharing great stories, especially with her younger sisters and brothers. After graduating with a piano degree, she taught piano to hundreds of young students, travelled, and loved spending time with friends and family. She was also an accomplished writer, with several published poems and a novel she began writing as a teen and continued working on for many years. That book is 'Ellyn'. Tragically, Rachel died in a road accident at age 27 in 2023. Her family and friends continue to be blessed by her creativity. We're sure you will be too. Enjoy.

9 781915 975065